BUFFALO DREAMERS

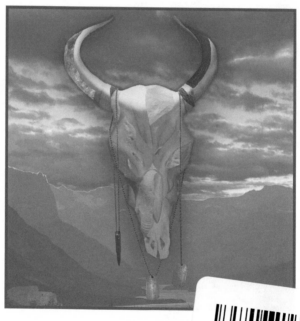

a novel

BY JOHN NEWMAN

sweetgrassbooks
an imprint of Farcountry Press

ISBN 978-1-59152-312-3

© 2022 by John Newman

Cover art by Jack Newman

Design by Steph Lehmann

For more information or to order extra copies of this book
call Farcountry Press toll free at (800) 821-3874
or visit www.farcountrypress.com

an imprint of Farcountry Press

Produced by Sweetgrass Books
PO Box 5630, Helena, MT 59604; (800) 821-3874; www.sweetgrassbooks.com

The views expressed by the author/publisher in this book do not necessarily
represent the views of, nor should they be attributed to, Sweetgrass Books.
Sweetgrass books is not responsible for the author/publisher's work.

Produced and printed in the United States of America

26 25 24 23 22   1 2 3 4 5

For Lisa,
Who believed, supported, humored,
and endured me on this journey

Chief Arvol Looking Horse, Spirit Releasing Ceremony, Gardiner, Montana.

FOREWORD

According to the U.S. National Park Service, so far this winter Yellowstone National Park and the Montana Department of Livestock have trapped and slaughtered 1,187 wild buffalo migrating from the Yellowstone plateau to winter range in the Gardiner Basin and upper Madison Valley. Hundreds more buffalo remain in a trap operated by Yellowstone National Park inside the park…

Mi-ta-ku-ye *(my relatives)… Let it be known that Yellowstone territory; the habitat of the last wild Buffalo Nation - is sacred ground; it has been a sacred site for the First Nations people, and for all humanity who hold deep respect for all Creation… These Buffalo that lost their lives in Yellowstone did not die by Natural Law, nor were their spirits honored with ceremony… we see this as an unnecessary massacre. We have known that this particular herd is the last original Buffalo Nation that still follows their migration pattern, the little that is left intact; they are the sign of our connection to our well-being of living in harmony…*

In a Sacred Hoop of Life, there is no ending and no beginning… Can-te Mi-ta-wa I-ta-han *(from my heart).*

— *Chief Arvol Looking Horse*
   19th-Generation Keeper of the Sacred White Buffalo Calf Pipe

PROLOGUE

It was a good time to be a wolf. The Yellowstone winter had been unusually harsh, with an early autumn and heavy snow, leading to exhaustion throughout the famished buffalo herd. The pack roamed from Old Faithful to Mammoth Hot Springs, at first culling the tough old bulls that struggled to keep up. Then, as the birthing season came to its frothy peak, the wolves feasted on the warm organs and still-soft bones and sinews of fresh-dropped calves, their bodies matted with the sweet fragrance of birth fluids streaked with blood, even licking clean the nesting pod of grasses where the cow dropped the calf it had carried all through the snows.

The buffalo swept through the forest, chewing the fresh tips off every tree limb within reach. As the snow was blown clear from the ridges by the steady Northern Rockies winds, they mowed the underlying grasses to the precise height that evolution had designed their lip to ensure regrowth. And when the first thaw of early spring opened the trails down from the wintering slopes, the herd pulsed with the innate knowledge that food supplies were over-grazed and hard times were ahead. They began to move, instinctually following ancient migration routes that knew no boundaries, down a network of streams and canyons to the confluence with the Yellowstone River, and from there, onward to the lush but forbidden pastures of Paradise Valley in the heart of Montana cattle country.

1

The late afternoon sound was unmistakable, a steady whup-whup that was a combination of powerful motors and huge blades cutting the high-altitude air. Sam Comstock, an Iraq war vet on contract with Montana Fish & Game to put his Marine sniper skills to good use, turned the beat-up government issue truck towards the chopper, half expecting to hear the shriek of war planes returning from a mission. But there was no smell of burning oil, no likelihood of an improvised roadside bomb here on the north side of the vast, nearly deserted Yellowstone National Park, only the disinterested shuffle and snort of a few elk on the ridge above and a small herd of antelope below, pawing to get at the meager grass beneath the crusty remnants of late-April snow. He took a deep breath to steady himself, ran his fingers through his thick auburn hair, and searched the horizon.

"What the hell's going on?"

Big John McLaughlin, a senior game warden and Sam's boss, leaned forward from the back seat and fidgeted with the scanner, trying to find the right channel to put him in touch with headquarters. He gave Sam's broad shoulders a squeeze. "Just what we came for. It's what pays the bills."

"That doesn't sound like any civilian chopper."

"Well now, I'm just not sure who besides us they got up in the air or on the ground. Lemme see here." BJ randomly hit a channel with a screechy voice backed by the roar of helicopter engines: "There's one, get him! Bring the ship in closer! And the little one, there! Smoke him!"

Sam's bloodthirsty associate, Oxnard, let out a war whoop. "Lock and load boys! We are fuckin-A in business!"

The forest opened up to a long, broad meadow with a herd of sixty to seventy buffalo stampeding down towards the north entrance of Yellowstone Park. And banking in hard over the ridge was an Apache attack helicopter, coming in low and fast.

"By god, you're going to catch us in friendly fire!" BJ barked over the radio. "Give us some goddam room! And who the hell are you?"

"This is Lieutenant Jack Walker, US Army Montana Reserves, 163rd Battle Streamers. Mission classified, but be advised, you are in harm's way."

Sam pulled in close beside the herd, steering with his left hand and holding his M40 sniper rifle in the crook of his elbow, aiming out the window while careening across the uneven range at thirty miles per hour. Oxnard was seated in the passenger window, getting set to blast away over the roof of the truck, while BJ angled for a shot with his .357 Magnum revolver. A buffalo calf had fallen behind and was in a direct line between the chopper and jeep. Sam saw the door gunner load his massive 30mm chain gun, and heard over the radio: "You want me to shoot a calf?"

"Get 'em now!" Walker commanded. "The nits grow up to be lice, don't they?"

The gunner took aim and unleashed a barrage of 1,200 rounds per minute, obliterating his target with Sam's jeep a scant ten yards beyond the zone of mayhem.

"What the hell is an Army chopper doing here?" Sam asked.

"They told me it'd be an inter-agency operation," BJ replied, "but I figured we were brought in to cull the old and infirm, not massacre the whole goddam herd!"

"Closer!" Oxnard shouted. "I'm goin' for a head shot."

The closest bull hooked its horn, shearing the driver's side rear-view mirror clean off.

"We get any closer you're going to be able to brush his teeth!" BJ growled. "Sam! Watch it, ahead!"

Sam swerved to miss two people on an ATV, coming straight at them, waving a blanket. The ATV passed between the truck and the buffalo, then skidded around and came right back to place themselves as a shield directly in Oxnard's line of fire.

"Get outta the way!" Oxnard shouted, practically climbing out the window to get a better line. In response, the passenger on the ATV stood on the back seat and pulled open his shirt to offer his bare chest as a shield. "By god, I do believe these are Indians!" BJ said, pulling up on his pistol.

Sam sped up as fast as he dared, but the ATV kept pace alongside, the herd pushing right on through a prairie dog town, several of the buffalo going down hard as their hooves were caught in holes. Up ahead, Sam saw several more figures angling in to provide a human shield: two on horseback, one on a dirt bike, here came another on an ATV. Now, from further down the hill coming up from the park boundary town of Gardiner, were a couple of pickups bristling with cowboy-hatted hunters firing into the herd.

"Getting kind of crazy out here," Sam said, as the military chopper came back around, the door gunner blazing away at everything that moved, which had the immediate effect of hazing the buffalo away from their preferred direction down the Old Yellowstone Trail towards Yankee Jim Canyon.

"Herd's turning!" Oxnard shouted. "Sonsabitches are headed right into town."

"And they're splitting up. Sam, leave the main body for the chopper, follow that gang over yonder."

Sam cranked the wheel over, powering through a four-wheel slide to fall in behind a group of eight buffalo that rumbled past the Roosevelt Arch and tore through a barbed wire fence as though it was gossamer, right down onto the high school football field where some kids were tossing frisbees

"Pull up," Oxnard said. "This'll be easy."

Sam slammed to a stop and Oxnard and BJ climbed out, reloading as they moved. A mother and calf were stopped beside a snack stand window, the mother panting hard but moving her head back and forth as she stared into the window. Sam noticed that she had a distinctive white star on her forehead, which was in sharp contrast to the craggy black mane of hair on the top of her head and around her massive neck.

"Sweet old thing is admiring herself," BJ said. "I've heard they do that."

"Last things she'll ever see," Oxnard said, raising his rifle.

Several kids ran over and screamed for Oxnard not to shoot. He hesitated.

"What d'you want me to do, boss?"

"Just hold on a sec," BJ said. "I'm thinking."

Sam felt a shudder go through his body. The presence of civilians, especially young people in the middle of a firefight, was deeply unsettling. They looked to be about fourteen to sixteen years old; in Iraq, you would have assumed most were armed and potentially lethal and fired at the slightest provocation.

"Take care, man. These are just kids."

"We got a mission to do!"

"Stand down, Ox," BJ ordered. "Sam's right, this is getting just a bit too… western."

A pickup truck came around the corner with four guys in cowboy hats, each holding a rifle.

"Looks like we'll have to rely on some Montana boys to get the job done," Ox huffed.

Three girls placed themselves between the truck and the buffalo.

"Chill out! We're not going to let you shoot them."

"Just back away, darlins, this won't take but a minute," one of the cowboys said.

"Easy does it," BJ said. "We don't want to make matters worse, now do we?"

The girls got between the mother and the calf, and the calf bolted twenty feet down the field. A guy in the truck immediately opened fire, tearing three quick holes in the side of the calf and dropping it in the grass. At this, all the students became hysterical, circling around the pickup and pounding on the sides. One of the cowboys got out, setting his rifle on the seat and motioning for the kids to step back.

"I'll do this my way," he said, buckling on a belt and holster that held a pearl-handled .45 revolver.

"You just doing that for your personal protection?" a girl asked.

The cowboy winked at her and walked right up to the cow buffalo, facing it head-on within an arm's length, then did a quick-draw, but his gun was empty.

"You dick head!" one of his buddies said.

"I thought you were gonna help it," the girl said.

"I surely am," the cowboy said, turning his back on the buffalo and removing a single cartridge from his belt.

Sam saw the old cow stiffen a bit, its curly tail straightening out into an upright flagpole. The animal must have weighed close to a thousand pounds, at least half of which seemed to be concentrated in that massive front assembly of head, neck, and shoulders—a perfect battering ram equipped with delicately curving, very pointy horns.

The cowboy placed the bullet in the clip, spun the holder, and kissed the shiny end of the barrel. "We'll do this Russian roulette style," he said. But before he could turn and pull the trigger, the cow bolted forward with a surge of speed and power that was truly astounding, especially for the cowboy, whose mouth grimaced open as the horn curved through his jeans and up into his rear end. The cow flicked him ten feet into the air then stomped twice on his crumpled body before dashing off at an almost immediate thirty-five miles per hour.

"Goddam it, she's gettin' away!" one of the guys shouted, rushing to help his fallen cowboy comrade. And in the commotion, the cow disappeared down the field and back up towards town.

Beads of sweat were on Sam's forehead. He gripped the steering wheel so tight his knuckles were white, his breath coming in short gasps.

"Let's get outta here," BJ said. "Ox, you coming?"

"Yeah, but I should go with those cowpokes, least they're not afraid to do what's got to be done."

Sam felt like he could barely breathe. He rounded the corner and saw the white-starred mother buffalo on a hillside above the football field, its plaintive, deep-chested bawling echoing in his own wounded heart.

BJ gave him a sideways look.

"You alright with this, son?"

Oxnard punched Sam hard in the shoulder and fired off two more quick rounds into the great beyond. "Let's hit it!"

The repeated gunfire now had a galvanizing effect on Sam, a combination of anger and excitement that provoked him to push the accelerator to the floor, setting all four tires in a dust-cloud creating spin. He clenched his jaw and laid a death grip on the steering wheel as they plowed towards downtown, Sam reflecting that there was nothing wrong with himself that couldn't be washed away by buffalo blood.

"Yes sir," Sam managed to say through clenched teeth, "all sorted out."

• • •

But Sam knew that things were far from sorted out. Long armed and muscular with angular, unshaven features, he appeared much older than twenty-five. He had inherited his mother's deep blue eyes and a lighter shade of her flaming red hair, the rare combination of which she deemed a providential sign. But it had been a while since he felt anything resembling providence.

He enlisted in the Marines right out of high school. It was a long ways from the Nevada backcountry town of Ely to far-off Iraq, a country he wouldn't have been able to find on a map before they put a sniper rifle in his hand. The evident tension in his shoulders, neck, and face were indications of a barely controllable, deeper trauma that he acquired in the deadly Tigris River Valley. Something was broken; he didn't know what exactly, nor apparently did the Navy doctors who removed a T-bone's weight of shrapnel from his shoulders and chest, leaving a few spiny fragments that were too close to his heart to be safely cut out. They proclaimed their operation a success and sent him down the hallway where a team of post-traumatic stress experts listened to him talk or admired the pictures they asked him to draw. It felt good to be paid attention, even though it seemed no different than jump-starting the battery of a side-swiped, rear-ended car you then drove off a cliff with the license plates removed: a wreck.

Soon after coming home he was told by his high school girlfriend, who had loyally waited for him throughout his long tour, that he was distant and strange. She dumped him within the month for a recent grad of the University of Nevada at Reno who had the good sense, in her opinion, to build a future for himself rather than go off and fight other people's wars. It made Sam raging mad and pushed him to an edge that he hadn't known was there, especially since his younger brother Blake had introduced her to the guy. He got in some serious street fights that should have landed him in jail, but he ended up a few drunken days later standing on the rooftop parapet of an abandoned four-story warehouse, considering a swan dive into oblivion. A strong gust of wind caused him to lose his balance and fall backwards rather than forwards. He hit his head hard and lay there, retching and nearly unconscious, unsure whether it was providence or bad luck that had saved him from himself. A snow flurry early that next morning shocked him awake and he stumbled down the stairs to the street, resolved to do a better job at self-destruction.

It didn't help that he also came home to a father falling fast into the darkness of Alzheimer's. The strain of caring for his dad caused his mother to leave Ely to be closer to Blake off at UNR. Sam had the house to himself and he would wander the rooms, feeling increasingly distant and strange. When that got to be too much, he'd go and sit beside his father at the rest home, neither of them talking. The doctor once thanked Sam for being such a loyal son, but when Sam asked if Alzheimer's was contagious, because that's why he mainly came to sit, hopefully to forget the things that had happened over there, the doctor strongly encouraged him to go get some counseling.

What seemed to work best was to go out alone to hunt the wide-ranging deer and antelope that roamed the surrounding valleys and mountains. He used his hazard duty pay to buy a fancy single shot M40 stalker rifle, tricked out with an even fancier scope. The 25-inch barrel and custom-charged and tipped bullets allowed him to stalk on foot over open ground with miles of uninterrupted visibility, both for himself and for his prey. Even with the expensive firepower, the odds were all on the other side, which was how he liked it: a nice change from Iraq, where men armed with World War I-era Russian rifles went up against laser guided missiles and satellite-directed drones.

Meeting BJ two months after being discharged was the first good thing to have happened. They met while Sam was scoping-in his rifle out at the shooting range. The meticulous care he gave to setting the scope for a thousand-yard shot—much longer by far than for any of the other Saturday shooters—attracted BJ's attention.

"I'm thinking you're not from these parts, and that you know just what the hell you're doing," BJ said.

Sam wrapped the shoulder strap around his right elbow, lay down on the ground, and created a tripod shooting platform with his left forearm braced in taut linkage to his right arm and shoulder. He took aim, fired, then carefully ejected the spent shell and put it in his shirt pocket.

"Load your own, eh?"

"Yeah, and I'm also from around here. Or at least was." Sam sat up and used a spotting scope to check the accuracy of his shot.

"None of my business, but I sure hope you're not fixing to shoot anyone important."

"No, the Marines paid me to bag my limit on that score. Now I only shoot to eat."

"Marines, huh? Well, son, that makes two of us."

BJ was a fellow vet, although from the much earlier Southeast Asian mud-hole of a conflict. A Nevada game warden, he recognized Sam's backcountry upbringing and USMC Scout sniper team skills as valuable assets for a special assignment he was about to begin with the State of Montana. He offered Sam a temporary job to come along on the month-long wildlife management project and Sam immediately signed on. In the weeks leading up to the trip, BJ quickly became something more than a boss: a kindred spirit who could speak with Sam in the secret language of a returning warrior. But there was a lot that Sam was not ready to tell any-one, especially about the 7mm bullet and two dog tags that he brought home from Iraq. The bullet hung between the tags on a chain necklace hidden beneath his t-shirt. The tags—his own and one of a fallen buddy—were a reminder of what he owed those left behind; the bullet was a deadly link to the past and an ever-present portent for the future.

For now, he was just glad to be in Montana with BJ and his lunatic, varmint-control specialist, Oxnard, and to try and forget as much of his recent past as possible. He put his hand over his heart, with the bullet and tags pressed against his chest, knowing that the choice was always there. It wasn't exactly sorting things out, but it was a way of getting through the nightmares that kept him awake at night.

2

The private luxury helicopter took up position directly above the town of Gardiner. Bob Smith, the forty-something president of the Montana Livestock Association, monitored the action below, occasionally spitting pistachio hulls out the small sliding plexi-glass window. He peered intently through a pair of industrial strength binoculars.

"What's the count, Larry?" he asked the chief veterinarian for the National Park Service, seated behind him in the four-person chopper.

"Oh, must be about a hundred," Larry replied. His uniform shirt was buttoned tight around his neck, forcing a ripple of pink flesh to bulge out below his sloping chin. "Got an extra nut or two there?"

"Need an exact, Larry. Only takes one to screw up the whole industry, know what I mean?"

"Well, let's see here," Larry drawled, raising his pocket mini-binoculars for a closer look. "There's one, and two, couple over there makes four."

"Shit man," Bob gasped. He turned to the pilot. "Duke, get another chopper in the air, now, with your best man, full digital photog equipment."

"Got it." Duke radioed in the order to headquarters over at Bozeman. "We'll have him here in forty minutes, max."

"Make it twenty. Use the Bell Jet."

"It'll cost a whole lot extra."

"Make it happen! We're talking a billion dollar exposure here!"

A copper-skinned young woman seated beside Larry leaned forward to hand Bob a sheet of paper. The bulky earphones and intercom microphone pressed close to her mouth made her appear larger than her slender face and figure would otherwise suggest. But the piercing intensity of her dark eyes set above high cheekbones gave her a gravity that was matched by the seriousness of her voice. "Frankly, you have little to worry about. There has never been even one documented case of cattle being infected by bison."

"Wait a minute Kate, have I seen that?" Larry demanded, reaching for it.

Bob briefly scanned the document. "I know all about this lame-brain hypothesis," he said, tossing it on the floor. "But this is no research experiment now is it?"

Kate Smith felt the chopper shell shrink-wrap around her soul as she waited for the inevitable negative burst from her boss. A recent PhD graduate from the wildlife management program at the University of Montana in Missoula, she was the youngest member of Larry's staff, and already his least favorite.

Larry grabbed the paper off the floor, crumpling it in his hand and not reading a word, but already in full command of the strongest possible opinion.

"Katie, this is simply all wrong. You know you need more field experience. This is hardly the place for theory."

"It's no theory, my data is derived from sound, empirical evidence."

Larry leaned close, speaking in a low voice as if intended for Kate's ears only, but that could be clearly heard over the in-cabin intercom. "You're a specialist in predators, not prey; wolves, not bison. And furthermore, you should know there is a time and place for this discussion, certainly not in the presence of a major taxpayer who happens to be *extremely well-connected.*"

Kate turned away, gritting her teeth. It was one thing to work for a boss who stood in stark contrast to her own values and mindset, but it was a whole other thing to constantly be at odds on entire paradigms, like saving animals versus slaughtering them.

As if in response to her dire thoughts, Larry tapped Bob on the shoulder and unmistakably mouthed the words: "Affirmative action."

Bob lowered his sunglasses to more clearly assess Kate. "So what tribe are you from, princess?"

"La-ko-ta," Kate said, precisely enunciating each vowel and syllable.

"A Lakota from Dakota! Hell, these diseased little creatures would be right at home on the Pine Ridge rez."

"Are you suggesting that might be an acceptable solution?" she asked.

"Oh, you big bullshitter!" Bob said, slapping and squeezing her knee, "That'd mean we'd have to transport 'em right through the middle of my Montana cattle. And we can't have that, can we? No siree, the only solution here is a *final one!*" He turned to Larry. "So, what's the count now, big guy?"

Larry raised his little binoculars and began counting again, using his fingers to keep track.

Bob shook his head and turned back to the pilot. "Bring us in behind Lieutenant Walker. I want to get a better view of our boys on the ground."

"Looks like a turkey shoot, if you ask me," Duke said, piloting the chopper in a long, sweeping turn above the river and bridge.

"That's what I'm afraid of. You can bag a turkey with one shot, but it takes a whole clip to bring down a buffalo."

3

The bus seemed to levitate, carried forward by the charismatic power of prayer and song, every pilgrim inside clapping hard and singing with an ear-splitting gusto that echoed across both sides of the vertiginous Gardiner Bridge.

"Nearer my God, to thee…" the voices rang out as the dilapidated, smog-belching vehicle rolled through Gardiner on Highway 89, leaving Yellowstone Park behind, and heading down Second street, its brakes squealing and ineffective.

"Buffalo are moving down to the bridge!" Ox shouted.

"Sam, cut 'em off before they make the grade. We gotta keep 'em the park side of the river."

"No room," Sam said, focusing intently on the churning mass of animals in front and to either side of the truck. He tried to scoot around the remaining thirty buffalo so as to block the narrow entrance to the bridge, but they were an unstoppable force; if the bridge had not been there, they would have run straight off the cliff. As they stampeded onto the bridge, Sam could see the military chopper hovering at eye level, with the door gunner sighting on a parallel line through the herd and right into the truck. Sam's stomach seized as he had an instant recollection of the friendly fire that had carried away so many of his buddies. "Incoming!" he screamed.

But a wave of natives ran onto the bridge just as Duke landed the chopper on the north side. A National Park Service SUV was waiting, doors open, as Bob, Larry, and Kate piled in and started south, Sam skidding to form a blockade to keep the buffalo on the park side, but they just pushed around, some of them crowded over the rail to a bellowing plunge to their death. The natives drove the herd forward, the bulk of the herd quickly moving past Sam's truck.

"Let's go!" BJ said, grabbing his lasso, "And bring extra ammo!"

They ran with the natives onto the span, with the river 200 feet below. Walker maneuvered his chopper right above the oncoming NPS SUV, laying down a covering blast of fire to keep the buffalo from trampling forward. Simultaneously, the church bus crunched into the right rear fender of Sam's truck and careened past onto the bridge, preventing any possible retreat. The terrified creatures had nowhere to go, circling helplessly with a horde of screaming people coming at them from every side. The cowboys jumped out of their truck and moved in, shooting the buffalo and finishing them off at point blank, the natives trying to shield the animals but not having any success. One native with a long knotted ponytail stripped off his plaid flannel shirt, revealing a hand-painted Ghost Dance design canvas tunic underneath. He grabbed a cowboy's rifle and held the end of the barrel right over his heart, screaming "Shoot!" Oxnard answering: "Do it!" By the time Sam ran to the center of the span there were less than ten creatures still on their feet, huddled now in a bellowing mass. One bull turned and plunged straight off the bridge, hitting the water with a tremendous splash then floating feet-up into the downstream rapids. Another pressed towards Bob and Larry, with Kate waving her sheaf of papers and hazing it off the upstream side of the bridge, close enough to the shore that it splattered onto a rock, splitting open and spilling blood and gore into the river. Oxnard brought down several more, the cowboys firing incessantly.

"What a massacre," BJ said, repulsed by the carnage.

Sam just stood there, his gun at his side, feeling like he'd seen all this before, the blood now flowing freely across the roadway, the men tracking it in every direction. The natives and everyone else on the bridge were shouting all at once in English, Cheyenne, Lakota, Spanish, and a variety of other dialects.

Kate took up position in front of the remaining few survivors and screamed at everyone to stop shooting, to no avail, the surviving buffalo down to four, then three, then two, and finally one last female with a light star on its forehead: the one that Sam had seen on the hillside.

"No!" Kate screamed. "This animal is my responsibility and therefore you have no right!"

Bob smirked and nudged Larry, who immediately stepped forward. "Kate, I want you to stand down, now, that's an order, and let these men get on with their very essential and important job. It may not be what we want, but..."

"You monster! You call yourself a protector of wildlife, and here you..."

Larry grabbed her hand and pulled her away just enough for Oxnard to step forward and fire point blank into the side of the cow's head, splattering brain matter everywhere. The creature lurched crazily and fell over at Kate's feet, its tongue protruding and an incredible quantity of blood gushing out. And there, exposed now and pressed tightly against the guard rail, its nose buried beneath its tail as if hiding in tall grass, was a pure white buffalo calf, shivering from fear.

A hush settled over the mob. A hunch-backed tribal elder woman was the first to move, creeping slowly towards the calf in a posture of reverential awe. "The sign we have been waiting for," she whispered loudly.

"But is it the end, or the beginning?" asked a teenage native girl.

She clenched her fists and stood with her back to the calf. "No one will hurt our sacred little brother!"

"Form a circle, quickly!" the elder woman commanded. "And join hands, shoulder to shoulder."

The cowboys regrouped and pressed forward, each trying to get a shot.

Kate threw herself at the now-porous circle in an effort to lay across the calf, but at this the animal lurched to its feet, dodged first to the left, then to the right, then turned and with a bleat and a fart, launched itself up to the railing and would have gone over to its certain death, but Sam, watching from the side and tremendously admiring Kate's determination and exotic beauty, pushed a cowboy aside, grabbed the calf at the top of the railing, teetering there for a moment's fateful eternity, one foot on the cement, the other raising up now to try and stay this side of doom, the realization of his folly spreading across his astonished face—when a looping cast of rope circled out from behind and over the mob and caught him around the shoulders and the waist of the calf all in one expertly thrown lasso, cinching tight and levering against the railing as the two of them pitched out, then swung ten then twenty feet below the bridge roadway, where they pendulumed safely if not for the desperate scraping for traction as BJ was pulled forward until he found his footing with his boots caught up against the curb. Sam let out an inarticulate howl of pain, the calf gasping for air, face-up with his own, the two of them staring wide-eyed at the bridge understructure with Kate leaning forward to stare back.

"Are you ok?"

"For shits-sakes, no!"

"Hold on there, Sam. I gotcha," BJ yelled.

"But what the fuck!" one of the cowboys said, drawing a knife to cut the rope.

The native with the knotted ponytail placed one hand on the rope, his other on BJ's shoulder. "We'll pull, together."

They threw themselves into the rescue, but when Kate dropped her papers to help pull, one older native with a scar across this cheek shouldered her out of the way, saying: "We don't need a white man's whore to save our sacred calf."

"What we need to do is work together!" she said, pushing back and pulling on the rope.

Sam and the calf were soon back up over the railing and onto the asphalt. Off to the Gardiner side of the bridge, a crowd of pilgrims from the bus along with a group of high school kids coming out to express their horror at the slaughter.

Larry, trembling and ashen faced, sidled over to stand between the trigger-twitchy cowboys and the calf. "Maybe we'll just take a moment to reconsider what comes next, ok boys?"

The minister from the bus, a bearded, large-girthed Southern Baptist—Reverend Jones—parted the crowd and confronted Sam laying on the ground with the calf in his arms. "Heathen! False gods!" he bellowed, pointing an accusing finger. "Worshiping a golden calf was the one heretical thing that brought down the wrath of god! Be warned! The end is near; signs and portents are at hand! You must reject this false god and turn to the one, true path. Do you hear me? All of you! Damnation and hell-fire!"

His legion of pilgrims, the women dressed in long skirts, the men a plainer side of Amish, all of them humorless, stern, and totally without sympathy for Sam's deep rope burns, broke into song, one particularly sturdy woman catching Oxnard's eye and holding his transfixed gaze.

The cowboys snorted in disgust and headed off in search of easier prey. Sam eased out of the lasso and nudged the calf over to Kate.

"You were very brave to do that," she said.

"More like a damn fool," he said. She looked even better close up, Sam thought, admiring her contrasts: the dazzling white of her smile against rich, smooth skin; her slim figure masking obvious strength. Neither of them said anything for a moment, the two of them scratching the calf and soothing its terrified attitude. "This little heifer's all yours."

"Right." She removed her belt and made a loop to lead the calf away. Sam watched her go, those tight Lady Wranglers not missing the belt one bit. "BJ, I want to thank you."

"Aw, it was nothing. Just a bit of lasso practice was all."

BJ followed Sam's gaze, the pure infatuation unmistakable in Sam's eyes.

"Well you know," Sam said slowly, "I'm just about done here. If you don't mind cashing me out, I think I'll forage my way back home."

BJ laughed, re-coiling his rope. "I believe you've already done your time in the Marines. You can do whatever you damn well please."

4

The Chiefs sat on folding chairs inside the relative comfort of a 1,000-square-foot, wire-taut Naugahyde tent, with a great fire in the middle, the snow falling more steadily as the day turned into an arctic-cold evening. They smoked quietly and patiently, waiting for Crazy Wolf to speak, while their sons and daughters sprawled on the ground on the outside of the circle, exhausted and bloodied from the carnage on the bridge.

"What is the future?"

"Tell us Crazy Wolf!"

"You have been to the grave."

"Beyond the night."

"And your power comes from all things."

"Where are you leading the nations?"

"Speak to us!"

The words and whispers stopped, and Crazy Wolf, a Cheyenne Suhtai of the warrior Fox society, faced west out the tent to the lengthening shadows over the Montana wilderness. Stocky, a bit bowlegged, his face deeply lined and acne scarred, he was younger than most of the chiefs by a full generation, but revered by all as wiser than seven generations.

"Garbage," he said after a while. "The future is garbage."

The assembly of chiefs and elders from across the High Plains, Rocky Mountains, and Columbia Plateau groaned as if gut-punched.

"Garbage," his father, Chief Standing Elk said. "What the hell do you mean by that?"

"He means to sign here," the Chicago representative for Landfill Management Industries said, holding out a contract and a pen. Dressed for Vegas, where he hoped to head on the very next available first-class flight out of the Bozeman airport, Tino Gugliardi shivered in his lizard-skin loafers and oil-derived polyester shirt and pants. "I didn't pay for this tipi to fight skin cancer."

The tent was normally reserved for NASCAR and professional golf corporate sponsorship events, but due to the size and scope of the commission that Tino expected to receive from the so-called Indian Nations Land Use Enhancement Project—a network of cut-and-fill dump sites on reservation lands bordering dozens of booming Western population centers—he had personally paid for the tent to be boxed, shipped, and pitched on the edge of Yellowstone Park for the express purpose of motivating a quick sign-off.

Crazy Wolf shook his head, shifting his knotted long black ponytail over his shoulder. The buffalo slaughter by white hunters bent on total and absolute genocide evoked feelings that were more fundamental than emotions: a pure hatred laced with the deepest disgust. The slaughter was an affront, an insult, a blood challenge. But competing with his strong desire for revenge was an aching longing to go home to his wife, Laura. Their boy would soon be five years old, and the long period of sacred abstinence between Crazy Wolf and his wife would be over. The chiefs knew this, and that was a large part of their respect; that a man would turn his physical power inward, in order to provide power to his child, and a stronger vision for the tribe.

"Nothing lives forever," he sang to himself, recounting the warrior song when facing certain death in battle, "except the rocks." He thought of the Buffalo Family Ceremony that he had pledged with his wife when their son was born, a ceremony that was manifested by his deep ancestors, the earliest Suhtai. The buffalo were sacred animals, essential to the Cheyenne. The animals had provided everything his people needed for survival: the destruction of the great herds had broken their living link to the earth, and soon after came the end of the old ways and a descent into the basest sort of concentration-camp existence on the reservation. The pain and shame of that experience was carried in the heart of every person who had native blood. Crazy Wolf felt his thoughts coalesce around this desperate, sad reality, and how the Ceremony, with its celebration of the bull, cow, and Yellow Calf, led to a new sense of harmony.

He shook his head again and turned back to the chiefs.

"The hoop turns between day and night. We go to the mountains for dreams, but it is in the valleys that we make our lives. Indians have land. Not enough and not what we had before they came. But we have some and that is our strength."

"We should press for subsidies," the Gros Ventre chief, Eagle Beak, said. "Our people need food and housing, not vision quest dreams!"

"Don't talk like a ration Indian. Listen to my son's proposal," Standing Elk said.

"Who you calling a ration Indian? I take offense!" Eagle Beak said, reaching for a knife.

"The one asking for subsidies—for rations! And don't act like you are going to stab me, your belt is empty."

"Sit down you old redskin farts," Yellow Thunder, the Nez Perce chief complained. "I can't see."

"Garbage is what *they* do best," Crazy Wolf said. "This proposal allows us to set aside a corner of our land, a fragment, and charge enough to send every child to language school. Reclaim our stories. Not as *they* say it, but the way of our ancestors, before *they* came. Their time is drawing to a close. Nothing can save them. I have seen it. We must be ready. You have chosen me to lead and now I will lead."

And with that he set pen to paper, just as a tremor ran through the structure. A sound like thunder backed against the late afternoon calm.

"Earthquake!" the Crow chief, Steven Silver Bear cried.

"Armageddon!" the Wanapam elder, Coyote Jim shouted.

"The end-time!" Yellow Thunder said.

Crazy Wolf closed his eyes and dropped the pen, arms slowly rising to embrace the world beyond the horizon. "They come!"

Tino leaned forward to sputter right into Crazy Wolf's ear.

"Don't pull that visionary shit on me! We got a verbal! You promised that once you signed, all the others would fall in line. This has to happen, today!"

The chiefs were on their feet.

"What do you see?" Chief Goes in Front, of the Peigan-Blackfoot asked.

"Ai-yee! The earth, it is shaking!" Victor Many Horses, of the Flathead tribe cried.

Crazy Wolf opened his eyes, unblinking and seeing nothing, and everything.

"Our brothers flee their prison. They seek sweet grass and fresh waters in a new land beyond the Whites. This is the start of the new time! If we stand with them, we shall be saved!"

And with that he stripped off his plaid flannel shirt, revealing a hand-painted Ghost Dance design canvas tunic underneath. The sons and daughters of all the chiefs stood, peeling off clothes to reveal their own similarly painted Ghost Dance shirts.

Crazy Wolf raised a fist high over his head. "We must save our buffalo brothers!"

"What about your garbage?" Steven Silver Bear said, the derision in his voice barely disguised. "Here the Whites bring us buffalo meat, and you want to put an end to that, but have them bring their garbage to bury on sacred lands. Is that the new way of the Cheyenne?"

Chief Standing Elk jumped to his feet, squaring his broad shoulders and turning a sharp nose to the Crow chief. "Take care of your words, Silver Bear. The *Votostataneo* are a singled-out people, and we do not take kindly to a Custer-lover questioning our honor!"

Steven Silver Bear laughed and blew a cloud of smoke in Standing Elk's direction. "You, the Gros Ventre, the Peigan Blackfeet, Nez Perce— everyone around this council is a singled-out people. Soon, we will all be standing on one another's shoulders, with our feet in garbage."

No one spoke as Crazy Wolf walked slowly around the circle to stand in front of the Crow chief. Steven's son, the scar-faced Medicine Dog, eased over to stand by his father's side, his hand resting on the bone handle of the knife he carried in a beaded sheath at his waist. Crazy Wolf lowered himself to a half-kneeling position, directly opposite Steven's face. "The first thing that unites us as Natives, is our tie with the earth, our mother. All our power comes from the earth. The second thing is our stories, how we know them and pass them on to our children, in the true language of our ancestors. The sacred buffalo is our link to the earth; we need schools and special tools to keep our languages alive. Both of these are possible; both are within our reach. But if we turn our back on the buffalo, or allow our languages to be lost, we will have nothing." He raised himself back up to full standing and held his arms out as though embracing the light of the roaring campfire. "This is a time of crisis! Our mother cries out in despair, rejecting her children with warming seas and skies. The Whites are lost, they are like the lemming that over uses the grasses of its own pasture, then runs with all its family into the ocean. And we are lost with them unless we lead the way to a new salvation. We are at war with an enemy that is everywhere, even within our holy circle. We must not allow the bond to be broken or our stories to disappear into the fouled air, never to be reclaimed. Tomorrow, when our father the Sun rises, we too shall arise. I see a great battle. We must call on our buffalo brothers to lead us to victory, into a future where the Indian way is restored, and our dead live again!"

By now, the younger natives had all stood and moved closer to the fire, the elders leaning forward, listening to Crazy Wolf's every word.

"Ha-ho," Standing Elk murmured, nodding his head. And each in turn around the circle nodded and murmured in agreement, while Crazy Wolf slowly lowered himself to a cross-legged position, staring into the fire and hearing an ancient herd of buffalo stampede through his mind.

5

The snow fell all night, cleansing the blood-stained ground and creating a white canvas upon which creatures large and small could paint the tracks of the new day. The morning broke clear and desperately cold, and Sam tossed fitfully in a too-thin sleeping bag, not sinking into the darker sleep where his usual nightmares flourished. He had made a rough little camp just down from the Gardiner Bridge on the Park side of the Yellowstone River, the first stop on an unclear route home. He'd been honest with BJ about his plan to forage his way back to Nevada. There wasn't much to go back to so he was in no rush; he might just lie here all day and wait for spring to roll around. His muscles were extremely stiff from the general thrashing he had received the day before, and the rope burns and cold steel of the rifle he held at his side numbed his hip and knee. He mind drifted back to the bridge, how that amazing girl had stood up to the mob and smiled back at him when he handed over the calf. But his first impression was a baptism of warm, wet kisses, until he awoke with a start, quickly brought the rifle to a firing position and saw that the white buffalo calf was licking the dried sweat from his face and neck.

"Go on now, get outta here!" He placed the end of the rifle barrel on the calf's forehead and tried to push it away, but it came right back, its dark brown eyes staring at him from beneath the longest imaginable eyelashes with an expression of playful curiosity and unconditional love.

"*Wohpe!* C'mere sweetie! Where are you?"

Sam rolled over to see the very same young woman from the bridge creeping through the sage in untied hiking boots with no socks, bare legs, and a saddle blanket over her shoulders that barely reached to her hips. He knew she was flesh-and-blood real, but in his injured and needing frame of mind, she seemed every bit an angel.

"Mornin'."

"Oh! It's just you," she said, standing up straight and pulling the blanket more tightly over her body, which had the effect of revealing her curves and sinuous length to an even greater degree. "You're not going to shoot that calf, are you?"

"No, she and I are buddies. But you can call me Sam if you want."

She looked away, pretending not to be interested. "Good morning then, Sam."

"Just gettin' to know my new gal," he said, setting the rifle beside a ten-pack box of bullets and scratching the calf's moist pink nose. "What's that you called her, 'Whoopi'?"

"No, it's *Wohpe,* Lakota for 'Goddess of Peace,'" Kate said, not coming any closer, but not stepping away either. "She grew up to become the White Buffalo Calf Woman, but I'm sure you knew that already."

"Oh yeah, all up here," he said, tapping his head. "But what'd you say your name was?"

She turned back to Sam, looking him up and down with all the subtlety of a cattle buyer. "I didn't." She seemed to like what she saw and made a slight move in his direction. "But it's Katherine."

Sam couldn't help but be flattered by her attention. "Well, OK then, Kate." They were quiet for a moment, Sam feeling proud that he had survived this small round of conversation. It had been a long time since he had engaged in even a hint of flirtation.

"You see any of the others?" she asked.

"Which others?"

"The bison herd. I was hoping some escaped. I made camp up there in those trees and figured they might have bedded down nearby."

"Not likely. Pretty efficient buffalo-killing machine yesterday."

"That's what your government does best." She stood there for a moment, looking around as if a bison might stumble out from beneath a sage bush. Sam rolled back the other way and winced from pain. "You ok?" she asked, taking a few steps towards him.

"Yeah; well no, not actually. The rope cut me pretty bad."

"Let's see." Now she came over and squatted down beside him, unzipping his sleeping bag and unashamedly running her hands over the welts on his chest and shoulders. "You with those Nevada boys?"

"Was," he replied, "but I'm done now." Her gentle touch was electrifying, and the sight of her up close—bright eyes and smile against that earth-brown skin—was mesmerizing. She had seemed so shy at first, but now Sam had the feeling that she was in complete control and he only needed to respond.

Her hand settled on his necklace. "What's this?"

He slapped his hand over hers and tried to move it away. "Nothing."

"No, c'mon, tell me." She was surprisingly strong and succeeded in pulling her hand up against his t-shirt, exposing the bullet and dog tags. She leaned closer to read the name on one of the tags. "Heydon Jones. I thought you said your name was Sam?"

"It is. Heydon was, well, he was a close friend."

"Was?" She let the necklace drop back onto his chest, slowly passing her hand over his collarbone and shoulders, feigning disappointment. "What, are you telling me you're gay?"

Sam linked his fingers, resting his head on his hands. "Not hardly. He was a war buddy."

"Oh, so you're some kind of vet?"

"Yeah. You ok with that?"

Now she took up the bullet and examined it closely. "I'm not sure I'm ok with this being live ammo."

"Well, you never know."

"Know what?"

"When you might need it."

She looked at him for a long time, holding his eyes with her own. There was a lot to like about this Sam, she thought: good looks, great body, but most of all, his eyes: a blueness that was deep enough to dive into. She had learned from studying wolf packs in the wild that staring was serious business, signaling mating attraction or a mortal attack. There could only be one leader of the pack, typically a dominant male that used his solitary strength to savage the others into submission, but occasionally it was a female who assumed total control through a combination of vicious wile and sexual favors, cultivating a subservient sub-group that kept even the largest male at bay. It impressed her that Sam met her stare. She could feel his vulnerability and desire, inviting her in at the same time as maintaining restraint from forcing himself upon her. It made for a powerful attraction; something she could work with. He looked away, then back, and she could tell that he was injured, and not just from the rope burns. "C'mon," she said, "I know what you need. Follow me."

She stood and jogged down towards the river. Sam pulled on his jeans, boots, and a wool vest, tucked the rifle and bullets into the sleeping bag, and with the calf at his heels, followed her down the slope to the banks of the Yellowstone River, where a hot springs poured out of the ground into a waist-deep pool bounded by a wall of boulders. Just beyond the boulders, the river flowed swiftly into a series of impassable whirlpools and rapids.

"Mineral water will do you good," she said, dropping the blanket and stepping naked into the steaming water, her body quickly obscured by the swirling mists. She immersed to a neck depth, treading lightly.

Oh yeah, it'll do me good, he thought eagerly. He tore off his clothes and followed her in, the necklace still around his neck. He crouched down to a depth where his body was submerged up to his neck and moved slowly over the smooth stones, feeling the warmth return to his muscles. The steam above the water was so thick he could barely see Kate moving on the far side of the pool. They circled around, keeping their distance. The calf bawled and pawed the frozen ground.

"That was a brave thing you did yesterday. I'm sure your white buffalo calf girlfriend is very grateful."

"More foolish than brave, but I guess there's not much difference."

Kate moved towards Sam, her eyes fixed on his. "You're not like the others, are you?"

"What do you mean?" The sun rose higher and with it the steam, intensifying in the relative humidity. He briefly lost her in the mist.

"A hunter, but not bloodthirsty. Like a wolf: selective."

Sam turned at the sound of a helicopter moving into, then out of, range. "Hear that?"

"Sure, a chopper, but probably ten miles away."

"I love that sound. Used to mean that reinforcements were on the way. *Hadji* didn't have no choppers."

She appeared out of the mist, moving slowly. She held her hands just above the water, palms faced to him. "And a *hadji* is?"

He brought his palms against hers, intertwining their fingers. "A hostile. The enemy."

He felt her loosen her grip and ease backwards.

"I wish you wouldn't say that."

"Hey, it's just a word."

"It's derogatory." She treaded away from him back into the mists. He followed slowly, then lost her. "It's real, at least over there."

"It's real here. I know all about being from a different background and lumped together in one convenient slur."

Now he saw her. He treaded closer, their eyes locked again.

"What are you anyway?" he said, breathing, blowing bubbles, then breathing again, "if you don't mind me asking."

"Sioux. Lakota. You know anything about the *Oceti Sakowin,* the Seven Council Fires?"

"Not a thing. But if that's what you are, I'm in."

She seemed to make up her mind about something and came right up to Sam, wrapping her legs around his waist and embracing his neck. "There was a time when the Sioux were about as hadji as they come." She bit him on the shoulder, not just a love bite, but hard enough that it seemed to Sam sure to draw blood.

"Jeezus! That hurt!" He tried to push her away, but she held on more tightly.

"Pain is good. The Sioux know all about pain. But I know about pleasure too." She released her legs from around his waist and lowered her head to go underwater, but Sam was afraid of getting bit down there. He pulled her up by her hair and she squirted water in his face, her hands pinching, fondling, squeezing. He drew her towards him, wrapping her in his arms and feeling her embrace him in return, when she suddenly pushed away with a scream and Sam turned to see five or six huge, dark animal figures emerge from the mist and move along the shore, with an equal number of long-haired men and a few women following the buffalo downriver on foot and horseback, then stopping to confront Sam and Kate.

"Look what we have here!" Medicine Dog said, riding a beautiful paint horse. "The mixed-breed whore and her white buffalo-killer."

Sam made a move to attack, but Medicine Dog pulled out his bone handled knife. Kate held Sam's arm.

"Don't be a fool," she said, then turned and spat at Medicine Dog. "Mixed breed yourself. I'm pure Lakota, but I don't suppose you ever even knew your father."

Medicine Dog laughed, appreciating Kate's spirit. "Ho! But he knew your mother. Come here and wash my feet, little sister!"

Sam inadvertently looked over at the sleeping bag, measuring the time and distance it would take for him to retrieve his rifle. Medicine Dog saw Sam's intent expression and in one swift move slid off his horse and pulled the rifle and box of shells from the bag. "Ha! I saw you with this yesterday and I wondered where you had it hiding." He fumbled with the safety switch and accidentally pulled the trigger, blasting a column of water right next to Sam. "Ho! Big recoil! What sort of cannon is this anyway?" He pulled back the bolt and the casing was automatically ejected. "Only one shot at a time? Now that's a bullshit gun!" He took one of the remaining nine bullets from the box and loaded it in the chamber.

"You want some help?" John Wilson asked, riding up on a Yamaha dirt bike.

"A Crow doesn't need help from a Paiute, especially one who travels on the war path with his mama."

Yura, the Indian elder woman, hobbled over to Medicine Dog. "John Wilson is my nephew. And we must go. You've frightened our brothers, and they're on the move."

"You go, old woman. I have a prisoner to take."

"Prisoner!" Joseph White Bird said. "Don't be crazy."

"Just what I would expect from a Nez Perce," Medicine Dog said. "It takes a Crow to put the White man in his place! We never miss the chance for a scalp." He aimed just over Sam's head, fired, ejected the shell, and reloaded. "This all the bullets you got, White man? But I only need one to blow you away!" He fired again just over Sam's head, reloaded, then vaulted back onto his horse and jammed the rifle and remaining six bullets beneath the blanket tied onto the back of his saddle. He took a leather thong from his pocket and tossed it to John Wilson. "Here, wade out there and give this to the whore, to tie up her boyfriend. Unless he wants to come out and get turned into a steer right here on this beach."

Several more buffalo came down the shoreline with Crazy Wolf on a horse following closely behind. "What's going on?" he demanded. "Who's shooting? Why aren't we moving?"

Shining Shirt skipped a flat rock across the river. "Medicine Dog wants to make up for burying his balls at Little Big Horn."

"Hey, stick it, Flathead!"

"Let's see you try."

"Stop it!" Crazy Wolf said. Then to Medicine Dog: "What's the meaning of this?"

"This is none of your business, that's what meaning it is. The white man is my prisoner. I'm going to tie his ass up and bring him along."

"I'm the one who's tying him up," John Wilson said. "That makes him my prisoner."

"You just do what I told you and hurry it up! He's *my* prisoner!"

John went out to Sam and grabbed his wrist. "This'll just take a second."

"You can all kiss my white ass!" Sam said, putting his hand on John's head and pushing him underwater, then let go and thrashed angrily towards shore. "You got that straight, chief?"

Several of the natives moved forward to stand with Medicine Dog. They all had their knives out now.

"Yeah," Two Suns said, "your ass is definitely white."

Sam stood there, not believing this was really happening to him. He looked back across the river: there was still some ice on the exposed boulders in the center, with a series of deep whirlpools twirling down the eddy lines. The river would be freezing cold and treacherous, almost certain death.

Crazy Wolf nudged his horse to Medicine Dog's side and leaned down to speak to him. "Why do you insist on doing this? The sacred buffalo are our business." He gestured towards Sam. "Not this *vo'estane.*"

"Because I feel like it," Medicine Dog said, "that's why. Because it amuses me."

"In other words, the same reason a dog licks its butt," Two Suns said, "because he can."

"Ha! Big tough Blackfeet! We stole your horses for a hundred years!"

"While we took your scalps and women."

"Ho, you want a piece of this?"

Crazy Wolf's horse wheeled around, confused as to why they were not staying with the buffalo. But Crazy Wolf knew that this was no simple matter. Custom allowed Medicine Dog to do as he would, and if Crazy Wolf insisted that he come along without his prisoner, it was possible that Medicine Dog would feel pushed into a corner, reject the group out of hand, ally himself with the police, and turn around in pursuit of the band. And it was not just Medicine Dog: under the right circumstances, any one of the group might do the same. "Well then let's get on with it," he said without any enthusiasm.

John Wilson looked more warily at Sam. He reached around Sam to hand the ties to Kate, who had stayed submerged up to her neck. "Sorry man, but if I was you, I'd let her tie this on." He noticed Sam staring out at the river and down into the rapids. "Unless you're Aquaman and can swim like a fish. Me? I'd drown, and I'm a pretty good swimmer."

"He's right," Kate said, turning Sam to face her and reaching for his wrists. "It'll probably only be for a short time. That guy's just trying to save face."

"No offense, but that guy's a *hadji*."

Kate tied the thong loosely around Sam's wrists, his hands out front of his body, and turned him back to John. John cinched the ties tight, noticing a skull and lightning bolt tattoo on Sam's shoulder.

"Nice tatt. What are you, some kind of gangbanger?"

"It's for my Marine sniper unit," Sam said. "We shot terrorists like you every day of the week." He tapped John on the forehead. "Right through the head!"

John led Sam on shore and helped him slip into his jeans and shoes. Kate hesitated, still submerged in the warm water. "All of you turn around. I'm coming out now."

"Why? Why should we turn our eyes?" Medicine Dog said.

"Because we are the sons of chiefs!" Crazy Wolf shouted. "We will be chiefs! Yura, help her out of the water."

Yura gathered up Kate's clothes and stood at the edge of the river. Everyone turned except for Little Bull and Medicine Dog. "What are you looking at?" Little Bull said.

Medicine Dog hesitated then turned as if he needed to sharpen his knife on a stone.

Kate quickly came out of the water and took her clothes from Yura.

"There is no shame in being who you are, my daughter. Shame only comes from living a lie."

"I am not ashamed!" Kate said. "Now leave me alone grandmother. I have this *tatanka* to care for." She went to the buffalo calf and set to examining its ears.

"*Tatanaka*," Yura repeated quietly to herself, nodding and watching Kate with a look of sympathy and sadness.

"I told my boss I was going to take some time off," Sam said to Kate, his back to Medicine Dog. "No one's going to miss me for at least a week."

"By then we'll have figured something out. You can count on these guys not working together. There'll be plenty of chances to escape."

"You think? I really don't like the looks of this."

Medicine Dog came over and tossed a rope over Sam's head, jerking it tight. "Let's go white boy, before I drag your face through buffalo shit."

And with that, the group began to move downriver, the mist hanging over the water and up the shore, twelve buffalo scuffing slowly through the brush, the white buffalo calf skipping at Kate's heel.

"Allow me to refresh your memory," Bob Smith said, leaning back in his full grain cowhide leather chair as the hammer spike came down hard on the forehead of a body-trussed steer behind him in the Smith Brothers Meat Packing slaughterhouse. The steer was dead on impact, then hooked, lifted, and conveyored away to be skinned, gutted, filleted, and plastic wrapped for the international market. "We had the English mad cow scare three years ago, the Canadian beef brou-haha just before that, and the Japanese ban right on the edge of the French embargo. Granted, they were orchestrated out of this-here office, and each one made me a fortune, but do you have any idea what those sons-a-bitches would do to get even, if they had half the chance? It'd be fearful—a massacre!"

Lieutenant Walker watched the slaughter with eager interest, leaning forward and ghoulishly giggling each time a cow was spiked, whereas Chief Veterinarian Larry Donohue covered his eyes and squirmed uncomfortably. BJ nodded back at Bob Smith but said nothing, his mind focused on the three empty shell casings in his pocket. After a long night trying to sleep in the Gardiner Hi-Ho Motel, he had arisen before dawn to drive down to the head of Yankee Jim Canyon on the Yellowstone, to try a bit of nymph fishing. While thrashing through the willows he came across a jumbled set of tracks heading downstream. He surmised they could have only come from a remnant group of buffalo that had survived the previous day's mayhem. BJ followed the tracks to a small clearing above a hot springs, where he found a few scattered items of clothing—a jacket, t-shirt, other odds and ends—that he immediately recognized as Sam's.

But most disturbing, half buried in the mud amidst a trampling set of horse and human footprints, were these 7mm shell casings, obviously recently fired, and uncharacteristically left without any intent of recharging. BJ knew Sam well enough by now to know that the kid simply wouldn't do that unless something was seriously amiss.

Another cow was elevated and spiked as Duke came into the office with a thick file and laid a handful of digital images on Bob's desk.

"Facts, in my experience, are for the most part nothing but BS," Bob said. "The meat business, no different than the flower, perfume, health food, organic, and whatever else high-end market, is all about perception. And if the perception is that eating a steak is going to cause you to foam at the mouth and your children to die screaming, then no amount of facts are going to prevent you from switching over to mac and cheese. Know what I'm saying?"

Walker and Donohue grunted and nodded their assent as Bob spread the pictures out. He picked one up and held it high.

"Which is why when I see that a baker's dozen of these black-plagued locusts busted out of the Park and are probably fornicating with my cattle even as we sit here on our sorry asses talking about it, knowing that some French speaking candy ass is going make dog food out of my hard-earned business, I get really pissed off!"

The grunting became sworn assertions; the nodding positively vigorous. BJ got up and went over to a side table that had a thermos of hot coffee. He poured a cup and stared at the chorus of bobbing heads, while cow after cow was spiked and gutted just beyond. He recalled that his first instinct was to call in the location and general direction of the buffalo the moment he saw the tracks. But as chance would have it, he'd left his walkie-talkie in the truck. And once he found those shell casings, a familiar if long-forgotten emotion had overtaken his sense of responsibility: to place his loyalty in a fellow soldier rather than to the outcome of an improbable mission. He leaned against the table, sipping his coffee and trying now to remember the details of another thing that had always seemed curious about Sam: the necklace with the bullet and dog tags that the kid tried to keep hidden. Why two tags, and why a charged and tipped bullet?

"So, tell me what we know about these guys," Bob asked. "Are they as bad as I think?"

"They're basically what we call eco-terrorists," Lieutenant Walker said. "The kind of folks who blow up dams and expect everyone to go back to living in caves. They sure don't care about bringing the black death to your cows."

"Easy does it on the black death, Lieutenant. Bad enough we're tagged with brucellosis."

"Let me put it to you another way," Larry Donohue said. "I look at these first-nation, indigenous peoples…"

"Hold on! You mean, when I walk up to a card-carrying, cigar store American Indian, I need to address him as: 'So what kind of first-nation, indigenous person are you?'"

"Correct, unless you know their particular tribal association. In any case, my premise is that they are subject to hereditary and environmental influences that have caused them to misunderstand the consequences of their misguided actions."

"Oh, I get it," Bob said, "like when I came home with bad grades and told my folks it was either because I had inherited their stupidity, or because Joey Wallace sat behind me and made farting noises with his armpit. Yeah, my dad had a stick with my name on it whenever I tried that argument." He turned and nodded to Duke, who removed a sheaf of papers from the file. "Now that we've heard from the government, fill us in on what private industry was able to find out."

"Well now," Duke said, "our detective did some work on the internet, made a few calls, and it seems like we got an alphabet soup of shit kickers and pot stirrers on our hands. I'll save the best for last, but the first thing we got to understand is that they care a lot more for these buffalo critters than just as a commissary for all their provisions. I mean, you think it'd be enough to get moccasins, robes, meat cuts of every kind, medicine, fish hooks, string, air bags from their intestines and gim-crack pouches from their scrotums; but no, they got to make them out to be some sort of god or such, their blessed link to the dirty old earth. I come from a ranching family, and if anyone ever told me that the cow-calf pairs were anything other than a couple of hundred dollar bills on the hoof, I'd a told them..."

"Just the detective report if you don't mind, Duke. That's all I paid for," Bob said.

"Right. Says here there's an old lady from some tiny, forgotten tribe on the banks of the Columbia. And get this: she's a dreamer. Connects directly to the buffalo through dream vision. Can you imagine such bullshit? Then there's a Flathead, a Blackfeet, Gros Ventre tough cookie, a Nez Perce. Don't know how they could all be together, they were always at one another's scalps in the past. And then one genuine pain in the ass: goes by the handle Medicine Dog; your basic genocidal maniac in a head dress. A Crow, straight line descendent to Custer's favorite scout, so you know that gets him extra respect with the native die-hards. But here this is interesting: he's related through an aunt to a family that was wiped out at Wounded Knee, so he has the worst of both worlds: Indian guilt, and Indian righteous wrath. Which leads me to Crazy Wolf, a real Cheyenne shit-kicker. Raised on the rez up at Lame Deer; the usual high school dropout gang-banger run-ins with the law, mainly harassing other tribes in about four states, stealing their cars and such, no doubt stole Medicine

Dog's crappy little Mustang. Says here there was a price on his head with just about every tribal gang in Montana, the Dakotas, Wyoming, Idaho. Then he went kind of silent for a couple of years."

"Probably ran off with his tail between his legs," Walker smirked.

"Not quite. He showed up in the Army, right after 9-11; Ranger school, got pulled into some super-select 75th Rangers Regimental Recon Detachment."

"No way! Not the 75th! Do you know how tough they are?" Walker said.

"We surely don't," Bob said. "Get on with it, Duke."

"All sorts of hi-tech, secret shit," Duke said. "Got credit for nailing some of the Al-Qaeda big-wigs, saved some buddies in a big-ass firefight up in the Afghani mountains. Nominated for a Medal of Honor, but I guess they already had an Indian that year, so he walked away with the Distinguished Service Cross." That hung there in the room for a moment.

"You got any Distinguished Crosses, Lieutenant?" BJ asked Jack Walker, who was busy fidgeting with a shirt button. BJ shook his head and turned away, trying hard to remember the significance of wearing more than one dog tag on the same chain. Then it came to him: the tragic Vietnam experience of a crazed loner, Miles Curtis, who had transferred into the unit after surviving the siege of Khe Sanh. Miles had carried the tags of four fallen buddies through three subsequent tours of duty, fighting like a maniacal one man army, dangerously without fear and causing everyone else in the platoon—BJ included—to keep their distance. A couple of years later, BJ learned at a Marine reunion down in Vegas that Miles had come home, holed up in a Detroit slum apartment, and shot himself.

BJ realized that one of the tags had to be Sam's, and the other must have been from a fallen close friend. He'd heard Sam vaguely refer to a couple of terrible incidents he'd been involved in while in Iraq. He knew that Sam had been physically wounded, but BJ also knew from his own

Vietnam experience that emotional battle scars went much deeper and caused the most serious damage.

"So he musters out about five years ago, a bona-fide war hero, although no one gives a shit. Not a mention of him anywhere until *wham-o!* He pops up as kind of a junior chief at the big Cheyenne Pow-Wow. Gives a speech, heads up a couple of ceremonies. Says here he had a vision off at their sacred mountain in Sturgis. Doesn't say if he was on a Harley."

They had a nervous laugh, joshing one another about the big Harley riders gathering that takes place every year in that rowdy town at the base of Bear Butte, the sacred mountain of the Cheyenne and many other tribes.

"And then he got everyone going on a return to the old ways," Duke continued. "Kind of a prophet. Oh yeah, he's got a wife and kid, and now get this: he's taken a vow of chastity for five years."

"Well there you have it!" Larry said, slapping his knee. "I haven't been laid in half that time, and no wonder he's on the war path!"

The others looked at him. Larry blushed.

"We're all glad to know that, Larry." Bob cleared his throat and took the papers from Duke. "Seems to me we got the real deal on our hands: a gang leader with tactical military skills and a group of followers who can use dreamer-radar to out fox our every move. I don't know how to factor in the chastity angle, but it makes me think he's not the kind of guy we can go to a strip bar with and cut a deal over a beer. Plus, if he pulls in the family kin from all his tribal hangers-on we'll have a regular Little Big Horn on our hands. So, let's all agree to keep this out of the papers. Last thing we need is for these redskins to come together as a grassroots force, with Crazy Wolf as a martyr hero. So how 'bout we expend some tax dollars to round up these magic bison and put an end to the madness before it begins. Are you with me on this?"

Walker tugged his watch cap down tight on his head. "My crew's gassed and ready to fly!"

"And we have top people—top!—working on the situation!" Larry said.

"Gentlemen, I am so reassured," Bob said. He leaned forward. "And where exactly are you going to fly?" he asked Walker. And to Larry: "Tell me again what your top bureaucrats are working on—no need for facts; just a general flavor of what they're doing?"

Walker cleared his throat. "Well, you know, scanning missions, concentric circles, fan out and find them, bring 'em to justice."

"Really! That warms my heart, thinking of you flying circles over all of Yellowstone and Montana. That might take, what, two, three months to locate them?"

Walker stared down at his feet. Bob turned his attention to Larry, who squirmed like he had a tick on his butt.

"We're taking more of a scientific approach, mapping and reviewing the historical record of where other bison might have gone in the past."

"Like, how long in the past?"

"Oh, past two or three hundred years, based on foraging data, tree rings, seed electron microscopy."

"Seed what?"

"From old stool samples. You know, buffalo poop."

Bob just stared at him, then at Walker, then he laughed out loud, as the hammer came down and another steer was hoisted up with a bright red splash of blood spattered onto the window. "It takes my breath away!" Bob said, pushing a button on his desk, which alerted a dark young worker to quickly come and wipe the window clean. "To think of the genius assembled right here at Smith Brothers Packing!"

The bullet was meant for Sam, BJ realized with a jolt, that's why he used a single shot rifle, and why he carried the bullet around his neck at all times. The Iraq War was still being fought, right inside Sam's head, with the dog tags a constant reminder of the high stakes, and the live ammo available to put an end to the pain if the trauma became too great. If indeed he had come into some sort of trouble out there on the banks of the Yellowstone, there was no telling how he might respond. If his internal trauma turned outwards, god help anyone who got in the way. But if something snapped and he turned inwards, the results could be self-destructive in the extreme. The key was to get to him before it happened.

"You been kind of quiet, boss," Bob said, turning to BJ. "You got any idea where those buff might be headed?"

Everyone in the room turned to him. BJ looked back, his mind made up, and shrugged. "Could be just about anywhere, couldn't they?"

Bob jumped up, enraged, and swept the digital photos off his desk onto their feet. "Get them! All of you! Are you waiting to be hooked and hung up on the line along with the rest of these brainless animals? Or do you expect me to be the one who's hung out and gutted? And believe you me, my competitors would like nothing more than to see my head shrink wrapped and stuck on a spike over their corporate headquarters. Now get the hell out there, and bring me the tongues, tails, and testicles of twelve dead buffalo!"

7

The buffalo grazed peacefully down the west side of the river, heading north through Yankee Jim canyon beneath a thin cover of stunted trees and bushes, their ruminant stomachs extracting abundant nourishment from this shabbiest of pastures. Even *Wohpe* seemed to sense the giddy freedom that came from leaving the park boundary behind. She kicked and pounced between Kate and Sam, licking any patch of exposed skin on Sam, or suckling on Kate's extended fingers.

"The only way to move them fast is slowly," Two Suns said, stopping on his dirt bike to cut a willow branch and idly brush the ground behind a plodding male, while Little Bull, also on a dirt bike, collected stones to throw at its massive hindquarters.

"My grandmother says the first people were born out of a buffalo blood clot."

"More like a buffalo chip for you."

"Hey, the Gros Ventre are a buffalo nation. We know how to get them moving." Little Bull skipped a stone off the animal's back; it swished its tail and twitched an ear as if dealing with nothing more than a bothersome horse-fly, then suddenly gave a convulsive burp and regurgitated a smooth, round hair ball onto the ground. John Wilson quickly drove over and picked it up. "Hi-ya! A magic ball!" He held it high over his head, shouting for joy.

"Cute kids," Sam said, stumbling along. His hands were tied together in front, with a leather braided rope pulled tightly around his neck and held like a leash by Medicine Dog, riding ahead on his horse. "Can't wait to see how they look in prison uniforms."

"They're just teenagers," Kate said. "I'm sure they don't grasp the gravity of the situation."

"That's no excuse," Sam said, recalling his recent experience with teenage kids, or even much younger, who were capable of the worst sort of mayhem and bodily harm. "Consequences go with the action. Isn't that right, boss?" Sam pulled hard on the leather rope, nearly jerking Medicine Dog off his horse. He wheeled the horse around and came right at Sam.

"Want to try that again, big man? Come on, show me how tough you are!" The horse stomped and reared right in Sam's face, threatening to crush him under its sharp hooves.

"You get down off that horse, I'll show you tough!"

"Oh, big white man! Look at you now!" Sam dodged and weaved, but Medicine Dog kept on coming, pushing Sam towards the main body of the buffalo herd, which was becoming very nervous at the close presence of a human. A feisty two-year old curved-horn male slashed at Sam, just missing his chest, when a fist-sized rock suddenly caught Medicine Dog full in the back of the head, pitching him over the horse's neck onto the ground. Sam quickly looped the rope around Medicine Dog's throat and would have choked him to death, but Crazy Wolf came over, jumped off his horse, and got Sam in a full-nelson.

"Leave it!" he hissed in Sam's ear.

"You're next!" Sam said, not letting go, Medicine Dog's face starting to turn from vibrant red to pale blue.

Crazy Wolf cranked down hard, and Sam very reluctantly lost his grip on the rope. "Untie him!" Crazy Wolf said to Kate, straining to keep the pressure on Sam. She came around to work on the knots holding Sam's wrist, and Crazy Wolf growled: "Not him, you stupid woman; Medicine Dog!"

"Don't call me a stupid woman," Kate said, stepping back and tightly folding her arms.

"Then you should know that this one," twisting Sam's face to hers, "is his prisoner, and no one has the right to release him other than Medicine Dog. You said you're Lakota, you should know that."

"If he's anyone's prisoner, he's mine. I had him under control."

Yura and Shining Shirt, both driving ATVs, came over from the sides of the small herd to see what the commotion was about. Shining Shirt stared closely at Kate.

"Who's your father?"

"My father is *Wi*, the supreme god of the sun; my mother is the Moon. I am sister to Ptesan-Wi, the White Buffalo Calf Woman."

Yura carefully approached Kate. She reached out to touch her cheek, but quickly withdrew her hand. "*Wakan, Lila Wakan*," she muttered, slowly stepping back with her head down in a posture of submission.

"She pretty much looks like one of us," Shining Shirt said. "Definitely enrolled-quality Indian."

Joseph White Bird dragged John Wilson over by the back of his neck. "I saw him throw the rock at Medicine Dog. The Nez Perce are not one to kiss up to a Crow, but I don't like a Paiute siding with a White."

"I wasn't siding with anyone. I was trying to save him from choking. Medicine Dog was damaging my prisoner!"

"He might be right," Two Suns said. "Medicine Dog claims the white man as prisoner, but it was John Wilson who brought him to shore."

"This is my captive!" Medicine Dog said, coughing, gasping, and staring hatefully at John Wilson. "His people are nothing, they scratch in the dirt for grubs. And now he has tried to free my prisoner. He will live to regret this." He grabbed the leather rope and pulled Sam away from Crazy Wolf, knocking Sam to the ground and laying one knee on his back.

"Don't you talk about the *Paviosto* that way! And give me back my prisoner!" John Wilson screamed, attacking Medicine Dog, fists flying.

Two Suns and Little Bull grabbed him from behind just as they all simultaneously heard the rhythmic chest thumping sound of a helicopter approaching from upriver. Everyone instinctually crouched down. Even the white buffalo calf ceased its frenetic bounding from Kate to Sam, and leaned forward on its front legs, listening intently.

"End of the road," Sam said, turning his face up from the dirt. "Maybe you should draw straws to see which one hangs first?"

But it was just a tourist flight, circling around the edge of the park, then continuing on to Cooke City. The deep, mechanical sound disappeared over the ridge, replaced by the rush of the river and the steady breeze high on the upslope forests.

"Tell me again where you're leading us?" Kate asked Crazy Wolf, who had come over to stare intently into the face of the white buffalo calf.

"He's not leading us anywhere," Medicine Dog snapped. "We're following a path of buffalo turds."

Crazy Wolf crouched lower, staring at the calf. "Yura, I need you." The Wanapam elder moved in her curious, stagger-stepped, hunch-backed way, seemingly not at all surprised that Crazy Wolf would want her assistance at this time. "You're a *yantcha*, descended from the great dreamer-prophets Smohalla and Solaskin, what do you see?"

"To see clearly would require an intensity of sacrifice and enthusiasm that is lacking. I haven't experienced a good dream since before I came."

"Not through you—her," Crazy Wolf said, gesturing to the calf. "We have a covenant with the buffalo. They are our connection to the earth mother, and this one is her sacred representative. Can you see what she sees?"

Yura half-closed her eyes and lowered her hands, palms outward. She slowly dropped to her knees in a posture of prayerful waiting. The dozen buffalo fanned out in a semi-circle with the opening to the east, grazing in a casual manner that suggested lazy indifference rather than earnest hunger. The white buffalo calf came and stood directly in front of Yura, then lay down, curled its nose beneath its tail, and fell fast asleep.

"John Wilson, give me the magic ball!" She reached out, her eyes still closed, and he came over and handed her the buffalo hair ball, which she rolled in her hand. The ball was slightly smaller than a baseball, but every bit as smooth, hard, and quite a bit heavier and denser.

"The *sama*—this one," she said, nodding at Sam, "came from out of the rising sun, and the world fell apart, torn to pieces by greed and murder. None of us were spared, not even him." The surrounding circle of Indians pressed in closer to listen to every word.

"But we survived," Crazy Wolf whispered, staring intently at Yura. "We've come this far. How much farther do we have to go?"

Yura leaned forward, her nose practically touching the calf's nose. "I see flames, burning bodies, death."

"Us? Which ones? Or is it everyone here?" Shining Shirt asked.

"And deep snow."

"In April? No way!" Two Suns said.

Yura shuddered and made a contorted, ugly face. Her words came out in a raspy squeak. "I see people eating—people, consuming their own flesh. Followed by flames, and a path through the snow."

"This makes no sense," Joseph said. "We're wasting our time here; we should be on the move."

Crazy Wolf ignored the fear in his own heart and continued whispering into Yura's ear. "What is our path, buffalo mother? You were there at our birth and have sustained us through endless winters. Where should we follow you?"

"We must go as one, even as we appear as many. The path is a holy road that our people have walked before. We must walk it again, through the Bitterroots, across Lolo Pass."

"North, to the Medicine line?" Joseph White Bird asked, referring to the Canadian border.

"No, into the face of your people."

"The Chief Joseph trail! I know that route like the back of my hand! Every Nez Perce does."

"But in reverse," Crazy Wolf said. "And they'll be searching for us with everything they've got. Especially since we have this one." Nodding at Sam.

"He goes where I go!" Medicine Dog said.

"Yeah, and if you don't, you'll be on their payroll by sunset," John Wilson said.

"You watch it!" Medicine Dog said. "My knife is singing for your blood!"

"Stop it!" Crazy Wolf said. Yura came out of her trance, appearing cold and disoriented. He placed his blanket over her shoulders and took the magic ball from her hand. He turned to John and held it up, as if about to throw it to him. "John Wilson, we need you to return up river, all the way to Gardiner. Tell everyone you meet that you saw the buffalo moving east, with a growing band of Indians. Tell them that you are trying to catch up with the escaped buffalo. Can you do this?"

"You give me my magic ball back, I can do anything."

"Good!" Crazy Wolf tossed it to him. "Go now! We will move north, then west; White Bird will show us the way."

8

"I know their plan," Lieutenant Walker told the assembled war room of Park service officials, livestock owners, and local police officers.

"Already? But we just got here," Larry Donohue said. "You haven't even looked at our maps, data bases, satellite surveillance."

"Plus, we got a pack of contract hunters standing by, at my expense!" Bob Smith added. "Isn't that right?"

BJ stood off to the side, holding up a doorway. "Locked and loaded."

Walker knowingly tapped the side of his head and dunked a donut in his coffee, allowing the buzz in the room to rise to a fever pitch. "To know where they are going, one must first know where they have been."

"Spare us the horseshit about walking a mile in their moccasins," Smith said.

Walker finished his donut, licked his fingers, and moved to the head of the table. "No, I'm talking about looking inside their heads: what motivates and drives them, why they get up each morning."

BJ snorted. "To get laid, eat, and get stuff, no different than you and me."

"I think that the bison are primarily interested in food and water," Larry said, "and when it comes to mates…"

"Not the buffalo, you moron!" Smith said.

"The red man is a fairly simple creature: a primitive; not much advanced beyond the cave man. They're no match for all this," Walker said, gesturing to the high tech paraphernalia crammed into the room, "but they can be wily, like their brother, the coyote."

"You ever met one?" BJ asked.

"Yeah, how do you know so much all of a sudden?" Smith asked.

"Let's just say, I stayed up last night and watched *Dances With Wolves* several times."

Bob turned to speak over his shoulder to BJ. "In other words, no."

"And after I fully absorbed the facts, I did what we should all do in a situation like this, I sat down and thought, and I recalled my studies at the Academy, where we examined a number of historical battles during the Indian Wars."

"Seems to me we generally got our butts kicked," BJ said, removing a toothpick from behind his ear and chewing on it, "except for when the cavalry had the chance to massacre women and children, while the warriors were away."

"It was a war of attrition," Lieutenant Walker said, dismissing BJ with a sniff, "and the non-combatants—well, there are always necessary losses. We definitely put the fear of god in them with our firepower."

"Yeah, but getting back to the bison," Bob said.

"No different than these natives: primitive, plodding, few moving parts."

"Pretty much perfectly adapted to their environment," BJ said. "You ever try to round up a buffalo? They're tough."

"Well that may be, but my hero, General Sherman, had it best when he said that to kill the Indian, all we had to do was exterminate the buffalo, which he called 'their commissary;' I think that's rather good: their commissary."

"Walker, you are a regular font of wisdom and information," Bob Smith said. "Now, what was that you said about knowing where they are? Because I've got a billion-dollar headache caused by twelve escaped animals."

The Lieutenant flipped a switch to unscroll a large map from the ceiling, then whipped out a telescopic pointer. "Strict military logic suggests that the savages would revert to their old war path and follow a route here and here"—jabbing with the pointer—"up what has come to be known as the so-called Chief Joseph Trail. We could intercept them anywhere along an azimuth from Yellowstone, to Billings, to the Bears Paw Mountains."

"I've hunted antelope up in that country," BJ said. "It's pretty rough and covers a lot of ground."

"This was the likely route," Walker said triumphantly, "but good soldiering always relies on boots on the ground over logic, and just this morning we apprehended one of the hostiles." He snapped his fingers, a door opened, and John Wilson was dragged kicking and fussing up to the front of the room. He was soaked from his waist up.

"Why, it's just a boy!" BJ said.

"Do you mind telling me why he's all wet?" Larry asked apprehensively.

"This bastard tried to drown me! What is wrong with you! And give me back my ball!"

"Standard military procedure," Walker said.

"He held me underwater until I thought I was gonna die!" John sobbed, trying to hold back his tears. "And the ball is mine! It's magic!"

"Probably a bomb," Walker said, removing the ball from his pocket and tossing it in his hand.

"Let me see that," BJ said. Walker tossed it to him. "This's a buffalo hair ball for chrise sakes." He went over and handed it to John Wilson, then came back and spoke closely to Walker. "You water-boarded a kid?"

"Jesus, Mary, and Joseph!" Larry said, crossing himself.

"Child combatants are common to all modern conflicts."

"Maybe oversees," BJ said, "but this is America last time I checked."

The various bureaucrats and officials in the room fidgeted uncomfortably or were simply too shocked to do anything but stare at John, or at their own feet.

"So, what'd he tell you?" Bob asked. "You get any good intel?"

"Damn straight! Kid sang like a bird. Dim the lights, please." He moved to the other side of the map, removed a laser light from his pocket, and made a series of sweeping red arcs. "The hostiles are moving in an easterly, southerly direction, possibly to seek aid and comfort from that nest of checkbook liberals over in Big Sky. But they won't get far. We can cut them off here, here, or here," the red laser dot jumping all across Montana.

"Not too many cattle up the Gallatin," Bob said, "at least they won't infect the whole state before we close 'em off."

"Exactly! The only good buffalo is a dead buffalo!"

"How you propose to do the job?" BJ asked.

"Maximum firepower! Apache attack chopper, 30 mm cannons, all guns blazing! Just warms my heart that the Army named our choppers after the Indians. What tribe are we going after anyway? Sioux? Cheyenne? Maybe we could change the name to one of those."

"I'm sure they'd love that," BJ said. "But speaking of which, there were some native guys acting as human shields last go-round. How do you propose to deal with them?"

Walker shrugged. "In a war of attrition, there are bound to be necessary losses. Lights please."

The lights were turned back up, everyone squinting and still in somewhat of a state of shock.

"Hey! Where's the kid?" Bob asked.

Walker looked around, under the tables and behind the chairs.

"He was just here a second ago" Larry said. "He couldn't have gone far."

BJ laughed. "Like you say, general, they're all just a bunch of wily, little coyotes!"

The sun rose higher as the cover thinned and the buffalo moved more slowly than ever, leaving the relative safety of Yankee Jim Canyon for the wide-open expanse of the Paradise Valley, the Yellowstone River surging northward, coffee-colored with early runoff. Crazy Wolf and the others did what they could to keep the herd close to the river, where the streamside willows provided some hope of shielding, but they were in full view of a dozen farm houses and country roads, and even the occasional drift-boat fisherman slowly floating past, startled to see a wild buffalo peering back through the brush like a vision from the Corps of Discovery.

Sam stumbled along behind Medicine Dog, the pace slow enough to maintain a bit of slack in the rope tied around his neck. Being captured had been a constant fear in Iraq; the reports by survivors and the tortured remains of those who didn't make it were used throughout the Corps to demonize the enemy, justifying any amount of retribution allowed within—or beyond—the Geneva Convention rules of engagement. Sam resisted the temptation to fantasize all the ways he might take revenge on his captor and set his mind to making a careful assessment of his situation, and to begin planning an escape.

"Hey, white man! You want some water?" Medicine Dog took a water bottle out of his shoulder bag and drank his fill, then spat a spray in Sam's direction. He laughed, returned the bottle to his bag, and gave the rope a stiff jerk.

Sam smiled back, as if Medicine Dog's baiting and humiliations meant nothing to him. He noticed that Shining Shirt and Two Suns were watching this exchange; Medicine Dog took note as well, and angrily jerked once more on the rope, then spurred his horse to walk a bit faster, forcing Sam into a slow, steady trot.

The river made a bend with an old steel bridge just downstream, the road leading across a field and up the hill towards a low bluff where a single antelope stood stock still, its hind legs thrust straight out behind, motionless head staring off into the distance. The buffalo stopped moving, pawing the ground and shaking their heads, then raising their nostrils to test the air. They seemed to be uncertain where to go, or perhaps they had caught a whiff of something in the vicinity that was gearing them up for a full-out flight response. For Sam also, the terrain and arrangement of features were reminiscent of some other place that filled him with dread: the river bottom, a bridge, a desolate road cutting across an empty field. The image of a black man flashed in his head; a friendly face; smiling and laughing with a heartiness that seemed to draw the world closer; then a bright fireball, and the face was lost in flames.

Sam shook off the image as Medicine Dog drew up his horse, not wanting to get ahead of the herd.

"Hi-ya!" he shouted to the others. "Where is Crazy Wolf? The buffalo are stalled."

Joseph White Bird pointed downstream and yelled something that was lost in the wind. Medicine Dog cursed, turned his horse, and circled back around the herd.

It was obvious to Sam that the group was led by Crazy Wolf, but that they held only a loose allegiance, if at all, to one another. They seemed similar to the complex tribal clans of the mid-East—the Sunni, Shiite, Kurds, al-Jaburi, Ubayids, Bakhatra, Bukeheet—united against a common enemy from outside their interwoven *khams,* or extended families, but inwardly nurturing ancient blood feuds or *al-tha'r* that predisposed them to kill one another's children if left to their own history and lethal devices. The thought of that stuck in his mind, blocking out his effort to rationally plan an escape. Why was it that people were so easily united in hate? The image of the black man reappeared: Heydon Jones, his good friend from boot camp right on through deployment; bunking together, sharing MREs—Meals Ready to Eat—"Eat it now, taste it later!" he'd say, repeatedly. Driving patrols through dusty villages where every chador-shrouded woman seemed more certain to be an enemy than a friend, providing coordinates and wind speeds for an improbable sniper shot. He hadn't thought of Heydon for months, and here his face had popped up twice in the space of a quarter hour, staring at him now from a distance, watching as Sam raised a rifle, aimed at a shrouded figure, Heydon's mouth open, screaming for him not to shoot, and fired. The recoil within the dream jolted Sam back into full awareness of his surroundings and the presence of the small band of Indians. None of them showed Sam any sympathy whatsoever; they barely looked at him or paid him notice; it was doubtful any could be persuaded to provide assistance. On the other hand, it occurred to him that they would be unlikely to come to Medicine Dog's aide if he provoked a confrontation. They might even welcome seeing Medicine Dog humiliated. He forced himself to consider the possibility of making a deal with Medicine Dog; maybe offer a payment, or try to become his trusted friend, then slip away into the night. Sam gave the alternatives their due consideration, but after about five seconds he concluded they were as unlikely to succeed as they were completely unappealing.

He saw a slender piece of driftwood on the ground, the horse heading straight for it. Sam made a loud yelping-yelp, attracting the attention of the others—Medicine Dog facing stoically ahead—and when the stick came within reach, Sam grabbed it and waved it over his head in a theatrical display of disdain, as if wielding a toy sword—Medicine Dog still not turning to pay any attention.

"The white man is about to count coup," Shining Shirt said to Two Suns.

"I think he may be losing his mind. Medicine Dog has brought him low."

"He's cute," Little Bull said, drawing stares from the others, "for a white man."

They moved closer to listen, and heard Sam shout: "Hey, mister big stuff, how 'bout you kiss my ass?"

Medicine Dog laughed, not even bothering to turn around, but speaking loud enough for the others to hear: "I'm up here and you're down there, walking in my horse's shit, so who's kissing who?"

Sam jogged forward and jammed the wooden stick far up the horse's butt. Immediately it reared, pitching Medicine Dog to the ground, Sam pulling the rope from his hand, looping it off his neck, then running as fast as he could away from the river and up the hill towards the antelope.

"Ha-ho!" Two Suns shouted. "Medicine Dog, you're losing his scalp."

The horse ran off, kicking madly like the wildest of broncs, trying to dislodge that piece of driftwood. None of the natives made a move to help Medicine Dog or to retrieve Sam, who was scrambling up the loose, alluvial gravel, the antelope strangely holding its ground, Sam moving fast and hearing the shouting behind him, then looking up near the top and seeing four gray-bodied, silver-tipped dog-like animals larger than any dog, the realization dawning on him that these were the real-deal wolves, a whole pack of them just over the brow of the hill, coming forward to check him out and see if he was perhaps more vulnerable and an easier meal than some muscle bound 60-mph antelope.

Sam was breathing so hard he thought his heart would burst, but now he turned and ran at a diagonal back down the hill, the herd starting to surge downriver, the natives yelping helplessly trying to keep them close to the cover of the streamside brush, Sam certain that the wolves were right behind him, and gaining. He aimed for the front of the herd, hoping that a hungry wolf would prefer a fat buffalo to a skinny white guy, when he suddenly felt a vice-like grip on the base of his neck, his feet leaving the ground, and the image of Heydon being blown to pieces, arms and legs disassembled, head coming off, flashing again in his mind.

10

Crazy Wolf saw the wolf pack up on the rim and thought nothing of them, other than to caution Kate to keep the calf close. "They're on the move with the season; it's been a tough winter; they have pups to feed." He walked slowly in front of his horse, loosely holding the reins, with Kate behind, the calf skipping along at her heel. The horse tossed its head and Crazy Wolf's hand brushed against his back pocket. Kate saw his wallet fall out. She picked it up, but rather than hand it right back, she took a moment to look at his driver's license with "Brian Thompson" listed as his official, anglo name.

"I know all about wolves," she said, struck by the grim, cigar store visage frowning back in the photo, which was in sharp contrast to his re-al-life vibrancy and personal power. She tucked the wallet in the back of her jeans and came to his side, sweeping the hair back from her face. "These are probably from the Swan Lake pack, or maybe even the Chief Josephs."

"How do you know that?"

"I've studied them—hunting, feeding, mating."

"That about sums it up for all living things," Crazy Wolf said.

The calf playfully bumped Kate in the rear and she grabbed it by the ears. "Oh, you, *Wohpe!*" she said, planting a big kiss on its nose. She straightened up to stare at Crazy Wolf full in the face.

He too was unsettled by their suddenly flirtatious contact. He looked away, then back, their eyes locked, then blurted out the first thing that came into his head. "Maybe we could call her something better than *Wohpe.*" The calf came over and nudged him in the crotch.

"Well, whatever you call it, that calf's having all the fun," she said, causing Crazy Wolf to blush.

He turned away out of modesty, feeling an inward turmoil that was entirely unexpected. He was a chief, and more importantly, a father and husband who had sworn to control and focus his power. He felt his mouth go dry, his heart pounding in his chest.

"Odd though, they don't seem to have any collars," she said.

"Who, people? Or do you mean the calf?"

"The wolves, silly!"

They both laughed and started walking again.

"Maybe they're ghosts," Crazy Wolf said. "They appeared; they can disappear."

"Is that how you got your name?" Kate asked, noticing—and admiring—the strength in his arms, body, and face. "Coming and going without a trace?"

He walked along in silence for a moment. "A name is a very personal thing. There are tribes where they never say their name. One of the most famous Indians ever, Ishi, never told anyone his name; it just meant 'man'."

"But you're Cheyenne, and I'm Lakota. Our names are public. My father brought the whole family together and shouted my name out loud: Katherine Little Coyote. He said it was because a coyote was wailing away when I was born, but my mother later said it was a wolf. I might even change it to that one of these days."

"You have a thing for wolves?"

"If you're digging for a compliment, no. But I got my doctorate in wolf pack behavior, especially the role of alpha females. I know all about them."

Crazy Wolf could feel her staring at him with an intensity that was so unlike his own wife. It made him feel very uncomfortable, but in large part because it stirred up feelings he thought he had controlled and pushed deep down. He tried to look back at Katherine, but the feeling was too strong, and he turned away.

"Yeah, I come and go. But my name, well, you would have had to know me back in the day. I was pretty crazy, and I guess you could say I roamed around like a wolf. I sure got in a lot of fights."

"Well, you're in a big one now," Kate said. "The cattle industry isn't going to stop until these buffalo are rounded up and probably killed. And I don't think they're going to care much if anyone gets in the way, especially a bunch of crazy Indians."

"You can leave whenever you want, if that's what you mean."

Kate flared. "I told you I'm here to protect my calf! No one's going to scare me away."

Crazy Wolf looked at her with a deadly serious expression. "Whoa, maybe your studies rubbed off. Sounds pretty alpha to me."

Kate couldn't help herself; she felt completely flattered. "Really?"

He looked away for a moment, fighting the rising surge of his feelings, then grabbed her arm and gave her a short quick shake. "Don't think I can't see what you're doing. I too have studied wolves, but by watching them, sitting with them, seeing how they live. I know all about what you call alpha females: the leaders who use their sexual favors to keep control of the lead male, and all the other members of the pack." He pushed her away. "But I am a chief, and I have sworn the Buffalo Family Ceremony with my wife and child."

Kate was too stunned to speak. She brushed the dust off her shirt and jeans, staring down at her feet, took a deep breath, then looked back up, forcing a smile. "OK, Brian." She took his wallet out from the back of her jeans and handed it to him. "From one alpha to another."

But before he could ask how she got his wallet, he saw Sam running for his life down the slope towards the now charging herd, which thundered past with the natives on their horses, dirt bikes, and ATVs trying to keep up. "Grab the calf! Yura, give them a ride, and stay with the herd!" He jumped on his horse and rode hard at an angle to intercept Sam ahead of the oncoming wolves and the onrushing buffalo, pulling in behind and seizing Sam by the collar of his vest and swinging him around onto the back of his horse, the lead wolf snapping at Sam's hamstring but catching a hoof in the face instead.

The buffalo were now in full flight, unstoppable and relentless as they charged through a rusted barbwire fence, across a road, through another fence, then on and on, the Yellowstone River always on the right, the occasional modest ranch house giving way to an increasing number of mini-mansions, as the wolves peeled off and turned back, sensing the downstream boundary of the Mill Creek pack, the buffalo not caring about anything but the ringing alarm inside their collective heads, energizing every fiber of their massive bodies to run and run, the natives beside and behind acting as a kind of surrogate pack, keeping the alarm at full power.

11

A Montana state trooper on a coffee break was the first to call it in. "Got some strange wildlife activity going on over near Emigrant. Buncha damn bison on the rampage."

"Musta got loose from Charlie Green's place," the local dispatch said. "He's raising about twenty head, says they're leaner than top sirloin, the idiots down in California and out in New York don't mind paying top dollar, but my brother Wally tasted it, you know him, don't'cha? Runs a cement mixer truck out of Belgrade, doing pretty well actually, except for his wife has a bad case of the croup."

"That's all good, Nancy. I'll swing by Charlie's, but how 'bout you make a call up to the park, see if some of their own got loose?"

"Now why would that be? They got plenty of room, besides you ever tried reaching someone in the park? My brother Wally tried to make a camp reservation last year, for Labor Day don't'cha see, and they put him on hold 'til practically Christmas, wastin' his precious time!"

And by the time the trooper had driven out to Charlie's place, found him on the back forty spreading hay, and determined that none of his dispirited domestic bison had jumped a fence, Nancy finally got through to the park switchboard and proceeded to wear down a long line of administrative gate keepers before finally being put through to Larry Donohue.

"What do you mean, rampaging buffalo?"

"Well that's why we're calling you, don't'cha see? There's hundreds of 'em stampeding over taxpayer property, fornicatin' with their livestock, chasin' the children off the bus stops, and what the State of Montana wants to know is, what're *you* Feds going to do about it? Cause this is *your* problem, don't'cha see?"

Larry hung up and thought for a long, hard moment before doing anything. The first priority was to figure out was how this might come back to bite him. If indeed the bison were headed north onto the rich cattle grazing ranges near Livingston and Big Timber, rather than the steeply wooded wilderness of the Gallatin River, then this was a disaster of potentially epic proportions. The cattle ranchers would call their farm extension agents; the agents would call their Livestock Association rep; the reps would work it up the ladder to the Association leadership; who would get right in to the USDA; then definitely to the Congressional delegation; from there over to Interior; right back down the chain of command to the Park Superintendent and plop onto his own desk like the soupiest of cow paddies. His only hope was to shift the blame.

He scooted his chair across the linoleum floor to a set of metal file cabinets and unlocked the one file door conspicuously marked "Secret." Inside, were three or four manila files that contained his past expense account receipts, plus one file simply marked "Kate." He brought the file back over to his desk and carefully examined the contents: her personnel reviews, education background, and way in the back, a one-page, federal pre-application form testifying that she self-certified to be a member of a qualifying minority race, entitling her to preferential hiring status. At the very bottom was her signature, with the words "Lakota, Pine Ridge" written in the margin. "Thank you Jesus!" he said to himself. "I can blame this all on her. I'm saved!"

12

The late afternoon regulars at the Stockman in downtown Livingston were the first to sense that something was up when the requisite Montana saloon sign—"Liquor Up Front, Poker In The Rear"—shook off the hooks and hit Jamie Matthews on the head.

"What'n the hell's goin' on?"

"The hell I know!"

"The hell you don't! Some sum'bitch threw somethin' at me! And you and Benny're the only ones here!"

"The hell we did!"

And so it went, the bottles above the keg-o-rators tinkling as they trembled on the shelves. When the lead female buffalo turned off Park Street and headed past the Bar and Grill onto North Main, the town took on a distinctly Pamplona-esque composure, everyone ducking for cover in doorways and alleys.

"I'm almost out of gas," Yura shouted to Crazy Wolf.

"Stay with them! We've got to find a way."

"There is no way!" Shining Shirt shouted. "Do you hear that? Sirens!"

"We're all going to jail!" Two Suns said.

"About time," Sam said, sitting backwards on an ATV, his hands tied behind his back, a blindfold across his eyes, Medicine Dog driving.

"Shut up, white man!" Medicine Dog said, laying a sharp elbow into Sam's kidneys. "When we get settled down, you're going to pay, big time!"

"When we get settled, you're going to be in a federal pen and I'm gonna come visit your roommate every week, to make sure he's getting enough."

"Look! It's John!" Shining Shirt said, pointing back down the street, where the kid was racing to catch up on his motorcycle, a broad smile on his face. He brodied to a stop, a brace of willow branches in his hand.

"Hello auntie!"

Yura was delighted. "My John! I knew you'd make it!" She turned to the others. "My great warrior!"

"I chased you all the way down the valley," he said, exuberantly waving the branches like flags. "They run like the wind!"

"They are the wind," Crazy Wolf said. "But we haven't much time. It sounds like the police are searching for us."

"No, we have some time."

"What do you mean?" Crazy Wolf asked.

Kate, holding the calf across her lap on the back of Yura's ATV, saw a line of fire trucks racing down a perpendicular street, with several police cars in pursuit. "Why aren't they coming this way?"

"It means I pulled fire alarms all across town," he said, stripping the leaves and smaller branches off the main stems of the willows. "Plus, one other thing."

"What thing?"

"I knew our brothers were in trouble, so when I came into town, right past the rodeo grounds, I saw many cattle trucks, loaded with bulls. The big ones, rodeo ones. And I did a bad thing."

"What sort of bad thing?"

John looked past Crazy Wolf and shouted, "Hi-ya!" just as the buffalo, which appeared to be headed to the city park down by the river, suddenly made a u-turn because a herd of fifty to a hundred prize brahma bulls came snorting around the corner the far end of the street, and stampeded all together right back up Main, a tsunami of bovine muscle fighting for shoulder and horn space within the narrow confines of the old west boulevard.

"Freedom!" John Wilson shouted. "Our brothers are free! I set them all free!"

And now it really was Pamplona in Montana: no one was safe; the store windows smashed, cars stomped, a chaos of wild buffalo and prize bulls feeding off each other's primordial panic and exhilaration, the bull owners huffing and puffing behind with their bullwhips and stun sticks, a crescendo of cuss words and whip cracks echoing off the ruined downtown. Plus a new, even more sinister sound: the chest pounding thump of a helicopter coming in fast and low to hover over the town.

"Hold your goddam fire!" Bob Smith shouted into his headset, as the door gunner in Walker's Apache got ready to lay the entire living mass to waste. "Those are hundred-thousand-dollar-a-head stock down there."

"But they're all mixed up with the buffalo," Walker answered. "That means they're infected, we gotta smoke 'em!"

"The hell you say! You hold your fire or I'll attach your wages for the next hundred years! Kee-rist! What a shit-show!"

The stampede split, re-joined, split again, a random combination of wild and domestic gene pools sloshing beneath the tree-lined streets, then moshing together in the intersections, impossible to predict where they'd go next, Crazy Wolf keeping his renegade band together in the unlikely event an escape route presented itself.

"Isolate the lead female!" Kate shouted to the group. "The others will follow."

"Where," Medicine Dog asked, "to hell?"

"If you're lucky," Sam said, fighting back nausea from the pitching and turning.

And on one of his passes through the sleepier, older section of town, Crazy Wolf looked down a quiet street and saw with clear certainty the escape route he had prayed for in his heart. "Go into the herd! Haze them out, and move this way," motioning with his hand towards the train tracks, where a line of empty boxcars, the doorways open and facing town, sat waiting like a rolling sanctuary.

But just then a fire truck pulled into the intersection and a team of firemen opened up with fire hoses, blocking passage and soaking the bellowing herd. The crap-stained street became slick as black ice.

"This way!" Kate motioned to the wide open doors of a garage that had been converted into an antiques emporium. She waved her arms and succeeded in directing the lead female bison, the others falling in behind, Kate leading down a long aisle bordered by the finest crystal and china.

BJ drove past just as the tail end of the buffalo herd passed through the doors. The sound of crashing tables and broken glass drifted out of the building. "I'll be damned! A bull in a..." But his truckload full of bloodthirsty cowboys were focused on the slip-sliding brahma bulls which had gained traction and aggressively faced off against their whip-cracking owners.

"Let us out!" one of the cowboys demanded. "We'll take 'em on foot."

"Be my guest," BJ said, tiring of the poisonous banter in the truck, the others passing a flask and describing in graphic terms how they'd kill the buffalo as slowly and painfully as possible. And as for the Indians, well, the more humane of the various passionately held opinions was that they should be cut up with dull, rusty knives and dragged back to the park behind the truck, to be fed to the wolves.

He turned down several streets, trying to get at the back door of the antique emporium, but by the time he circled around the buffalo were nowhere to be seen. He knew that the rodeo bulls would stand and fight, while the buffalo would run in flight, as was their prairie-bred disposition over many thousands of years. That was really the only way to survive in the face of organized hunters, whether from nomadic wanderers down from the Siberian ice bridge, or from the wolf packs that had evolved to pick off the too old, too young, too sick, or foolishly brave. Staying with the herd and keeping ahead of danger was the only way to go.

And, so, he worked up one street, down another, wondering how a whole herd of buffalo could have disappeared in such a tidy little town. They were nothing more than mortal animals and the Indians were surely lawbreaking renegades, but he couldn't help feeling impressed that they had come this far. It seemed they had good luck bordering on the supernatural, unless maybe they really were enchanted.

He heard the buffalo before he saw them, the Indians calling out in a way that steered them down a backyard alley and onto a street aimed straight to the rail yards. It was getting dusky now and seen from behind the buffalo were moving in that rhythmic up-down motion of a pre-historic dream: dark, wooly, unstoppable. They'd been on the move for many hours and were running with a steadiness that could outrace a prairie fire.

The chopper was overhead, combing the streets with powerful search lights, but it was off the mark by half a mile. He heard the occasional gunfire and wondered if the cowboys in their drunken frustration had taken to shooting the rodeo bulls, or maybe a stray dog or cat.

BJ saw the Indians drive the buffalo right up a cement ramp and into a boxcar, slamming the door shut, then hurrying to load their horses, ATVs, and cycles into the next car up the line. And there, in the dull glare of a single overhead industrial light, he caught an unmistakable glimpse of Sam, standing beside the pretty young National Park scientist who had been on the bridge. It all now made perfect sense: why Sam had taken off on sudden notice. He'd gone over to the other side, surely more for the girl than to ally himself with a bunch of criminal natives. But BJ didn't really care. He was glad Sam was in the middle of such a raucous mess; it would take Sam's mind off his wartime stress and worries and keep him from doing harm to himself. And as for the buffalo escaping town, it seemed the perfect solution to a problem he no longer had the heart for. When the train slowly pulled from the station, BJ tipped his hat and turned back towards the bright lights and madness, resolved to keep things to himself and protect Sam any way he could.

13

Tino Gugliardi couldn't remember ever having been so pissed: first from the nearly hysterical anger he felt at being stiffed by Crazy Wolf on the garbage contract, and second from being laid low by the relentless drinking binge he went on later that same day. The combination of cheap vodka chased by abundant tequila, washed down with a toxic local white lightning served in jam jars, made for a black-out night and a long, bitter morning. Once he got his head out of the toilet, he headed back towards the Bozeman airport, stopping at a coffee shop in what he considered to be the absolute middle of nowhere to retch on the ground and grab a cup of joe to brace himself for the last desperate miles. He walked out of the café to his car, passing a cop sprawled in a cruiser in the parking lot, a radar speed gun in his hand pointed lamely at the ground, and his radio turned up loud.

"That's right, Nancy," he was saying, "like I told ya a hundred times already, they were goin' downriver to Livingston; no, not *in* the river, but on the road, well actually, kind of at the side of the road. Which is my jur'sdiction."

And then her screechy voice: "But don't'cha see, they're already there, my cousin Beth says it's like a tornado came through, isn't a building left standing! So don't'cha think you should get on up there?"

"But like I said, it's not my jur'sdiction, you want me to screw up the way the whole gov'ment works? How'n the hell I know it isn't the Park that should be steppin' in, it's their damn buffalo!"

And when Tino heard the magic word—"buffalo"—he sobered up quick. "Excuse me, officer," he asked, keeping his distance for fear of smelling like the bottom of a spittoon, "but are there some wild bison in the area?"

"How'n the hell I know?" the cop said, disinterestedly. "I look like Smokey the Bear?"

"Yeah, but I overheard you saying something about buffalo."

"Oh, I get it, you're spyin' on what law enforcement has to say in private? That your car?"

"No," Tino said, not quite understanding what alternate universe he had suddenly strayed into.

"'No? You're drivin' a late model, convertible, outta state, twenty-six inch wheels, muscle g-car that's not your own?" He clicked back on his microphone. "Nancy, run me a license plate will ya," reading off the numbers and letters on Tino's rental. "And stand right there, I got my eye on you, don't you move a finger!"

So Tino stood there, listening to these two morons go back and forth about the plates, the jurisdiction, the weather, and how it disproved all notions of global warming, except for maybe last week when it was a bit warmer than usual so that was probably global warming, with her cousins and their various health issues thrown in for good measure, until the cop finally said, "Shit, a rental, I figured as much. You wanta see buff, you gotta go thataway," waggling his speed gun, "back up to the park. They got more'n they can handle. But if you hurry down that-a-other way you might catch the show in town. Group of 'em got loose and are runnin' amok. Now let me get back to police work." And proceeded to get into an argument with Nancy concerning the proper way to make bean dip.

Tino struggled to get his priorities in order, the desire to leave Montana forever being paramount. But that aside, maybe there was still a chance to cut a sweet deal, assuming he could track Crazy Wolf down and get his attention for half a second. It just didn't seem possible that a human being, even an Indian, would value worthless, empty land crawling with four-legged lawnmowers and poisonous snakes more than a state-of-the-art, cash-cow dump, especially when Tino was offering such familiar and favorable terms, consistent with the Nevada gaming interests that controlled virtually all of the Indian casinos: one for him, one for the tribes, two for him. What could possibly be wrong with that?

14

"They were carried straight up to Heaven!" Jaimie said. "I saw 'em with my own eyes, every one of them sacred as an angel!"

"What's he been drinking?" Bob Smith demanded of the bartender.

"The usual: old fashioned with a beer back."

The other Stockman regulars nodded vigorously, mumbling the slurred speech of all-day imbibers.

"Seems like they should be seeing devils," Bob said. He grabbed some beer nuts, went outside and thoughtfully chewed while he looked up and down the now-dead quiet street, which was covered from curb to curb with a fragrant schmeer of bovine crap. "Damn, where could they've gone?"

• • •

Over the rainbow was definitely one possibility, but west on the Montana Rail Link, rumbling up the Bozeman Pass was a better bet. With the blindfold tied tightly over his eyes, Sam couldn't see anything, but he could feel the increasing cold surround his body and his ears pop from the altitude. The whoosh of the air brakes and whine of the cantilevered boxcar wheels as the train followed the twisting contours of the mountain, was deafening. All the long day he had felt strong, ready to fight back if the opportunity presented itself, but now he was tired and sore, and he craved Kate's touch. Their brief moment together in the hot springs had opened a trap door that he thought was closed forever; he could smell her nearby; his heart ached.

Two Suns made a fire with some pieces of wooden pallet. John Wilson was crouched close, working to shape a small basket at the end of one of his willow sticks. Medicine Dog stood across from him, loading, ejecting, and re-loading each of the seven remaining bullets into Sam's rifle. The dim light flickered in the rocking, rolling space, casting shadows on the graffiti sprayed interior, lending a cave-dwelling appearance to the otherwise grungy, industrial space.

"So, where were you a sniper?" John asked Sam.

"Who wants to know?"

"Just me, John Wilson."

"What kind of name is that? Why aren't you like these others with some dumb-ass animal name?"

"Hey, watch what you say!" Medicine Dog said. He loaded one bullet and placed the six free bullets in a pouch and tied it to his belt, then looped the rifle strap over his shoulder. "Our names have meaning."

"Oh yeah? So does mine, Sam, purely biblical. Plus, I'm named after my father. What are you, named after a dog?"

Two Suns leaned forward and slapped Sam across the face. "Your prisoner has a foul mouth!"

"I could take his tongue out right now! And maybe I will." Medicine Dog pulled the knife from its sheath and made a show of testing the sharpness of the blade and point.

"He's my prisoner and if anyone cuts his tongue out it will be me!" John Wilson said.

The others laughed at Medicine Dog's expense.

"You're a boy and a Paiute. Watch your tongue or I'll cut yours out as well!"

"The Paiute are a great people," Yura said, gazing into the flames. "They have been on their lands long after most others ceded everything." She stared now at Medicine Dog and spoke slowly, "And became ration Indians."

"Ha! Then answer the white man—why doesn't your boy have an Indian name? Who gave him such a name as John Wilson!"

Yura blew onto the fire, causing the flames to flare up. "I gave him this name, after his great, great grandfather." Her voice lowered to a rasp. "Wovoka!"

Crazy Wolf turned sharply. "The creator of the Ghost Dance?"

"Wovoka," she repeated, the flame flickering more brightly.

"That's a pretty powerful name," Shining Shirt said. The others grunted their assent.

John Wilson was satisfied with his handiwork. He placed the buffalo hair ball in the basket at the end of the willow branch and whipped it around. "There! That seems ok. We can play some good lacrosse now."

"We are here to save the buffalo, and this child is playing games!" Medicine Dog said.

"Lacrosse isn't a game," John Wilson said, "not Indian style, the way it's meant to be played."

Sam turned to John's voice. "Did you say lacrosse?"

"Sure. I just made a stick, all natural. Ever played it?"

Once again Sam could see Heydon Jones clearly in his mind. Sam had played some football in high school, which was the tough-guy sport of choice back in Ely and had tried to get some of the local kids near their base in Iraq to learn how to throw and catch the football. It was a challenge, because their inclination was to kick the ball around on the ground, soccer style. Heydon, on the other hand, was an east coast preppie and had played lacrosse in the summers, ice hockey in the winter. Ice hockey wasn't much of a sand lot option in the Mideast, so he arranged to have ten lacrosse sticks shipped over and got the kids throwing and whacking, mainly whacking.

"Yeah, I know a little bit about lacrosse."

"Where are we?" Joseph White Bird asked, briefly opening the boxcar door to peek out at the streaming, featureless darkness.

"Where are you leading us?" Shining Shirt demanded of Crazy Wolf, who squatted on his heels beside the white buffalo calf, one hand on its flank, where it lay curled between Sam and Kate on a bed of thick packing cardboard.

"Shut the door, it's freezing!" Yura said, her hands stretched out to the fire, trying to capture some of its fleeting warmth. "The snow is getting in."

"No! Open it wider. It is time to throw the white man out, along with his whore!"

"Don't you call her that! Don't you even speak to her!" Sam said.

"Sam, it's ok," Kate said, placing a hand on his arm, his head jerking around to follow her voice, his anger replaced by a screaming need to break free of the blindfold and wrist ties.

"You got to get me out of this, Kate." He felt a growing sense of claustrophobia, the darkness behind his eyes spreading throughout his body. "We need to leave here, now."

"Do not speak to him!" Medicine Dog said. "He is my prisoner and I will do the talking."

John Wilson didn't look up, he just kept working the ball in the hoop, making little adjustments to its construction. "I don't know, but I think Sam is *my* prisoner. We were all there; I was the one who tied him up and brought him to shore. Anyone see different?"

Medicine Dog angrily tossed his knife into the wooden siding. "He is my prisoner and anyone who disagrees must fight me!"

The others mumbled their opinions then fell silent, stealing furtive glances at Crazy Wolf, who shifted position, knowing that this was an important test of his leadership. It seemed to him that the first thing to accomplish was to reduce the level of anger. "We have an old tradition," he said carefully, "that comes out of the invasion, when the black robes were trying to take away our stories, our language, our culture. We were forced to come into the churches, to enroll as reservation Indians, and if we gave our true Indian name, they would beat us until we gave a good Christian name."

"Why are you telling us this bullshit?" Medicine Dog demanded, in no mood to be played with.

Crazy Wolf motioned with his hands for Medicine Dog to take it easy, to be patient. "After a while we figured out that 'John' was a good name. So we all signed 'John.' And after that, the people would walk around greeting one another 'Hello John. Hello John.' I propose that we give John Wilson the very good name of 'Hello John.'"

The others laughed, grunted their assent, murmuring "Hello John," which the former John Wilson took in good stride, nodding to each greeter in turn. "But I'm going to get a real name of my own."

"When you find it," Two Suns said.

"When you earn it," Shining Shirt said.

"When the power rises within you and connects to a power outside you, and the secret of your personal power is revealed through a vision," Yura said.

"Hello John. Are you kidding me?" Sam said, twitching from anger. "That's supposed to be a name?"

"Shut up!" Medicine Dog said. "No one has spoken to you; you have no right to speak!"

"I spoke to him!" Hello John said. "He asked about my name, and now I have one to tell him! And he is my prisoner! You ask me first for permission to speak to him, even to look at him!"

"Child! Paiute!" Medicine Dog screamed, furious that Hello John was challenging him in this manner. He jumped up, holding the knife low and ready.

Crazy Wolf took his hand off the calf. The cold intensified, and the noise outside lessened as they neared the top of the pass. "Think about it," he said, not stepping in to restrain Medicine Dog, but subtly shifting his feet to establish a stronger base.

"Think about what?" Medicine Dog moved to stand behind Sam. "About the pain and suffering caused by my prisoner and his insect relatives? Your people call the whites *vo'estane*, the spider. In my house, we step on spiders." He brought the knife point to Sam's ear, and ever so lightly touched the inner canal. Sam immediately snapped his head away.

"Goddammit, what are you doing!"

"No!" Kate screamed, but Crazy Wolf restrained her.

Medicine Dog used the blade to gently trace along Sam's hair line. "The white invaders are a plague that never goes away. Just there, all the time, eating the foods provided to us by the Creator; first the buffalo, then the fish, then the antelope and deer. Now they take even our water and air, the snow has melted from the mountains, soon there will be nothing. Our world is ending, and this one is to blame!"

"You can't punish him for all that," Kate cried. "That's ridiculous."

"It's a start. If we don't kill them all, they will kill us. Our earth dies and you just sit there. You should be begging for his blood!"

Crazy Wolf, cat-like, moved onto his toes. "Easy, Medicine Dog. We're all warriors here."

"Ha! I know what you think, that we held the horses while you fought the battles."

"No, the Lakota held the horses, while you scouted," Little Bull said.

"For Custer," Two Sons said.

"Both of you, dead!" Medicine Dog screamed, slashing with his knife. "The Crow were there before the Gros Ventre, or Blackfeet, or Cheyenne ever saw a buffalo. We were eating their tongues and hearts while you scratched the ground, and this one," gesturing furiously to Hello John, "was eating bottom fish from his salt lake!"

"We are many tribes, but one people," Crazy Wolf said. "We're in this together."

"No, but his suffering can pay the price, at least a few coins." He grabbed Sam by the hair, raising him up to his knees, making a Crow counting-coup song that was an immediate prelude to taking a scalp.

"Get your hands off me!" Sam said.

"Ho! Listen to the white man. What is your manifest destiny now? To lose your hair, that's what!"

He would have made the slashing cut from Sam's forehead right across and back to his ears, tearing the bloody swath off at the roots, but Crazy Wolf leapt forward and grabbed Medicine Wolf's hand before the blade could do more than make a narrow straight line gash, the blood seeping down to Sam's eyebrows just above the blindfold.

"Aggh! You cut me!"

Kate screamed and jumped across the calf. "I've had it with you!" She untied the blindfold and tried to wipe the wound, but Medicine Dog continued to hold the blade right at Sam's forehead, he and Crazy Wolf nose to nose, their muscles tensed, veins and sinews standing out, Sam's face pressed between their thighs. "Don't do this," Kate implored Medicine Dog.

He answered with a slow, hateful, vengeance: "This whore, tells me, what to do?" And then with a burst of energy, he lifted Sam up and pushed him towards Crazy Wolf, spinning around to seize Kate and hurl her at the boxcar door. He flashed his knife at Joseph to move away and for Crazy Wolf to keep his distance, then used his foot to pry the door open just enough to push Kate's head out. In desperation she placed her hands on either side and managed to keep from falling to her certain death, a bright light and deafening sound sweeping down along the train towards the boxcar.

"Chopper!" Joseph White Bird said.

Hello John took careful aim and threw his ball straight and true at Medicine Dog's head, knocking him silly and allowing Crazy Wolf to pull Kate back inside and slam the door shut just as the helicopter flew past. They turned to face Sam, who was holding a split piece of wood with a sharp point, his hands still tied, a war paint of blood all across his eyes, nose, and mouth.

"Open it!" Sam demanded. "I'm outta here."

"No!" Crazy Wolf commanded, holding the door shut. "They'll find us."

"Maybe, maybe not," Two Suns said. "But by then he'll be long gone."

"He stays, we can't let him jump."

"He's my captive," Hello John said, coming forward to stand in front of Sam, facing the others and holding his lacrosse stick like a weapon. "I can do with him what I want."

"If he jumps he'll die, and when they find his body, they'll know he was on a train—this train—and they'll know where to look. He stays!"

Medicine Dog sat up, an egg-sized contusion forming on his forehead. "Where am I? Where are we going?"

Sam backed towards a corner of the boxcar, still holding the sharp stick, the taste of his own blood strong in his mouth, the shock of this alien environment resurrecting memories he had fought to repress. "I didn't stay alive over there to come back to this! Do you hear me?"

"Sam, put the stick down," Kate said, afraid of what might happen if Sam provoked Medicine Dog any further.

"I fought for my life, it's not yours to take!"

Crazy Wolf watched him carefully, but not out of fear. He sensed a spirit in Sam that connected strongly with his own: a warrior traumatized by the past. He held out his hand. "Come. Sit."

Sam slashed the air in front of him. He imagined there were people on all sides, with knives and spears. He dreaded moving his feet for fear of mines or roadside bombs. "No! You stay back! I'm not alone! I've got guys everywhere; they're calling in a strike now. One minute, or less, you *hadjis*'re all smoked. You hear me? Smoked!"

"White man's kind of loco," Yura said. "He been eating jimson weeds?"

Sam made stabbing noises, inarticulate gasps, terrorized by the shadows, the taste of blood.

Kate stood to go to him, but Crazy Wolf gently held her back. He stepped towards Sam, holding his arms down, palms open, staring straight into Sam's eyes. "Easy, Sam. This is a tight space, we're in this together."

"You're *hadjis!* Terrorists! I kill terrorists!"

"I don't know what a *hadji* is," Hello John said, "but it can't be good."

"We're all warriors here, you most of all."

"Stay back! I'm not alone."

"That's right, we're here. You're not alone."

Kate pushed past Crazy Wolf and Hello John, and reached out to Sam, but he stabbed at her with his stick.

"Back! *Hadjis!* Terrorists!"

Kate burst into tears. "No, it's me! Don't do this! Sam!"

He rushed at her with his sharp stick and Hello John whacked it away with his lacrosse stick, body checking Sam to push him back towards the corner of the boxcar. Kate turned to Crazy Wolf and buried her face in his chest, sobbing uncontrollably, while Sam sank to his knees, breathing hard, then rolled onto his side and curled into a ball. Hello John sat protectively in front of Sam, his lacrosse stick across his lap.

"Can you still hear the chopper?" Crazy Wolf asked Joseph, who stood with his ear to the door, listening intently, trying to separate the roar of the train from the threat of being discovered, the train rumbling over the pass on its long descent into the unknown.

15

"Good news, I've found them!"

"Tell me you're on the Gallatin River, away from my cattle," Bob Smith radioed back to Lieutenant Walker.

"Negatory. I'm up the Bozeman Pass. Got a positive sighting, night vision's coming through crystal clear."

"Oh, for shits-sakes!" Bob exploded. "You assured me they were over by Big Sky, not practically in downtown Bozeman." He swiveled around in his chair and slammed his hand on the window behind his desk. Larry fidgeted nervously, staring at his back, with the cattle slaughter conveyor line moving along at full speed through the window. Bob barked over his shoulder at Larry: "Can't the Park Service do anything right when it comes to managing your own goddam wildlife?"

"Now Mister Smith, you know we're doing our best here," Larry stammered. "But I've got a problem employee on my hands, this Katie girl. Y'know, she's one of those Lakota tribespeople. I had no choice but to hire her."

Bob cut Larry short. "You're her boss, right? That makes her your problem, so cut the crap!"

Duke came into the office, accompanied by Tino Gugliardi.

"Hey boss," Duke said. "I've got someone here who says he really needs to talk to you. Says he has a vested interest in this whole mess."

"It's way beyond a mess!" Bob said, turning back around.

Tino quickly introduced himself and explained that he absolutely needed to get in touch with Crazy Wolf as soon as possible, if not sooner. "Do you have any idea where they are?"

"Between here and Bozeman, somewhere up the pass," Bob said, immediately wondering where in Montana this Tino guy had acquired those reptilian shoes, and a shirt that seemed to have shreds of aluminum foil woven together with lint balls. "It's not gonna be warm and pretty, I can promise you that."

"Well, that's your chopper isn't it? Let's get a move-on, I'll take up front, you get in back."

"I bet you will," Bob said. "Tell me again why you've got such a heat on to catch them up?"

"Business," Tino said, as if that one word was sufficient to make his case to any hayseed in a cowboy hat. He pulled a hundred dollar bill out of his pocket and magnanimously offered it to Bob.

"Huh, now you're talkin'." He took the bill, pretended to admire it for a second, and came to the conclusion that nothing Tino was wearing came from anywhere north of the Platte or West of the Missouri. A creepy little guy like this might be of some diabolical use down the road. He wadded the bill and tossed it over his shoulder.

"Well then, since you're obviously a man of action, how 'bout you come along for the ride. Duke, show this *businessman* to the chopper and strap him in! Larry, we need you to come along and get your employee back with the program. Because you know how important it is to stick with the program!"

The cloud ceiling was low, pressing down on Bozeman Pass with its spooky high voltage towers and dinosaur-like rock outcroppings raking the sky. "I don't like the looks of this," Duke growled, carefully piloting the chopper.

"Where the hell is he?" Bob asked.

"Hold on a sec, there! Three O'clock! Jeezus! I haven't seen anything like that since Kuwait!"

An explosion of laser-guided tracers illuminated the unleashed, full force of Lieutenant Walker's hi-tech firepower.

"So much for those buffalo," Bob drawled appreciatively.

"Yeah, but what about Crazy Wolf? I fucking-A need his signature!"

"Might have to be posthumous," Larry said, then muttered to himself, "and I'm going to need a new assistant."

But when they landed, the smoking carcasses soon revealed themselves to be a herd of sheep, the Basque shepherd and two cowering dogs terrorized and huddled in their little jeep-pulled, cloth covered wagon, a hundred animals obliterated by the 30mm cannons into steaming mounds of mutton.

"Nice work, Lieutenant," Bob said, while Larry and Tino stepped carefully amid the bloody carnage. "You sure showed 'em what our tax dollars can do."

"They were right in my sights," he stammered. A few surviving sheep wandered among the dead. One stood behind Tino and bleated pathetically. Walker turned on the door gunner. "Corporal, how could you have been so stupid. So irresponsible! I'll have you court martialed for this!"

Bob exchanged glances with the very disgusted Duke. Then, to Tino: "How's about you pay off this *hombre*," gesturing to the sheepherder, "and you and Larry can bury the evidence. I'm sure the good Lieutenant will also lend a hand."

"What?" Larry said.

"No damn way!" Tino said.

Duke found a shovel and a pick in the shepherd's supply wagon and pressed them in their hands.

"Oh yes way," Bob said. "Unless you want to walk home. Price of a chopper ride just went up. Strictly business, you understand." He gave Larry a strong and encouraging slap on the back. "We still have a herd of infectious vectors somewhere out there in the darkness, and if we get distracted bringing justice down the chain of command, there'll be a Japanese or Canuck embargo on my cattle before you can put your first subordinate in front of a firing squad. We all OK on that?"

Walker hesitated just enough for Duke to throw in: "And I'd sure hate to be in your shoes dealing with the either the media, or the military justice system. You know how tough they can be on lower level officers who got nowhere to hide, no one to back 'em up."

Upon a quick, further reflection, Walker was definitely OK with that.

"Seems to me he should be the one getting court martialed," Duke said to Bob as they walked back over to the chopper, "for being an incompetent, horse's ass."

"Oh, I don't know," Bob said. "All three of those guys seem pretty competent at being full blown horse's asses." He stood beside the chopper stared off towards the Paradise Valley. "Damn! Where in the hell did they get to?"

16

The train rolled through the night, heading west to the great headwaters confluence of the Gallatin, Madison, and Jefferson at Three Forks, then north to Helena, stopping in a switch yard for a lengthy series of uncouplings and hard jolt re-couplings as the train was reconfigured, sending some cars north on the Burlington Northern Santa Fe and picking up some others for the journey to that den of iniquity in Missoula. None of the locations were apparent to the natives, huddled in the boxcar darkness. There was one last jolt just before dawn, followed by an hour of bad track then a last decoupling and slow glide to a bumping stop on a spur line. Joseph opened the boxcar door a crack.

"Where are we?" Shining Shirt asked.

"Nowhere," he answered. He opened the door wide to watch the engine disappear beyond a broad snow covered plain bordered by scrub trees, with high mountains to the north and east, and a much higher, thickly forested range to the west. They climbed out and set to sniffing the air and taking their bearings. Sam jumped down and started walking slowly away from the tracks, his feet post-holing in the deep snow almost to his thighs.

"Your prisoner is making a run for it," Little Bull said to Hello John.

"The prisoner is mine!" Medicine Dog said, pointing his knife first at Little Bull, then at Hello John. He brought the rifle into firing position, aimed, and fired into the snow beside Sam. The gunshot echoed off the hills. "And if you take one more step," Medicine Dog called out to Sam, "my next shot will be in your back." He took one of the six bullets from the pouch on his belt, reloaded, and watched as Sam stopped and sank to his knees. His wrists had remained untied from the night before, but the sun off the snow was blinding, and his few plunging steps were exhausting. Medicine Dog grunted, looped the rifle back over his shoulder, and turned away.

Kate opened the door on the next boxcar and one after another the buffalo leapt out. The calf was last. It stood in the doorway, glorious in the morning light. Everyone turned to stare at it. Yura held her hand out and whispered a prayer that repeated the word *tatanka,* looking each time at Kate, encouraging her with her eyes to repeat the word together. After ten or more repetitions, Kate finally mouthed the word. Yura immediately snapped her fingers and the calf jumped out of the boxcar as if winged, sprawling and rolling in the snow, then bounding straight over to a sturdy cow with a singular blaze on its forehead. The cow turned and the calf nuzzled to nurse, indicating that a successful adoption had been made.

"Where are you leading us?" Two Suns asked Crazy Wolf, who carefully watched the buffalo as they began to sweep away the snow and graze on the underlying brown grasses.

"Nowhere," he said after a minute. "Our sacred brothers are leading us." He fell in behind the lead group of buffalo, which worked their way across the field towards the high mountains.

"That's the Bob Marshall Wilderness," Shining Shirt said. "I'd know those mountains anywhere. We must have come down through Choteau. The Flathead Rez is right over that highest peak."

"No, you got it all wrong," Little Bull said. "These are the Bears Paw, west of Fort Belknap. The Gros Ventre have hunted there for a hundred years. I know them like the back of my hand."

The two began to argue about the relative merits of the mountains adjacent to their respective reservations, including the abundance of hunting, fishing, herb gathering, and places to seek visions.

"Why don't you vote on it," Medicine Dog said, "like good little white people. That way it won't matter which mountains they really are or where the hell we are. Isn't that right, Crazy Wolf? Isn't that the way you want us to be? Good little white people?"

Crazy Wolf paid no attention but continued to walk slowly behind the buffalo with Medicine Dog pestering him on one side, and Joseph White Bird on the other, speaking quietly and using his hands to outline the mountains and the pass cutting through. The buffalo meandered in that direction, everyone following except for Hello John and Sam, who remained kneeling in the snow.

Hello John had constructed a second willow branch lacrosse stick during the night. He tapped Sam on the shoulder, "Hey there."

Sam stayed on his knees, not turning around.

"Sniper man. You wanta play some catch?" He stomped through the snow to get around and face Sam, who stared ahead, his mouth half open. "You have to get up and get going. We need to follow our brothers." He placed the stick in Sam's hands, put the hairball in the pocket, and helped him rotate his wrists to cradle it without dropping. "Just like holding a gun, without the trigger." He let go of Sam's wrists, and Sam slowly made the motion himself.

"This is no gun," he said. "That was the whole point. Heydon wanted to turn it all around, get 'em started a new way."

"Get who started?"

"The *hadjis*."

"Those again. Well, they're over there, you're here." He stood beside Sam and struggled to get him up into a standing position. "And we're Indians, not *hadjis*, and the *tatanka* are leading us. You don't want to get left behind, plus you are, after all, my prisoner. Here, throw it to me!" He ran awkwardly through the snow, motioning with his stick for Sam to pass the ball, which after a stunned few moments, Sam did. "Yeah! Nice pass."

Sam took a deep breath and squinted up at the high mountains, rising to a stunningly blue sky. He scooped some snow to wipe on his face. Hello John threw the ball and he caught it, cradled it for a second, and tossed it back. The stick felt whippy and comfortable; it would make an adequate weapon if he was pursued. He caught another pass, a strong sense of freedom and new possibilities building within him, then deliberately passed it back far over Hello John's head.

"Hey, try to get it to me, OK?"

Hello John stomped off through the snow and set to digging for the ball, while Sam started post-holing towards a nearby stand of trees. No one was looking, they were all trying to make sense of the mountains. He figured he had a good two minute head start. But when he came closer to the trees he saw the snow move in a strange, unnatural way; more movement to the left; a gray apparition, then a black one; the muted colors coming clearer as Sam saw sets of eyes and the emerging outline of first one animal, then another, then a full pack of wolves. They were watching him intently; it seemed they were begging him to come into the forest with that willow branch to see who owned this part of the world, the loser sure to be served up for breakfast.

Sam stopped, turned slowly, and moved back to be with the group. Kate came towards him, then she too stopped, shading her eyes to look past Sam into the trees. The clear air, snow, playing catch, and now the awakening shock of fear brought Sam back to a fully alert state of mind.

"You see what I see?" he asked.

"I think it's the Nine Mile pack; that distinctive pair of white wolves is a sure sign. They must've drifted down from east of Missoula. That would make those," she turned to examine the mountains to the west,

"the Bitterroots. We might as well be on the Lewis and Clark expedition."
She came closer, Sam wishing that she would hug him, touch him. He
reached out to brush his finger against her arm.

"That would make you…" he tried to remember the name.

"Sacajawea? I don't think so." She looked towards the others just as
Crazy Wolf turned back, meeting her gaze. She stepped closer to Sam,
placing her hands on his hips and drawing him tight, her eyes still on
Crazy Wolf. "They've picked up the bison scent, but you would have held
them over for a snack, even if there's not an inch of fat anywhere on this
fine body of yours," she said, pinching him all over.

Sam felt his muscles contract, his world focusing on the woman in
front of him. "Kate, I just wish, somehow, this could be different; we
could be somewhere alone. There's a lot I need to tell you."

She saw that Crazy Wolf had turned back to the bison. She put her
finger to Sam's lips then took him by the hand. "Come on, *kemo-sabe*.
Let's just bide our time and see this through." And led him along the
beaten trail towards Lolo Pass.

17

The buffalo pushed over the first of several high plateaus, with steep declines on the other side followed by ever-rising slopes, higher and higher, the snow deeper but the animals intent in their purpose. For three days they pressed on, sorting themselves out in a kind of matriarchal hierarchy, one tough old female in the lead, two sisters close behind, several hard-breathing stud brothers shouldering themselves along, gangster-style. The white buffalo calf dashed from the center to the margins of the herd, never far from the protection of its new adoptive mother, with Kate always watching to make sure she was within the unmarked boundary of the herd's zone of safety. But in stark contrast to the orderly and harmonious progress of the buffalo, the only harmony within the pack of humans following to the sides and behind, was a sense of everyone united against Medicine Dog.

The more he failed to follow through on his dire threats—to scalp Sam, eviscerate Crazy Wolf, slash the buttocks off Little Bull, hang Kate headfirst in a yellow jacket nest—the more Hello John felt emboldened to challenge and pester him with little insults and claims that Sam was his prisoner alone. He even took to mimicking Medicine Dog, saying "Ho!" and Ha!" before expounding on the progress of the buffalo, or the weather outlook, or even the condition of his shoe laces, as in: "Ho! Broke another one. What will I do now, ha!" Everyone understood the biting significance of these pronouncements; they struck Medicine Dog to the core and enflamed his resolve to seek justice, mainly at Sam's expense.

For his part, Sam kept a close eye on how many bullets Medicine Dog had shot and where he kept the rifle. Once, Medicine Dog went to sleep at night with the rifle tucked under a rolled jacket that he used as a pillow. Sam crept over and ever so gently tried to slip the rifle out. He knew that one bullet was in the breech, which was all he would need to put Medicine Dog permanently to sleep. But in the last moment before he had the rifle in his hands, the wolves set up a chorus of howling and Medicine Dog stirred. When he saw what Sam was up to, he beat him severely and fired off a shot at close range, just missing him in the darkness. Crazy Wolf and the others were able to restrain Medicine Dog from firing again, but Sam felt that he had won this little skirmish, bringing Medicine Dog down to five remaining bullets. Unfortunately, Medicine Dog also took to keeping the rifle strap on his shoulder, so Sam knew he had to be vigilant. Sooner or later, Medicine Dog would have to set the rifle down, and Sam would be ready.

He also kept a close eye on the wolves. They were always there in the shadows, like the faintest of stars: if you looked directly they were nearly impossible to see, but if you looked to the side, their subtle movements and colorations revealed them as lurking predators, inescapable as death. It was the same with Kate. When Sam first saw her and Crazy Wolf locking eyes on one another, his natural inclination was to deny it completely. She remained attentive to Sam, checking to make sure his wrist ties were not too tight and that he had water and a share of the meager portions of bulbs, seeds, and small game gathered along the way and passed around the campfire at night. If he watched her directly he saw nothing to be alarmed about. Only when he looked away, with Kate and Crazy Wolf on the periphery, could he see how they held each other's piercing stares. His impulse was to charge him with the lacrosse stick and deliver a death whack. Either that or offer himself up to the pack, knowing that suicide at the teeth of the wolves would be swift but painful. Escape seemed out of the question. Medicine Dog and Hello John were vying for ownership, so instead of one guard he now had two extremely jealous wardens. It was clear to Sam that Medicine Dog was spoiling for a fight; for any excuse to cut him to the bone. Sam felt that Medicine Dog's anger was a sign of weakness and could be turned against him, no different than his own anger at Crazy Wolf was eroding his will to live. But the prospect of being torn apart by the wolves was too grim to seriously consider. For now, he focused on self-preservation.

The morning of the fourth day broke with unsettled weather and a feeling of unease within the herd as well as with the group of natives. The tension between Medicine Dog and Hello John had become a festering sore that was ripe for bursting. They came to a sharp juncture on the ever rising trail to the pass. A cross-mountain ridge led to a shallow, hanging valley that drew the buffalo to the smell of open water and green pasture. The lead female stopped snuffling for forage and pushed heavily through the snow, the others falling in behind, until she came to a precipice where she stopped short, her hooves less than a meter from certain death over the cliff.

"Why aren't we moving?" Little Bull asked.

"How can we know?" Shining Shirt said. "We're in the rear of the parade, scooping up the shit. I used to have to do this with our Boy Scout troop at the Fourth of July parade in Kalispell. We never knew what was going on at the front until we got there, and by then, everyone had gone home."

"Wait. Look at Yura. She's having one of her seizures."

"Idiot! That's no seizure. She's seeing through the eyes of the buffalo."

Yura took Crazy Wolf's arm and stood with one hand reaching forward. "Walk carefully, I see death in this place, a river pouring over the edge of the earth, with a spray of blood rising up. *Tatanka!*"

The calf seemed to respond to Yura's voice and stopped playing to stare at her, suddenly nervous and unsure of herself.

"What's the matter, *Wohpe?*" Kate asked, also keenly aware of the sudden change in temperament, and not just with the calf; the whole herd seemed to be on edge.

"Take me there, grandmother," Crazy Wolf whispered. "Where is this place?"

Yura walked slowly, passing through the uneasy herd, then down a steep slope at the edge of the cliff into a jumble of boulders at the bottom. She got down on her knees and scraped at the rocky soil.

"There's a cave, here!" Hello John said, crouching down to peer into a dark crevice leading back from the base of the cliff.

"Don't go in there," Two Suns cautioned. "This is the time of the bear awakening."

"It's too narrow for a bear. I can just fit if I squeeze sideways."

"Then of snakes," Sam said. "They curl in a ball for the winter and come out altogether, their poison concentrated after their long sleep. Trust me you don't want to be there when that happens."

"I'm going in. Stand back, you're blocking the light."

"No, those are our brothers," Two Suns said.

The shadows of the buffalo fell across the cave entrance as they moved slowly down the slope, each in turn stopping to stare nervously at Yura digging in the ground, then running wildly through the brush to get past the base. Only the white calf stayed at the edge, watching Yura with great curiosity.

"Crazy Wolf! We can't stay at this place, the buffalo are moving," Joseph said.

"No, wait. Yura has found something."

"*Tatanka,*" she said, over and over.

"What's that she saying?" Sam asked.

"The Sioux word for buffalo," Kate said, staying close to the calf.

Yura let out a shriek just as Hello John emerged from the cave and called, "Everyone come here! You've got to see this." He went back inside. Yura stopped digging and raised a cracked, fully formed buffalo skull over her head, offering it to the sun.

"*Tatanka!* This is a place of great death for you, life for us. We bless your gift of life!"

Crazy Wolf leaned close to stare at the stone. "A buffalo, you're certain?"

Yura nodded vigorously. "All underneath these stones are the bones of our ancestors. This is a sacred place."

"A buffalo jump," Kate said excitedly. "No wonder the herd was agitated. Who knows what memories they hold locked in their genes?"

"Crazy Wolf! We need you in here!" Two Suns called from the mouth of the cave.

"No," Joseph said. "The buffalo are leaving us."

The calf darted to follow the herd down the slope, then came back to watch Yura.

"The white buffalo calf knows," Kate said.

Medicine Dog seemed confused by the activity pulling the group apart. He stood with his arms outstretched. "Do not be afraid. I know where to go. We must gather together!" This, as everyone moved in three directions at once.

Hello John stuck his head out of the cave. "Look at Medicine Dog, he's finally found his source of power. We now know that the Crow warrior is really just a scarecrow."

Everyone laughed, and not just a little, but with deep, belly breaking peals of mockery. But Medicine Dog stood his ground for a moment, then dismissed the group with a sweep of his knife and followed the buffalo down the slope.

The calf turned to the cave and picked its way carefully through the boulders. Two Suns and Hello John had already gone back inside. The calf hesitated and then followed them in. Kate reached past Sam and took Crazy Wolf by the hand. "Come with me! Hurry, this is special!"

Sam saw how Crazy Wolf's face filled with light, even as he disappeared into the darkness of the cave, leaving Sam alone in the harsh midday sun. He turned his face to the sun, staring straight into it, feeling a powerful sense of healing from the blinding pain. He let out a high, piercing scream that came from the bottom of his soul. When the echoes of his scream had settled over the trees, Little Bull popped her head out of the cave.

"What's with you, white man? Get your cute ass in here. You gotta see this!"

Sam crawled on his knees into the cave. The others crouched in a long narrow chamber, the light slanting off the walls, casting their shadows on a montage of primitive line drawings: of horned beasts and fantastical antelopes; armed warriors with spears and bows, villages with tipis and sweat lodges, buffalo pitching off the cliff above. Sam's first impression was that it was a wall of graffiti, no different than a Reno alley way. But as his eyes grew more accustomed to the dim light, he saw the raw power in the images and felt a stirring sense of connection. The others were awed into silence, gesturing wordlessly to the hunter-prey relationships spread across the rock.

"Crazy Wolf, come quickly!" Joseph White Bird called from outside. He was the only one other than Medicine Dog who had not gone into the cave.

The words were muffled by the stale air, but no less urgent. Yura turned to face the entrance, her eyes stricken from what she saw beyond the light.

"Go! There is death! Danger!"

The calf ran to the entrance, Crazy Wolf crawling as fast as he could out of the cave, followed by the others. Sam went behind Kate, grabbing her ankle just as they left the darkness.

"Kate, I need to speak with you."

"No! Didn't you hear Joseph? We've got to see what's happening."

"But I need you here, now. Leave them."

She struggled to get free of his grasp. "I didn't come this far to leave *Wohpe* to the wolves. Is that what you want?" She used her free foot to kick Sam in the face. His head jerked back; they stared at one another for a moment. "Sam, I'm sorry. But I've got to go."

And she scooted out of the cave, leaving Sam to wipe the blood from his nose, the salty taste strong in his mouth. The others clambered over his half-conscious body; the cave fell silent. Sam lay in the dust, curling into a fetal position. He felt an irresistible urge to cry like a baby, and after a moment of intense resistance, he let go and allowed wave upon wave of sobbing convulsions to sweep up through his body, the tears streaming down his face. After it passed, he lay prone in the dust for what may have been five minutes, or five years; he couldn't tell. The stick figure images on the stone wall came alive and moved with a graceful elegance that was every bit as real as life itself: the hunters launched their spears; the horned wolves brought down an antelope; the village pulsed with preparations for the buffalo hunt. One image stood out above all the others: a radiant drawing of the sun, with lines extending to the village and to the buffalo. Sam felt himself drawn to it; he reached to touch the stone, when a shadow fell across the cave and he had a sudden sense that a wolf was coming in to eat him whole.

"Sniper man, there's no time!" Hello John said. "Follow me now!"

18

Medicine Dog stood on the ridge, aiming his rifle at a little farm homestead down in the valley, the smoke curling up from the chimney, and said,
"These dogs are mine! I will cut their livers out and eat them raw. Who is
with me?"

The others shuffled their feet. "I don't know, man," Two Suns said. "I
hear they have a special low-voltage electric chair just for Indians, cooks
'em slow. You really want to risk that?"

"Coward!" He jumped up on a fallen tree trunk and pounded his
chest, raising the rifle high over his head in one hand, his knife in the other
hand. "I am Medicine Dog! First son of Chief Silver Bear of the Hidatsa-
Absaroka. I am a great warrior; we are a great people! I will count coup
today and color my knife with the blood of these invaders and drive them
back over the waters to return our people to greatness. I swear this on the
souls of my ancestors!"

Sam heard this last part just as he saw the family come out of their
cabin and look up to the ridge: a lightly bearded father, a pretty young
pregnant wife, three children under the age of about eight. The children
pointed and waved; the mother and father rushed back inside the cabin.
The children started scrambling up the hill towards them.

"He's probably going for his gun," Sam said.

Crazy Wolf placed himself in front of Medicine Dog. "I can't let you
do that. We have no quarrel with these people."

"Cowards! All of you! If you won't do this thing, I will count coup
alone! I am not afraid!"

The children were laughing and calling out, "Come down! We want to play!"

"They're kids, man," Two Suns said. "No one here's afraid of kids."

The veins stood out on Medicine Dog's forehead; he was building himself into a blood rage. "Listen to them! Our sacred ground! And all you do is stand there letting this happen! I am Medicine Dog!"

"We don't really know exactly where we are," Little Bull said. "This might not be sacred at all. It could be like, just some ordinary place."

Medicine Dog slashed the air and let out a war whoop; the children were not more than fifty yards down the hill now; he could get to them in seconds.

"He's gonna do it," Sam said. "And I swear, if he hurts those kids I won't rest 'til he gets justice."

"Don't do this," Shining Shirt said.

"Make him stop, please!" Kate pleaded.

Crazy Wolf pulled out his knife and set his feet for Medicine Dog's attack. "Do what you must. I will do what I must."

But when they came back out, the woman was holding a steaming hot pie and the man was waving a paper over his head and motioning for them to come on down.

"Do you see that?" Hello John said. "They mean to feed us." He took off down the hill with the others quickly following. Two Suns picked up the youngest child and carried it to the cabin. Little Bull took the others by the hand and ran with them. Joseph was the first to the cabin and called back, "The buffalo are in the barn! Get down here!"

Crazy Wolf and Medicine Dog hadn't taken their eyes off one another, their knives still ready in their hands. Medicine Dog stepped forward off the log, right in Crazy Wolf's face, but he didn't back up. After a long, tense moment, Medicine Dog turned quickly and grabbed Sam by the wrists and threw him to the ground. He wrapped the leather rope around his neck and jerked him upright. Without a word, his face white with shame and fury, he led Sam down the hill. Sam didn't resist, but out of the corner of his eye, he saw Kate step close to Crazy Wolf, the two of them touching foreheads, his hands on her shoulders, hers on his hips.

The taste of blood was still strong in Sam's mouth when Medicine Dog dragged him into the barn and tied him to a pole, his hands behind. Sam could hear the buffalo feeding on a fragrant bale of alfalfa.

"Kill me now!" Sam said.

"Shut up!" Medicine Dog rummaged through drawers and shelves, throwing a variety of tools, solvents, and horse tack onto the dirt floor.

"Then hang yourself. You can probably get that right."

"I said for you to shut your white mouth!" He came over and smacked Sam with the back of his hand.

But it didn't matter to Sam. Nothing mattered. He laughed in Medicine Dog's face, spitting blood. Medicine Dog went back to rummaging around and found a can of Lysol and a half-empty bottle of soda. He pierced the can with a rusty nail, the aerosol shrieking out, then poured the 90-proof liquid into the bottle and shook it up.

"Cheyenne champagne!" he said, taking a huge gulp of the vile concoction, immediately retching and grimacing, then drinking again. He gasped for air, let out a whoop and fired the rifle into the ceiling of the barn.

"Look at you," Sam said, realizing that Medicine Dog was now down to four bullets. "Drinking all by yourself. What a loser."

"Oh, I'm gonna kick your white ass!" Medicine Dog came over and laid a foot right across Sam's ribs, then tied a greasy rag over his eyes. "I'll be back later to do to you what your soldiers did to my grandfathers. Ha! You're going to like that!" He went outside, leaving Sam in a private world of darkness and pain.

Sam tried not to think, but his mind was filled with Kate's face, looking up at him from the steaming water. He could feel their bodies pressed against one another, silky smooth, the contours of each fitting like puzzle pieces into the other. He shook his head, forcing the image out, and thought of BJ, what he might be doing now. It was still too early for him to realize Sam hadn't returned from the contract hunt; maybe tomorrow. What day of the week was tomorrow? Sam tried to count back the days but it was all a blur, fading into an earlier time, the sand and smoke blowing across a barren horizon, a spider the size of a large crab crawling out from beneath a pile of spent cartridges. Sam saw Heydon Jones just over there, surrounded by a group of kids, each with a lacrosse stick. He could hear Heydon speaking in that well-bred, clipped voice he had, the good choice of words. Being black made him more familiar and acceptable to the kids, they hung around him like a father, smiling and attentive. Heydon had the ball in the pocket and he was showing them how to bring the stick back, elbows in tight, rotating at the hip to get maximum torque, the kids eagerly imitating his motion to earn a nod of approval, all of them huddled in close. Sam didn't like the look of that spider, but it was simply too big to step on, so he let it go, skittering across the dusty yard to a gate where a woman in full chador, only a narrow slit for eyes, came through, heading for the kids. Sam didn't think anything of her, figured she was probably a mom, although she was kind of bulky, with a sharp edge or two at the waist, the realization suddenly building that these kids were orphans, that's who Heydon was committed to working with, the lost and forgotten kids of a ruined country, their parents gunned down by the allies or shot through the head by one of their own, kneeling beside a ditch. No way this was a mom! He tried to call out a warning to Heydon, screaming his name, but the word stuck in his throat, and there was only silence until the woman pulled open her gown, issued a screechy "*Allahu Akbar!*" the sticks of explosives strapped around her body a lethal dull color, the blasting caps shiny copper, then all was brightness as she pressed the hand detonator and a ball of flames, body parts, and shrapnel ripped the day into little pieces.

Sam felt water streaming down his face, but not from sweat. Kate had a wet cloth and was bathing his head. "Oh baby, did he hurt you?"

"Kate! I'm fine. Oh, I'm so glad you're here."

"Me too Sam. Oh, you poor thing."

Sam could feel her moving the cloth over his neck and shoulders. She gently pulled his shirt back. "You've got so many hurts."

He could smell her hair and skin. "Untie me."

"I can't do that," she whispered. He felt her kiss beneath his ear. "You're Medicine Dog's prisoner. He's over in the cabin, making a big show of that."

"Did he leave my rifle?"

"Oh no, he's waving it around, threatening everyone."

"Well then take this blindfold off."

"No, it's better this way. Quick, there's not much time," she said.

"What?" Sam could hear her fumbling with buttons, then the sound of a zipper, and now she straddled his lap and he could feel her bare breasts against his chest.

"Here, how's that feel?"

"What are you doing?"

"What does it feel like baby? I thought you wanted me."

"But Kate, I don't…"

She silenced him with a deep kiss, her hands running down his chest, waist, and below, his pants coming off, her on him now, moving, grinding, her breath coming in short gasps right in his face, him not caring and kissing, biting, gasping in return, then she made a loud moaning "Brian!"

over and over several times, before slowing and climbing off him, Sam in darkness, the feeling receding.

"Oh baby, we both needed that." She wiped him clean, tugged his pants back on. "You OK? I'll get you some food."

"Kate, what are you doing?" He heard her footsteps move away and he leaned his head back against the pole, unsure what was real and what was not.

19

The man and woman were homesteaders of a sort who had garnered a collection of trust funds, annual bonuses, and stock options from their urban lives as internet programmers, and re-created themselves up in the mountains, raising vegetables, goats, and siring a bevy of children, all the while borrowing down their equity until they, too, were foreclosed on like common tract-home commuters. It didn't matter. Since leaving the city and settling under the sun and stars, they had become disciples of a midwest ex-Baptist who convincingly preached that the end was not only near, it was any day now, most definitely before the next full moon, which put Armageddon at less than a month away. They greeted the Indians with open arms, inviting them to come along to a gathering of the faithful where they would all be raised up into Heaven as one, but when they received a polite decline, the dad handed over the deed to the place, and the family got in their bio-diesel mini-van and headed off, literally into the sunset.

The house was simple and fully stocked, the farm animals long since sold off or eaten. The fellow apparently was an amateur taxidermist: there were mounted heads of deer, elk, and bear, a variety of fish leaping out of clear plastic water courses, there was even a buffalo robe rug in front of the fireplace and a highly illegal mounting of a golden eagle standing on a fence post with a rattler clutched in its talons. Yura made a blessing over each animal, rearranging them in a sacred circle with the buffalo skull that she had carried down from the cliff positioned in the center.

Crazy Wolf, Shining Shirt, and Two Suns found a set of maps. They determined once and for all that they were now in the heart of the Bitterroot

Mountains, near the crest of Lolo Pass. They considered various routes to safety, although the extent of the threat seemed pervasive, nearly universal, so there didn't seem to be a safe haven anywhere. Joseph and Yura discovered a set of rock-and-roll drums, which they used to accompany a Grass Dance chant. And Little Bull and Hello John rummaged through the kids' rooms and came across a simple laptop computer, powered by a battery attached to a small array of photovoltaic cells, and connected through a long cable to the top of a receiver on a pine tree, allowing access to the worldwide web.

"Let's see if there's anything about us in the news!"

"Gotta be," Little Bull said, checking several search engines, but nothing turned up.

"You keep looking, I have to take a leak."

"Down the hall, left, and hold your nose. You won't believe it: an indoor outhouse."

Hello John followed his nose and found Medicine Dog in the bathroom, applying a war paint of lipstick and nail polish across his sagging, drunken face. By now, he had gone through several cans of aerosol and was in the darkest of moods.

"You, little one!" He grabbed a set of cuticle scissors from the cabinet and threatened Hello John with them. "I'll eat your, your..." but he couldn't quite get his mouth around the word he wanted.

"Fingernails?"

Medicine Dog tried to swing the rifle around but in the tight space the long barrel got hung up on the mirror. He pulled the trigger, shattering the mirror, the recoil knocking him back and over, nearly headfirst into the toilet. Hello John left him there and went back to Little Bull.

"Check this out," she said. "It's Kate. I googled her name." She pointed at the screen. "The girl's full-blooded Lakota alright, but she's not, y'know, one of us."

"What's that supposed to mean?"

"I mean, well, too smarty pants."

"Hey, grandmother says smart is good. Indians are wily like coyotes, but we need to be smarter, like a fox. Or better yet, an owl."

"Ok, but she's too full of herself. I can smell it."

"Ha, she'd like that, a she-wolf marking her territory. You better be careful."

Little Bull splayed her fingers and pretended to scratch the air. "She's the one who better watch out, I'm Suhtai-Cheyenne, like Crazy Wolf, and that makes me just a little bit more…" She paused to think.

"Dangerous! Definitely more dangerous."

• • •

When Medicine Dog got himself upright, he recalled that there were at least two more cans of Lysol out in the barn. He gave a whoop, kicked the bathroom door down to get through rather than turn the handle and pull it inward, and pinballed off the hallway walls and out the back door. The sun had long since set and it was getting cold, but he tore off his shirt because he felt way too hot. Boiling hot. He stopped to stare at the sky and felt a sudden sense of relief, then looked down. "Ho! Peed on myself!" He heard a skitter on the snow and saw a weasel chasing a new born rabbit. The weasel caught it after two bounds and shook it dead. "Ha! Just like my White man!" He removed one of the last four bullets, fumbled to reload, and slung the rifle back over his shoulder.

Sam was asleep when Medicine Dog came into the barn. He heard Medicine Dog grab an axe hanging from some hooks on the wall, and whack the pole three inches above Sam's head, cutting it nearly all the way through.

"Yeah, White man! I'll chop you to pieces." He took a big swing and missed Sam but almost split his own foot in two. Sam had a brief sense that all this was part of a continuing nightmare, but now he was fully awake, struggling up to his feet against the pole, rubbing the blindfold partially off in the process. As Medicine Dog wound up to try again, Sam jumped as high as he could and pitched forward, breaking the pole at the cut, rolling away now from Medicine Dog who saw that Sam was free and came at him like a windmill, one wild swing just missing Sam's face but cutting the wrist straps, and chasing him out of the barn. He threw down the axe and swung the rifle around, firing from the hip, the bullet caroming into the forest a half-mile away. Sam tore off the blindfold and ran across a field down a sloping valley with a winding creek in the middle. Willows were jutting through the snow, which was decomposed mush despite a night freeze setting in. Sam took three steps on the surface, one down to his groin, then up, down, his foot caught in willows. It was worse for Medicine Dog who moved sideways as well as forward, whooping and cursing and swearing that he would eat Sam's intestines. He tried to reload, dropping and losing the bullet in the snow, removed the last two from the pouch, and bit down on one bullet while he struggled to load the other.

The people back in the house heard the sharp report of the gunshot and the immediate bellowing of the buffalo in the barn and rushed outside. It was impossible to see Sam further down the valley. It appeared that Medicine Dog had been overcome by personal demons.

"Ha! Look at him, trying to shoot himself!" Little John said.

"Good thing the buffalo are bedded down," Joseph said.

Kate felt a sense of elation after her encounter with Sam, although she realized how strange it must have been for him. But that didn't matter. With Medicine Dog challenging Crazy Wolf for leadership of the group, she knew she needed Sam to be devoted to her and available to do her bidding, no matter what the sacrifice. She wanted Crazy Wolf to be the undisputed leader, with herself at his side, orchestrating his every move.

Now, with Medicine Dog running wild down the valley, she decided to go check on Sam and the calf again. She resolved to untie Sam and remove the blindfold this time. He had performed admirably while tied up; he might be even better with the full use of his body. She went out to the barn and was surprised to see that the doors were open—the calf up on its feet, the bison agitated and uneasy. The broken pole was the only clue she needed to know what had happed to Sam.

"He's after Sam!" she called back towards the group outside the house. "Medicine Dog'll kill him!"

"Well, he's his prisoner after all," Two Suns said.

"He's my prisoner!" Hello John said. "He has no right."

"It's a waste of a perfectly good man," Little Bull said. "The White man, that is."

Crazy Wolf ran over to the barn and looked inside: the tracks on the ground, the bloody discarded blindfold, the shreds of wrist ties. A pitchfork and pry bar were leaning in a corner. He went to grab them when one of the buffalo made a false charge, the others forming a protective circle around the calf, as if Crazy Wolf was a predator. He quickly grabbed the tools and backed outside.

"That's all you've got?" Kate said. "But he has a gun, he'll shoot you dead!"

"I don't want to fight him, just slow him down. He has a battle going on inside his soul that is much more violent than anything he can do to me. I'm more worried about getting him back here."

Kate hesitated, then came closer. "And what about Sam? What are you going to do with him?"

"His wrists are untied. He's free to do whatever he wants."

"Good." She held his eyes for a second, but he looked nervously at the others, not wanting to display his feeling.

"All my relatives," he said as a form of blessing, then began running across the field, the snow firmer now, not breaking through.

Sam felt the cold increase, quickly realizing how weak and hungry he was, the wind in his face, the layer of sweat acting as a very effective refrigerant. He stopped to look around and saw that the snow field was bounded by high, forested slopes, leading down to a narrow canyon that disappeared in darkness. There were no lights anywhere, no roads, no power lines. "Can't stay here," he said to himself, his jaw tight, teeth chattering. He could hear Medicine Dog slogging through the snow, his curses audible. "Can't go back." Sam saw movement on one side of the field. His first thought was wolf, but this was smaller, blacker, and he realized it was a bear cub. He dropped to his knees. "But where's mom?" Then saw a much larger dark mass at the edge of the trees on the other side of the meadow.

It appeared to be face down, probably digging for insects in a buried stump. "Can't go between them," he chattered, realizing the likelihood of an attack. An outcrop of willow branches lined this side of the frozen creek and Sam suddenly saw his opportunity. He stayed low, moving as silently as possible, dashing in behind the willows, following the curve of the water course. His foot broke through and it felt like hot knives piercing his ankle and toes. The cub was just above and saw him now, standing in front of a winter den. It bawled for its mother and Sam knew he had no time. He kept moving, faster, lower, hearing the deep answering grunt, Medicine Dog whooping and cursing, mindlessly coming directly between them.

By the time Sam got to the first tree at the end of the meadow, the mother had charged across the snow. Medicine Dog fired his last bullet to no effect, the bear swatting the rifle from his hands before he had any chance to reload. Sam heard a choked scream as the bear bit him across the face, then a tearing sound and Medicine Dog staggered backwards, a hideously bloody, gaping, toothy grin where his face should have been, then the bear was all over him, knocking him like a football, biting behind his neck and flinging him rag-like ten feet then back on him, tearing him to bits. After a minute of this, the bear was done. It nosed the lifeless remains, then dragged the carcass up to the den, roughly tugging it inside, followed by the cub, and all was silent again.

Sam realized he hadn't breathed throughout the attack. He sucked the cold air, holding his hand over his mouth to keep from coughing. He backed into the trees, the light silvery flat and shadowed, his feet crunching on the hoarfrost that had developed over the snow. The stream was deeply buried here, but it re-emerged in a smaller meadow, with a thermal rising from the hillside, the steam billowing into the low spots where it hovered like a spiritual mist. Sam waded into it, the cold now much more intense. He saw movement in the trees. Bear? No, there was more than one; a dozen, grey against the snow and darkness. He looked around. The movement was everywhere. The wolves knew now that they were in control and came forward out of the sheltering trees, unafraid, heads hanging low, eyes fixed on his wherever he looked, the steam issuing in small bursts from their nostrils.

Sam recalled the first rule of an ambush: to attack in one direction and hold your course, knowing that the perimeter was thin and once outside you could counter attack: sound advice for a company of fully armed, pinned down soldiers. But that rule didn't apply here. He tried to think of an alternative. The wolves were on all sides, some sitting on their haunches waiting for a sign to attack; a casual, easy prey at the center, no rush, this one wasn't going anywhere. "What did I ever do?" he said out loud, wondering how he had come to this, the prospect of being eaten alive so immediate and unavoidable. He sank to his knees, giving himself up, and answered his own thought with the recollection of a mission not long after Heydon's death, his spotter beside him on a rocky ridge, a group of friendlies advancing on a rude hut where some soon-to-be wasted unfriendly was holed up. Sam's job was to smoke anyone who intervened on this little display of military justice. "*Hadji*, three-o-clock, six hundred meters." Sam brought his rifle around and carefully bolted the cartridge. "Wind?" "Two knots, southeast." Sam made the adjustment, focused the scope, tuning it in to a woman in full chador, something bulky underneath, scooting down a side street, behind empty shop stalls, a tethered goat. "The woman, right?" "Affirmative." Sam applied pressure to the trigger, waited for her to emerge. There she was, in the open, stopping now, her hands not visible inside her robe, head down as if saying something. "What are you waiting for, drop her!" his spotter whispered. And Sam did as he was ordered, the rifle recoiling, a briefest moment before the bullet found its mark, passing right through chador, body, and out, the shock dropping her like a rock, the gown falling open and a dead baby laying against her breast, the accuracy of the scope so sharp that he could see the slow-bleeding hole through both child and mother. Sam gasped, sucking air like a drowning man might suck in water. "Come on!" he spoke, holding his arms out to embrace the wolf attack. "Do it!"

He saw the alpha turn its head, the others standing now, heads turned in the same direction. A loud "Hi-ya!" followed by a yelping yell, and suddenly Crazy Wolf was right at his side, pulling him up to a standing position, handing him a pitch fork.

"Back to back, circle, make noise! Hi-ya! Noise!"

Sam tried to shout, but it was more of a bark. His hands were numb and he could barely hold the handle; one foot was completely useless, numb to the knee.

"Hi-ya!" Crazy Wolf lunged forward with his pry bar. The wolves seemed indignant and scarcely moved back, looking at one another for the sign to get this over with. One wolf, a younger more aggressive sibling to the alpha, came in fast and Crazy Wolf set the butt of the pry bar on his foot and caught it full in the chest, pitching it to the side, another right behind coming at Sam. He stabbed it through the eye and nostril and it backed away, yelping shrilly, bleeding hard and pawing at its face as if it had a foxtail in its eye.

"We move, together! One step, now; another. Hi-ya!" Crazy Wolf kept the count and slowly, surely, they moved back up the meadow, past the blood spot and track where Medicine Dog had been dragged away, the crumpled skin of his face still on the snow. Sam stumbled against something hard and long, and in the dim light he saw the rifle at his feet. He grabbed it and slung the strap over his shoulder.

"What do you want that for? Medicine Dog took all the bullets."

"It's mine and I need it!" Sam said, thinking of the bullet of last resort that he kept around his neck.

The light soon faded to blackness, but a twinkling bright spot off in the distance marked the homestead. The wolves melted back into the trees and began to howl. Crazy Wolf lowered his weapon. "They are laughing at us." He mimicked their howl with a well-practiced, very accurate version of his own. "But I laugh at them! We live to fight another day."

Sam used the pitchfork as a brace and held himself up. "I shot her," he gasped.

"Who?"

"The woman and baby. Saw them fall. Bullet passed right through both."

"Huh."

Sam grabbed Crazy Wolf by the shirt, staring wildly into his face. "Didn't you hear me? She was nursing it and I shot them! You should've let them take me. It was my time!" Sam broke into waves of sobs, barely able to stand.

"Hey." Crazy Wolf placed his hand on Sam's shoulder. "I'm with you. Come on. You're almost home."

Sam pushed him away and held the pitchfork out. "*Hadji!* This isn't my home. You have no hold on me. Stay back!"

Crazy Wolf stood his ground. "You're free to go or stay, whatever you choose."

The wolves broke into a new round of howling. Sam tried to cover his ears with his forearms, still holding onto the pitchfork. "Aagh! The child is calling me! I shot her. It's my time."

Crazy Wolf came slowly forward. Sam held the pitchfork out against his chest.

"Get back!"

"There is no time, Sam."

"No! *Hadji!*"

"No time other than what we make of it."

"Heydon was blown to bits, and I got even. I shot her; a baby!"

"You have to let it rest, put it past, move on." He came right up to the pitchfork, held the tines to his bare chest. "Blood on blood. We're from different worlds you and I, but our blood runs the same. I'm still your brother."

"Brother?" The pitchfork trembled in Sam's frozen hands.

"I was there, spilled the same blood, lost the same friends. Move on."

The wolves howled. Sam lowered the pitchfork. "I'm cold, man. I want to go in."

Crazy Wolf put his arm around Sam's waist and helped him stagger the last bit across the field to the homestead where they found everyone in the main room, the men in a semi-circle with the women in the center, Kate and Little Bull at each other's throat.

"What's the meaning of this?" Crazy Dog said. He helped Sam to a chair.

"It's because of her they ran off!" Little Bull screamed at Kate, holding her by the hair and neck.

"I was the one trying to save them!" Kate grabbed her arm and scratched, drawing blood.

"There is pain and suffering here," Yura counseled. "We must seek healing."

Little Bull wound up to deliver a left upper-cut, but Two Suns grabbed her fist. "Easy now, let go! Someone's gonna get hurt."

"I'll kill her! She thinks she's so much better!"

"Who ran off? The buffalo?"

"All of them are gone!" Hello John said. "We looked, but the trails go in every direction. There were wolf tracks everywhere."

"I am better, you little grasshopper! I'm descended from the Seven Council Fires! Not even a half-blood *iyeska*. My father is Henry Weasel Bear. My mother's people were keepers of the Sacred Pipe."

"Let her go," Crazy Wolf said.

"Oh, I've seen you making eyes at her," Little Bull said. "And you of the Buffalo Family!"

"That is enough! We are all a family here! You are breaking the circle."

"But the circle is already broken," Yura said quietly. She placed a hand on Little Bull. "Come, child."

Little Bull let go and they separated to opposite sides, making the circle complete, with Crazy Wolf and Yura in the center.

Sam rubbed his feet to make the blood return, aware that Kate had not yet looked at him. Crazy Wolf told them about the confrontation with the bear and the wolves, which led to a long argument about what to do next, about the need for healing and renewal after Medicine Dog's death. But Sam knew that Kate could come to him at any time if she chose. Crazy Wolf had told him that he was free to leave, that he was no longer anyone's prisoner. But the only place he wanted to be was near Kate. Why didn't she look at him? They were all talking about healing, but he felt that he had the biggest wounds in the room. The only healing he needed was Kate's love.

"I call for the healing tree!" Kate said. "The buffalo left because we have failed to earn their power. Our group is in conflict. We need to be reborn. I call for Crazy Wolf to be the Pledger and Yura to be the Instructor for the Sun Dance. They both know the ritual. I am the Sacred Offering Woman. You others will be the military societies and the Thunder assistant. We all come from Sun Dance tribes. The Sun Dance is the only way we can be healed and earn back the buffalo. And without them the world is lost!"

A hush settled over the room. Yura looked up at Crazy Wolf and nodded.

"You know what she is asking?" he said.

"We have all the necessary sacred elements. It is unusual for this time of year and under these circumstances, but our power needs to be renewed. When I found the buffalo skull I knew it was a sign. Performing the Sun Dance is our only hope."

The others nodded their agreement, each aware of the obligations and commitment required. Sam, watching from the side of the room, felt the life return to his feet, and with it came pain. He unslung the rifle from his shoulder and slowly removed the bullet from the necklace, carefully reloading. The weapon gave him a new sense of either power or vulnerability. The choice was his.

"I'm not leaving," he said to himself, hearing the wolves fading into the night.

20

BJ tried to recall what he did when he got back from Vietnam. He remembered thinking that he never really left, that it was so deeply embedded inside him that he carried it everywhere, 24/7. He'd worked mainly in the supply chain, keeping the frontline warriors armed and ready to wreak havoc. When his convoy came under fire and he became shell shocked and was sent home on the next flight out, he felt that the world had ended. But it hadn't of course. He got a job, a life, and got over it, eventually. But when he went to the reunions in Pensacola, Detroit, or Las Vegas, there were always a few who were still blasting away in the door of a Huey chopper, or waiting in a trench at Khe Sanh, ready to slash the throat of the first poor soul who stumbled out through the fog. He hoped that Sam wasn't one of those.

As a sniper, Sam would have had the experience of seeing his victims at the exact moment before, during, and after the onset of death. He could separate himself from the experience by aligning his mind to the military code of conduct: friend or foe; enemy or ally. What was done to an enemy was acceptable, after all, they would certainly do the same to you given the chance. But for a sniper the pain inflicted was personal, delivered on a retail basis, one at a time, not like the B-52 bomb squads who rained wholesale death from ten thousand feet. BJ could imagine that the pain stored up within Sam was greater than just about any other branch of the service.

There seemed to be only three ways to deal with such pain. The first was to go inside yourself and allow it to tear you up until such time as it became too much and you did yourself in. The second option, closely related to the first, was to simply explode in rage at some random, unrelated provocation, venting like the hottest volcano, thus ensuring an equal and opposite response from the authorities, which was just another way of killing yourself. The third option was to lose oneself in some place or thing. That's how the walking dead survived. BJ had tried to stay close to his war buddies, but for a long time everyone was drifting, some away to places like backwoods Idaho and the desert canyons of Arizona, others staying in place but shrouded in their own private world of pain. Everyone suffered, but those who seemed to suffer most were the ones who had inflicted the most. He couldn't be sure what Sam had done immediately upon returning from Iraq, maybe a combination of the first two options. But if, as it appeared, he had gone over to throw in his lot with the Indians, then that not only made perfect sense, it was also a strong act of self-preservation. Saving the buffalo was just another way of saving himself.

BJ's rumination was interrupted by a loud harangue from the gang of cowboys emerging from the Timber Bar. They'd been driving around for the morning, having a fine time looking for Indians or buffalo to shoot. As far as they were concerned this was the greatest of all possible adventures, a point of kinship with great grandfathers and long lost family three generations removed: a return to the Old West, with the promise of blood and scalps before sunset.

"I see one a them sonsabitches, I'm goin' for a gut shot, make 'em die slow!"

"I say we run 'em over, then back up and do it again."

"Fool! We oughta tie one arm to a tree, other to the hitch, pull 'em apart!"

BJ let them run on like that, figuring that if they were lucky they wouldn't come within ten miles of the renegades. He knew how skittish and powerful those buffalo could be, and with a group of armed and passionately committed Indians as their allies, it would be a bad case of Little Bighorn disease to encounter them on even terms. Plus, you couldn't be sure how Sam would respond. BJ had a healthy respect for the deadly one-on-one skills Sam would have learned in the Marines. These candy-ass cowboys talked big, but they had no idea the wrath they'd be up against if they squared off with the likes of Sam Comstock.

There was a chance that Sam had indeed foraged his way back to Nevada, but not likely, given the way he had responded to that girl's smile. BJ had practically felt the heat given off in the exchange. Still, it was a possibility.

"You boys hang tight here a minute. I got a call to make."

"Take your time old man. We'll save you a scalp!"

"Yeah, you do that." BJ went around the corner and made a cell phone call to Sam's house: no answer. Then to Sam's mother up in Reno. She answered the third ring.

"Missus Comstock?"

"Yes? This is Betty."

"I'm John McLaughlin of the Nevada Fish and Wildlife Service. Your son, Sam, was with me on a special assignment up here in Montana."

"Well is everything all right? How's my Sam? Where is he?"

"Well now nothing to be alarmed about, but that's why I'm calling, to see if you know his whereabouts. He mustered out a few days ago and I figured he might've passed your way. Just want to ask him a few questions, about maybe working with me back in Nevada." Which wasn't exactly a lie. BJ liked Sam and figured he'd make a solid game warden, although he hadn't actually talked to anyone about it yet.

"I'm sure he'd like that. My Sam is searching, y'know. He needs something to take his mind off things. Blake!" She called into another room. "Blakey, have you heard from your brother?"

Sam heard something that sounded like a "Hell no!", then Betty came back on the line.

"We surely haven't. But I do hope he's ok. You never know about Sam, the state of mind he's in. You be sure and call me when you find him, will you?"

BJ assured her that he would. Next up he called Oxnard. The phone rang ten times before his whispering, throaty voice growled back.

"Can't talk, keep it low!"

"Well hello there Ox, how'n the hell are you?"

"I said, I can't talk! Are you deaf?" His voice rising to a decibel range just short of shouting.

"Sounds to me like you talk fine. But here's the thing: you seen or heard from Sam?"

"Why'n the hell would I hear from that little weasel? Last time we were together he was jumping the truck to foul my shot. Worthless bastard!"

"Yeah, well, I was figurin' on giving him a bonus," BJ lied, not liking Oxnard's tone. "Sign of appreciation for his dedicated hard work."

He let that hang there, feeling Oxnard fume on the other end. "Naw, I'm just jerkin' your chain big guy. I need to talk to him about something is all. You seen him?"

"Bonus, huh?" This, in a perfectly straight voice.

"I said I was kiddin', ok?"

"Cause I could use a bonus, know what I'm sayin'?"

"We all could Ox. Now about Sam…"

"Cause where I am right now, is one shitty place. I could use a vacation. Somewhere warm and friendly, not like this shit hole."

BJ could see that it was going to be a long haul with Oxnard. "Well if you don't mind me asking, where might that be?"

"Can't tell ya. It's secret."

"What, you playing hide-n-seek? C'mon, Ox, fess up!"

Now he spoke again in that menacing throaty way of his. "I followed that girl up here to the end of the world, that's where. And I'm talkin' about *the end!* Know what I'm saying? The absolute be-all end-all end-time. Arma-fuckin'-geddin time, that's what!"

BJ didn't know what to make of that and didn't want to either. "Now would that be on planet Earth, or are you in some other dimension?"

"How 'bout Nevada? That Earth enough for you?"

"Well why didn't you say so? If you're in Nevada, then you're home. Now about that Sam…"

"Nah, this ain't hardly home. People are walkin' around half dead, and don't even ask me what happens when they're full and all dead. No siree, I ain't goin' there."

"Ox, if you're in Nevada and you haven't seen or heard from Sam, then I guess that's all I need to know for now. But you get some good luck up there, where-ever-the-hell you are."

"Hell, ain't even half of it," Oxnard said, his voice sinking to a new level of dire and desperate throatiness.

BJ hung up and went back out to the truck. By now, the cowboys weren't just hankering for a fight, they were full-out begging for one. "How 'bout you boys get settled in the back of the pickup, keep your eyes peeled for any of those Injuns?"

"Oh yeah! That's what I'm talkin' about!"

So, they loaded up, and BJ drove over to a meeting scheduled at Bob Smith's office. It was a cool evening, and the cowboys nearly froze standing up in back like a pack of sheep dogs, flexing their muscles and waggling their rifles as if they owned the whole West rather than working for minimum wage. BJ left them out there shivering and on the lookout for hostiles and went inside. Bob was very concerned that a shutdown of the Montana cattle industry was imminent due to the possibility of a brucellosis epidemic caused by the escaped buffalo, so he had the slaughterhouse ratcheted up to double time. Whereas before the cattle seemed to be strung up, bonked, stripped, and gutted on a metronome scale, the pace now was disco, or maybe even hip-hop. BJ could hardly keep track of the freeway of death rolling past right behind Bob's desk. But when Bob came into the room, the first thing he did was to push a button that sped up the assembly line still more.

"Talk to me," he said to Lieutenant Walker, fidgeting and nervous in front of him. "You been burning gas all over Montana, what have you found?"

"Oh, I've been on the move, alright. It's been constant, night and day, up and down. We've pushed our choppers way beyond scheduled maintenance. But this is combat, and we got what it takes to get 'er done!"

"Get 'er done, eh?" Bob looked at Walker for a moment, then snapped his fingers in Duke's direction. "Yo Duke, hand me the print out." Duke handed him a map of north western Montana that had a flurry of squiggly lines drawn all over it.

"This look familiar, Lieutenant?" He held it out and Walker stared at it as if they were a set of Egyptian hieroglyphics.

"Nope."

"No? You don't recognize the GPS confirmed record of your flight pattern? I'm talking about a Google-certified map of exactly where, and when, you flew that gas-guzzling helicopter of yours. Now don't say it, but I know it looks all crazy, like some kind of maniac was at the controls. Who could have flown from here, to there," Bob pointing at the various locations, "then back to here, and way up to there. In fact, I asked the Google master what these random lines and trajectories had in common, and I bet you'll never guess. You want to try?"

Walker looked at the map like it was an original of his birth certificate. "Where the buffalo might be? I mean, based on our military theories of course."

Bob slapped his knee. "Well isn't that exactly what you'd think! Of course it is! But let me give you a hint: what your flight pattern has in common is the exact, precise, unmistakable location of every topless joint in Montana. You and your boys were out for a good time, weren't you? And all at the taxpayers expense! Way to go!"

Walker looked down in an expression of profound guilt, shaking his head in amazement that he'd been found out. Bob turned his attention to Larry.

"So how you doing there, Larry? Don't think I've forgotten about you."

"Oh, I'm sure you haven't."

"Cause I have some photos here that should be of interest. Duke, you got those photos?"

Duke laid out a peacock tail of 8-by-10 photos as if they were cards in a deck. Bob picked up several and held them out to Larry.

"Here you go. Take a look at these."

Larry held them up and stared carefully at images of Kate in the middle of the buffalo stampede, of Kate walking with Crazy Wolf, of Kate cradling the white buffalo calf.

"See anything of interest there, Larry?"

Larry had already started to sweat, the little beads glistening on his chin and the channel of pink flesh right below his nostrils. He bought some time by squirming around to remove his glasses and hold the photos up to a different, brighter angle to the overhead lights, as if that might make the images go away.

BJ looked over his shoulder at the remaining photos on the desk. He saw one that had a sideways view of Sam on an ATV, headed up a ramp into the railroad boxcars. BJ idly reached down and shuffled the photos on the desk. "May I?" he asked Duke, who shrugged. BJ turned to the side, removed the photo of Sam, and carefully slid it under his shirt while the others were focused on Larry.

"Looks to me like, well, there are about ten bison here, and here, a mix of females and males, they all seem to be healthy, nice spread of horns…" he went on like this for a minute or two before Bob exploded.

"Moron! Don't you know a technicolor case of Stockholm Syndrome when you see? Or maybe we should call it Bozeman Syndrome. That's your employee in the middle of all this. There! Do you see her? What's her name?"

"Oh, her? Why, that's Katherine."

"No shit it is! And what I want to know, is what are you doing about it? Look at her, right there as if she was one of them."

"Which technically, I have to say, is true. Although that's something I have no control over. I was forced to hire her, affirmative action you understand."

"Don't give me that crap. She's your employee, your problem. You got it?" And with that he tapped Larry hard right on the forehead, while a cow was strung up and spiked in approximately the same spot, emphasizing Bob's point with a brief convulsion and a spray of blood.

BJ, turning back to the group with the photo concealed under his shirt, was startled out of his shoes when Bob jumped up, his face draining of color, and screamed: "Do you think I'm going to let the likes of you ruin me? Duke! Get me the file!"

Duke handed over a sheaf of papers, which Bob rifled through, pulling out a yellow sheet with a series of columns and numbers.

"Do you have any idea what these are?" Larry and Walker looked at the sheet and shrugged, mumbling incoherent expressions of ignorance.

"You'll never guess, not in a million years. So I'll tell you: they're numbers of individual, actual bison that have a very special thing. Are you ready for this?" Looking back and forth, trying to encourage a reactive grin of appreciation for what he was about to tell them. "Computer chips! Radio activated computer monitoring chips, put right into their shoulder for the express purpose of monitoring their coming and going, and believe it or not, where they are at any given moment! Isn't that a great idea? In case they wander off the reservation! All we need to do is plug them in and track them down. Now why didn't I think of that?" His voice rising to a shriek: "Why didn't you think of that! It was your own goddam government agency that put them there in the first place!"

Larry stared dumbly at the paper. Walker took it from his trembling hand and read some footnotes at the bottom of the page.

"Says here the monitoring is only good for a five mile range."

"I'm on it, chief," Walker said, glad to have an excuse to get out of the room.

"Keep us posted," BJ said, following Walker. He could hear Bob laying into Larry as he rounded the corner and went back outside to the cowboys.

This raised the stakes considerably, BJ realized. The photo proved that Sam had thrown in with the natives, and in all likelihood he was still out there now, roaming the countryside without a clue that it was only a matter of time before he was found out. BJ knew that he had to get there first. He wasn't sure what he could do to save Sam, but he'd make an effort, that was for damn certain.

21

Sam couldn't be certain if he was dreaming or awake. He lay in the hay, feeling Kate curved against him, their bodies so tightly spooned that it seemed their hearts beat as one. A warm wool blanket covered his shoulders and feet; the hay, while not fresh, carried a musty smell that evoked spring rather than winter. It was very quiet, much too quiet in fact. For the past several days the sounds and smells of the buffalo had been with him every minute. His hands were free to move and the leather thong that had been tied around his neck was gone.

"Kate, I can't help it, but I love you," he whispered. He pulled her closer, but in the moment the dream evaporated, and he found that he was alone, his arms clutching a thatch of dry, bunched hay matted against his rifle. He sat up. Light streamed through the slatted boards in the barn and he could hear from outside the voices of his native captors. He jerked the rifle to a ready position and put his finger on the trigger, thumb on the safety switch. Their shadows passed across the slats, breaking the streaming light. Hello John pulled open the barn door and stared in at Sam.

"Ha ho, you hungry? My grandma's making some corn cakes, you can have some if you want."

Sam stared back at him. The boy shrugged and turned away, leaving the door open. I can make a break for it, Sam thought. He rolled out of the hay and crept over to the door. John and Little Bull were playing catch with their lacrosse sticks and the hair ball, the others came and went without even a passing glance to the barn. Sam eased out, his rifle still at the ready.

Crazy Wolf came out of the house, saw Sam, and made a gesture as if to sweep him away, like a pile of dust. "Go on, get! No one wants you here."

Sam stared at the house. Through the kitchen window he could see the back of Kate's head. She turned at the sound of Crazy Wolf's voice and made eye contact with Sam. She nodded and turned back to whatever she was doing. He walked slowly across the yard. Several natives went to the barn with crowbars and sledgehammers in hand, examining and pointing at the configuration of walls, roof, and supporting beams. Yura and a couple more emerged from the house carrying piles of blankets and quilts and set to building a small dome of arched willow branches which they covered with the blankets. No one paid him attention, it was as if he was at a zoo, observing the natives in their natural habitat.

He walked right out of the farm homestead. A road led up the valley, away from the meadow and forest where he now recalled he had escaped from Medicine Dog. A fresh layer of snow covered the ground, but it was easy walking. He had no idea where the road led but it didn't matter. He felt like he was floating and that if he spread his arms he might just fly away.

A mile up the road he stopped to examine two sets of tracks: one set appeared to be from a small sized cow, the other from a very large dog. He bent down and examined the direction and pattern of tracks. From the occasional placement of one on top of the other, it was easy to see that this was probably a wolf in pursuit of a solitary buffalo. He followed it a hundred yards off the road and saw where several more sets of wolf tracks converged on the buffalo, the increasingly smudged tracks indicating that the animals were running rather than walking. He felt a hunter's surge of excitement, wanting to see where the tracks led, not caring that he might be walking into a trap. He crossed a hill and heard a distant sound of dog-like barking, interspersed with the pathetic bleating sound of a calf. Now he broke into a run, holding the rifle at the ready. He knew he had only one bullet, but it gave him courage. The wind was in his face, he knew that the wolves would have to see or hear him rather than catch his scent, but with their focus on a kill he would be able to come up behind.

The trees were thick, the tracks zig-zagging around the trunks and low branches. Sam held the rifle in front of his face, pointed skyward, to keep the branches from slashing across his eyes. The trees spaced apart a bit, and up ahead he could see a clearing in the forest. In the middle of the clearing the white buffalo calf stood with legs splayed, while ten wolves sat around a loose perimeter, waiting for the right moment to make the kill and get on with a feast.

Sam crouched down on one knee, breathing as quietly as possible, trying to sort out his feelings on what came next. He saw a wolf stalk out of the circle, head low, moving sideways towards the calf. It surprised Sam that it didn't go straight ahead to make the kill. The wolf seemed half again as large as the calf, a full head and shoulders taller than any of the other wolves. But something held it back. It turned to look at a slender, lighter colored wolf, which sat on its haunches, head held upright in an almost regal bearing. The light-colored wolf made a sharp yelp and two other wolves stepped out from the perimeter and dashed towards the big male, which immediately curled its tail between its hind legs and returned to the perimeter. The calf made a quick move towards the far side of the clearing, but the closest wolves cut off any chance of escape, all the wolves pulsing inwards towards the calf. It began bleating loudly and continuously, running as fast as it could around the closing circle of wolves, every one of them staring first at the calf, then at the light-colored wolf, then back, tongues hanging out, heads carried low. Sam realized that his one bullet should be used on the light wolf, if he was going to use it at all. He had saved the white buffalo calf from certain death on the Gardiner Bridge; he could save it now.

But just as he raised and aimed his rifle, the trees on two sides of the clearing shook and shuddered as if a great wind blew down from above, or an earthquake was rattling them from below. The wolves ceased stalking and assumed postures of full alert. And suddenly, eleven buffalo came crashing out of the forest and formed a protective circle around the calf, their heads low and horns ready. The light wolf yelped again and now the large male made his attack. It tried to break through the circle and get the calf in one fast swoop, but as it passed between two buffalo they turned and pinballed the wolf between them, tearing a gaping wound in each side of the animal. It delivered a passing bite onto the hindquarters of the calf, but another buffalo whipped around and drove the wolf deep along the ground, flipping it into the air. The buffalo snorted and returned to the circle, while the wolf, mortally wounded, staggered through the perimeter and into the forest.

Sam felt exultant. He raised the rifle high over his head and let out a piercingly loud cry of triumph. The wolves turned as one. Sam ran forward, shouting his loudest, and when he came into the clearing they ran for the trees, the buffalos shifting guard to square off with him instead of the wolves. Sam stopped twenty yards from the nearest buffalo, held the rifle in the crook of his elbow, and applauded. "Yeah, we showed 'em, didn't we!" He could see the calf through a narrow cleft in the protective circle of bulk, horns, and hair. It looked so small and white compared to its menacingly dark elders. Sam lowered to his knees and watched the buffalo.

It had never seemed like wasted time to watch wildlife when he was growing up. He remembered seeing a bear tear into a rotted log and feast on ants; the sound sand hill cranes made when they rose as one and set off on another's day journey; the purposeful work of beavers; the rush and splash of ducks settling on a wetlands. He could tell that there was a family hierarchy among these buffalo. They seemed to communicate in an unspoken voice that was audible only to them. The twitch of a tail, quiver of a shoulder, flick of an ear all seemed to have meaning, and the deep breathing that formed clouds of steam emanating from their nostrils like flames from a dragon, held a secret rhythm and enunciation. Sam watched them for a long time. The sun was not visible behind a grey layer of clouds, but the light was fading.

Sam stood stiffly, arching his back to restore feeling. He wondered if they might follow him. He made what he thought were some friendly, consoling sounds—clicks and low whistles—then moved slowly back along the path towards the road. He went into the darkness of the forest and looked back: the buffalo hadn't moved. But he saw a flash of white, and here came the calf, squeezing through the circle and running right up to the edge of the forest. "Yeah, *Wohpe,* you know who you can trust." Sam kept moving and the calf followed, a hulking line of buffalo falling in behind.

It was a long slow walk back to the farmstead, and by the time they arrived it was very dark and cold. Sam could hear chanting, but he couldn't tell from where. He opened the barn doors and scattered some hay to draw the buffalo back inside. Whole sections of the roof had been removed, exposing the web of beams that pointed towards the tall center pole.

He walked into the house: empty. The rooms were an organized mess, clothes and discarded boxes of food everywhere. No one's ever going to accuse Indians of being overly tidy, Sam thought. He went into the bathroom to take a leak. A towel was draped over the shower curtain and he caught a familiar whiff. He drew the towel to his face and smelled the unmistakable odor of Kate. He kept the towel and went back outside.

The chanting came from a low dome that had a smoldering fire out front, piled high with burnt logs and large stones underneath. A small mound of dirt stood between the fire and what appeared to be a draped doorway on the east side of the dome. A bucket of water was to the side of the door. Sam drew the blanket back from the dome, a cloud of steam drifted out, and the chanting immediately stopped. It was very dark inside, but he could see a rich golden glow from heated stones in the center of the floor.

"Go away, now!" an angry voice said.

"Whatever, but I got your buffalo back," Sam replied.

A figure emerged from the darkness, wrapped at midriff in a towel; Crazy Wolf. "Where?"

"Should just about be in the barn, settling down for the night."

"Yeah for the white man!" a young voice said; Hello John.

"So, does this mean we don't have to go through with the Sun Dance?" Joseph White Bird asked.

"No, we have made the Pledge. And it is a white man who brought them back. They left because our power is diminished. We must restore the broken circle, or we will lose them again forever."

"You must be freezing, let him come in," Little Bull said. "He can squeeze in next to me."

"And if it gets too hot, just tell Crazy Wolf to pour more water on the rocks, to cool things off."

Everyone laughed, knowing that the steam made the heat nearly unbearable.

"No!" Crazy Wolf said. "We are preparing for a Sun Dance. The purification will be ruined if we allow him in. He's not a prisoner anymore, we need to be separate from white people. He should get out of here."

"He saved our *Wohpe*, we owe him a debt of gratitude," Kate said. "Here, take your clothes off and wrap that towel around yourself. Circle around to the left."

Which was the custom in a sweat lodge, with the men on one side, women on the other. Sam came in and was the last man in the circle at the back of the lodge, Kate beside him across a small gap. The sparks off the heated stones cast blue shadows against the roof of the dome. Sitting upright, the heat above was twice or three times the heat closer to floor, and whenever the water was poured over the rocks, the superheated steam created an enveloping cloud that drew out pain, replacing it with an intensity of feeling that was neither pleasure nor pain: the experience of being in a womb, about to be reborn.

At first, Sam was afraid he might burn his toes on the rocks. He crossed his legs and held his back straight with his butt tucked tight against the bottom edge of the dome. He was keenly aware that his left hand was inches away from Kate's right knee. But once the door was shut and Crazy Wolf began to chant, all other concerns or thoughts disappeared. There was only this eternal moment, with the heat and the chant. It went on and on, Sam sweating profusely. At one point he felt a hand on his knee, then moving up his thigh, across his waist and chest. The hand settled on the chain and dog tags around his neck, but he made no motion to resist. Very slowly, he reached out to place his hand on hers. She twined her fingers in his then drew his hand to her mouth and kissed and sucked on each finger. She guided his hand over her bare chest and body, beneath the towel across her lap.

The chanting stopped. Kate nudged Sam's hand away. The door flap was opened with a whoosh of steam, the darkness outside relatively light against the pitch black inside the sweat lodge. Sam felt haggard on the outside, energized within. Everyone shifted position, breathing in the refreshing air.

"So what, now we jump through the ice into the river?" Sam asked.

"That's the first of four sweats, my friend. We got three more pours to go."

And on it went, the cool stones pushed out, red-hot sparking ones dragged in, Sam feeling the chanting pulse move within his body and take hold. He had no idea what the words meant, maybe nothing. It all seemed to come straight out of the earth, a deep rhythm that made everything since birth irrelevant, both the good and the bad but especially the bad. It felt so good to have Kate beside him, holding and touching him like that: a secret within a mystery. There was so much he wanted to forget, but this had nothing to do with stepping back and starting over; it was a complete wiping clean; a rebirth.

When the final pour was complete and the door thrown open for the last time, Sam knew that he was here to stay.

"You going to be ok out there?" Kate asked.

"Come with me. Sleep with me."

"Maybe, we'll see."

That was good enough for Sam. He wandered back to the barn and settled into the hay, the sound of the softly breathing buffalo a reassuring presence in the darkness, and the scent of Kate on the towel beneath his head a powerful reminder why he might not need that one last bullet.

22

The preparations for the Sun Dance began at the moment the sun rose over the eastern ridge of the mountains. Yuraeechen began by demanding to know when the moon times would come to Little Bull and Kate. Satisfied that the special woman's power would not occur until later in the month, she next directed Little Bull to be her Thunder assistant and to collect grasses to stuff into the eye sockets of the buffalo skull, cedar bark for incense, sweet root for the "Throwing it at Him" ceremony, paints and clay for the straight pipe and for coloring the dancer's bodies. She directed Kate to remove feathers and bones from the mounted golden eagle for use as fans and whistles, and to loosen the springs and paint the sides of a snare drum found in one of the children's rooms. The new sound was much deeper, less raspy; she tied a small piece of leather around the drumstick which softened the sound further. The buffalo robe was shaken, the dust beaten out, and the underside rubbed by Yura until it was soft and pliable. She instructed them to perform their tasks in complete silence with eyes turned downwards in a posture of contemplation and submission, then she fell silent herself, her lips moving in a quiet, continuous prayer.

Crazy Wolf and the young men set to dismantling the barn in such a way that it resembled a Medicine Lodge. Normally, they would have searched for a proper willow tree, cut it down, and dragged it to a field where a whole new lodge would be built. But the circular design of the barn, with twelve supporting beams radiating out from the center was acceptable. The walls between the main structural supports were pulled off, exposing a network of beams that generally opened to the east. The floor was cleared for dancing, and ropes were fixed to the top of the center beam, leading down to the ground where large fishhooks were sewn into the rope ends. Crazy Wolf used a cigarette lighter to burn and purify the hooks, and a small metal file to sharpen the inside edge of the hook shank. None of the younger tribe members had undergone the ritualistic torture. They said nothing but watched in nervous fascination.

"You are men, but tonight and in the next few days, you will become sacred warriors. To be a warrior is to know pain, both given and received. I have counted coup in battle in Afghanistan. Someday you will have the chance as well. But here in this place, you will fulfill the visions you received as young men."

"What about the white guy?" Shining Shirt asked. "Does he get strung up as well?"

"No! Listen to me, all of you: the path for our people is to stay clear of the whites. Nothing good has ever come from mixing with them. They are a lost people, and they have infected us from the very start: disease, alcohol, war, destruction of our sacred lands. We must live apart, especially when it comes to our sacred rituals."

"My sister married a white," Joseph White Bird said. "At least he doesn't kick her ass the way my other sister's husband does, and he's a pure blood."

"But that's exactly my point! Your pure blood uncle is infected by historic trauma, by the consequences of Manifest Destiny. Only by a return to the old ways can he be reborn and saved. There's no mixing with these Europeans. Everything about them is contrary to our ways. Look what they did to our last buffalo, massacred them! They'd do that to all of us if they were given half the chance. And in the end, they will destroy themselves. Mother Earth is on a rampage even as we build our lodge. The world is heating up, dying, just like our great prophet Sweet Medicine predicted."

"But you joined the Army. Why'd you do that if you didn't want to mix?"

"I wanted to follow my warrior path. It's in our blood to be warriors. I have no regrets, but I never thought I was carrying a gun for them, only for my people. Now let's go into the forest to gather branches and stones for the altar. All this must be complete today, before sunset."

"Is that when we start dancing?" Hello John asked.

"Yes, the drum beat begins when our father the sun goes down."

"And the hooks?"

"On the third day."

"For the whole day?"

"Until the hooks tear out, until they pull free from your flesh, on that day or the next."

The walked in silence then began prying up stones and ripping foliage free from the trees.

"And what about you and Kate?" Two Suns asked. "Isn't there something kind of weird that happens between you two?"

Crazy Wolf was silent, but his face darkened. He was having trouble pulling a bough down from a spruce.

"She's the Sacred Offering Woman. What does she actually offer?"

Crazy Wolf pulled the whole limb down, sending a shiver up the trunk. "She offers herself. This is a renewal, new life, fertility. The lodge becomes a place of rebirth and power flowing out. We need that power to survive. Now go grab some stones. There is much to be done."

• • •

When the buffalo stirred and began to move just after dawn, Sam awoke as if in a trance and moved with them, slowly and with complete indifference to wherever they might lead. He felt invisible, an observer that no one could observe. He saw Crazy Wolf and the young men, tearing at trees and the earth. It made no sense but that didn't matter. Then he saw Little Bull scraping bark from a cedar tree, her pockets bulging with grasses.

He considered waving or speaking, she had seemed friendly, but she never looked at him. He heard an erratic drum beat and saw Kate beating on a drum as if trying to find her voice. He watched as she set the drum aside and tore the eagle into pieces, feather and bones removed, the bones scraped clean and hollowed out to make a piercingly loud whistle. The sound disturbed the buffalo and they moved away from her, he with them, circling around the farmhouse towards the sweat lodge. Yura was there, adjusting the blankets and sweeping the dirt floor. She watched Sam carefully, her face lined and concerned, then she moved slowly towards him so as not to alarm the buffalo.

"The *tatanka* have accepted you," she said simply.

"Guess they know that I accept them. Probably smell like them by now," he said without any intention at humor.

The buffalo grazed to either side of Sam and Yura, heads and tails down, muscles twitching in a natural feeding rhythm. Sam held one arm out and a large male grazed slowly beneath his hand, allowing it to glide across the massive shoulders and haunch.

Yura kept her gaze on Sam's face. "You have pain. You are in need of healing."

"I know all about pain," Sam said. "But I don't think there's any cure for what I got. There isn't a medicine chest big enough for what I need."

"You need to go inside yourself, draw out the pain, replace it with a vision."

"A what?"

"You've taken the first step. The sweat last night was a purification. It's a start. The next comes breathing. You must breathe to enter the dream-state."

"I dream when I'm asleep."

"This is different: deeper. Listen to your breathing; it will lead you into a dream, and from there, to your vision."

"Hey, I'm no Indian and I'm never gonna be." His gaze strayed over to where he had last seen Kate. "Even though there're things I like about you people."

Yura picked up a long willow branch that was not needed for the sweat lodge. She curved it into a circle about ten feet across, twined the ends together, and placed it over Sam's head and onto the ground. She stepped back out of the willow circle and held out her arms as if embracing him across the space that now separated them. "You stay in that circle and the vision will come to you, taking the place of all your pain. You have the power to do this."

Sam looked down at the willow circle. "For how long?"

"Two, three days; maybe four or five. And no food or water!"

"And that's supposed to be a good thing?"

"It depends on what you choose to bring on your journey. If you listen, the voice and vision will come. If you resist and fight, there is nothing that can be done, and your pain will consume you."

Several buffalo came towards Sam, grazing peacefully. Without breaking stride, they moved around the circle, not stepping across the branches on the ground even though there was good grass poking up through the thin patches of snow. As they moved past, Sam took a step towards the edge of the circle, then stopped. He felt a strong tug within himself, between acceptance and anger. His hand moved to the chain and dog tags around his neck. He wanted to be with the buffalo, not this creaky old woman. He stepped quickly out of the circle and almost immediately the buffalo turned, their tails flipping up and heads raised in a posture of alarm. He started to follow but they broke into a trot away from him, the big male turning to confront him, ready to charge if he came any closer.

"The *tatanka* know," Yurareecheen said to Sam. "You must choose."

23

Crazy Wolf found a good stone for the Sun Dance altar, a relatively oblong piece of granite with one flat side for the top and a curving face for the front. He rolled it up a small steep slope out of the creek bed, but there was a thick crust of ice at the lip of the slope and the rock slipped and nearly crushed his leg rolling back down to the bottom. He pushed it up again, grunting and calling upon the spirits and his ancestors to give him strength, but just as the rock seemed certain to make one last roll and settle squarely on the flat surface at the top, the ice gave way and the rock slid over his foot and skidded down into the muck and crud at the base of the hill. Crazy Wolf let loose with a series of curses intermixed with bear-like growling from frustration and pain. His toes felt crushed, but not as badly as when he stomped down and gave the rock a stiff kick.

Sam heard the ensuing howls and moved quickly in that direction, assuming something terrible had happened. He unslung the rifle from his shoulder and kept the barrel low and forward, ready to pull up and shoot from the hip if the situation warranted. As he got closer, he could hear the howls tone down into some very colorful swearing in both English and Cheyenne, the combination of which seemed much more potent than either one alone.

"You okay down there?" he said from the top of the slope. Crazy Wolf was down below, sitting on the rock and rubbing his bruised toes.

"Ai-yee. Leave me be, white man. Last thing I need to is to have you around." He put his boot back on, hunched his shoulders, and began rolling the rock up the hill.

Sam watched Crazy Wolf struggle for a few moments, then he set the rifle down and went to his side.

"No!" Crazy Wolf said. "This is for the Sun Dance ceremony; I don't want any part of your help."

But the rock started to slide. He put his shoulder against it and briefly held his ground, then was slowly pushed back down. Sam laid his shoulder into the rock, and together, grunting, farting, cursing, and breathing like animals possessed, they managed to get that rock up over the brow and onto level earth.

"Yeah! Got it." Sam flopped down and leaned against the rock, breathing hard.

"Just don't think this is your ticket into the Sun Dance."

"Your deal, chief. I got my own salvation to sort out."

"Is that what you think? Salvation?"

"How do I know? For all I care you're in there having sex with one another or who knows what."

Crazy Wolf didn't say anything. Sam felt his stare and returned it.

"Course, the word on the street is that you've taken a vow to not get mixed up with women for some crazy long period of time. It's not you I'm worried about. Just do me a favor and keep things civilized with Kate. Case you didn't notice, I got some feelings in that direction, ok?"

Crazy Wolf looked away. Sam could sense his sudden unease.

"There a problem with that?" Sam asked.

Crazy Wolf let out a slow gasp of air. "Oh, you poor, stupid white man. Why is it the Indians have to explain everything to you?" He bent down and rolled the rock out from behind Sam's back, then again and again, moving the rock in a haphazard fashion in the general direction of the farmstead.

Sam slung the rifle over his should and moved slowly beside Crazy Wolf, pushing the rock with his foot at the top of each roll.

"Explain what?"

"The difference between salvation and renewal, for one thing. You white people are so caught up in leaving this world behind, for some better world off beyond the clouds. That's the root of your problems; why you find it so acceptable to ruin Mother Earth. This is just a place to leave, a campsite. Which is why our two peoples can never co-exist. We don't want what you want, but you'll use up everything we have and leave us with nothing."

Sam didn't know what to say in response. "So what about Kate?"

"What about her? She's the Sacred Offering Woman, I'm the Pledger. If you knew anything about the Sun Dance that would tell you everything."

"I don't know shit, and I care less. What are you saying?"

Crazy Wolf gave a big burst of exertion, rolling the rock five successive times, then he turned away in a barely restrained rage of emotion. He held his hands high and called out to the sky: "I have fulfilled the Crossing of the Four Ridges – pledging the Sun Dance, the Sacred Arrow, the Sacred Buffalo Hat. I have fasted, sought visions, sacrificed my body, and undertaken the Buffalo Family Ceremony. I implore Maheo and all the Powers to bless my relatives! But now, here, I am just a man, and this thing is not something I asked for, but is forced upon me." He breathed deeply to avoid crying, his eyes shut and face in a terrible grimace of internal conflict.

Sam let him go on like that for a minute. "What thing? What are you talking about here and why does that involve Kate?"

"Renewal!" Crazy Wolf shouted. "It's all about fertility, the Earth giving birth, the start of creation. Don't you see? Kate is offering her body, and me as the Pledger must fulfill the offering in order for the Earth to be reborn. All our power comes from the Earth, this place you whites treat as one big cesspool. When we lay down together the power will be restored, but my Buffalo Family promise will be broken."

The truth dawned on Sam, slowly and then with the force of a tidal wave. "You're actually, like, going to do it with Kate? As part of this Sun Dance thing?"

Crazy Wolf couldn't speak. He nodded jerkily, his whole body spasmodic.

Sam turned away from him and walked straight into the forest. He could hear the buffalo pawing the snow to get at the new blades of grass underneath. Their snorts and the sound of them scratching up against a stump or tree came from every direction. He shut his eyes and breathed deeply through his nose; the earthy smell of them was unmistakable and reassuring. He stopped in a small clearing and stared up into the first slow twirl of snowflakes. The weather was changing for the colder, a storm was on the way. Maybe he would just stand here and let it take him, he thought. That would be the easiest way out of it all, just let the wind pass through and freeze him standing upright. The rifle was heavy on his shoulder. He slowly brought it around and rested the butt on the ground, the barrel pointing straight up into his chin. That would be easy too. All he had to do was lean down and press the trigger. He felt tired. Kate had seemed like such a good way out and now she was gone. Given over to this Pledger and Sacred Woman stuff. Sam couldn't make sense of it. Nothing made sense.

He dropped down to one knee, as if genuflecting at church, and switched the safety off, his finger on the trigger, the barrel brought slowly to the soft, accepting spot between his chin and neck.

24

Yura placed the buffalo robe over Kate's bare shoulders then came around to bring the edges together in front to conceal her nakedness. The robe had a rich odor of blood, sinew, and hair, and instantly created an aura of warmth embracing Kate's entire body.

"You must give thanks to this *tatanka* for making you such a beautiful wedding dress. But remember, it is worn in strictest modesty. It will become your wedding bed."

Little Bull stood to one side, watching the preparations with a look of deep distaste and jealousy. "I got the feeling this isn't your first time, nor maybe even your hundredth, with a hundred guys."

"Go away, grasshopper!" Kate said. "Don't you have something important to do, like hang the feathers on your Thunder bed?"

"I'll hang 'em off your butt!"

"Shh! Women! We are near the time of the initiation. Your minds should be pure, not bickering over meaningless disagreements. And Kate is right, you need to prepare the Life Tree. Take ten feathers and bring them to John, tell him to place them at the top of the pole. We haven't much time."

"Blindian!" Little Bull muttered at Kate as she left the room.

"Bitch!" Kate muttered in response.

"Shh," Yura said quietly. "Now is the time of reflection before the great struggle ahead. This is an ordeal, for the women as well as the men. And you have a most special role to play. Our power must be renewed, and the power will flow through you and the entire Medicine Lodge."

"So, what do I actually do?"

Yura leaned close and held Kate's hands in hers, staring intently into her eyes. "At the appointed time I will call for the renewal ceremony. Normally we do this at the start, but because the snows are still here we will do it at the end. You will enter the Lodge, the robe held tightly. You will come to the Sun Dance altar, make a prayer to the Buffalo skull, then spread the blanket on the ground, to the west. The Pledger will come to you and lay with you."

"Right there in front of everyone?"

Yura had been the Sacred Offering Woman many years before. She knew the feelings in Kate's heart. "The lights will be low; it will be sunset. The men will have broken free from their torture, their minds on their vision and their pain. The Pledger will be hungry and without water. You must make him want you. You think that is easy, but that is the hard part."

But Kate, thinking of her feelings for Crazy Wolf, realized that would not be difficult. Still, in front of the others. "Will I be painted?"

"Oh, my goodness, yes! We must do that now. Quick, let down the robe."

So, Kate dropped the robe and Yura made a potion of clay and water, red and blue juices from dried berries. She blessed the paint with cedar smoke, then proceeded to paint Kate's entire body, from a circle around her neck, down her shoulders, arms, breasts, waist and legs. A chalky substance was used for a series of white dots and circles; a line down the bridge of her nose, a spot on each cheek, and a flash of color extending back from each eye.

Kate had seen pictures of the painted Sacred Offering Woman, but other than little decorations at childhood rituals, she had never before been painted in this way. "Can I wash it off?"

"In four days. You must use your body to paint the Pledger. The paint is sacred and will give power to him or to whoever receives your color."

She placed the robe back over Kate. "Now go, into the forest, clear your mind of impure thoughts. When you hear the drum, you will know that it is time to begin."

Kate felt tremendously special and excited. This was all working out exactly as she had hoped. Her years of academic training had virtually eliminated the capacity to believe in anything other than pure reasoning and science. The very notion of renewal associated with the Sun Dance seemed trite, but she knew it had the power to bring a group together, and most importantly, to bring Crazy Wolf to her. She relished the opportunity to make him want her. And what could he do? It was his ritual responsibility to take the offering of her body. And once he got a taste of what she had to offer, she knew he'd be back for more.

She walked slowly and ceremonially into the forest, placing one step precisely in front of the other, her toes pointed straight ahead. The robe was so warm that the increasing cold and flutter of snowflakes made no impression. She felt powerful and alive, her heart filled with song.

The trees gave way to a slight clearing, and there on the other side was Sam, kneeling as if in prayer. Kate stopped, considering the implications of proceeding. She liked Sam, but she knew that her power over him was complete. She could do with him as she wished. Or not. At least he wouldn't be there for the big moment with Crazy Wolf.

"Sam!" she whispered loudly. He raised his head but didn't turn. "Sam!" she called out again. Now he turned and very slowly she opened the robe as if it was a great set of wings and moved towards him.

Sam had been at the moment of pulling the trigger, and his impression when he saw Kate was similar to his first thought when he saw her back in Gardiner: that she was an angel, sent to redeem him from his miseries. Maybe he had he already pulled the trigger and was now in heaven? He couldn't be sure. But as she came closer he stood and felt her embrace him in a strong grip, her body pressed against his, the robe pulled over his shoulders, the two of them together as one. He let the rifle fall to the ground and wrapped his arms around her body. Her lips kissed him at the very spot where he had held the rifle barrel. Her lips were so warm and soft.

"Do you want me?" she asked, kissing him.

Sam felt a deep weariness that went beyond desire. He was glad to hold and feel her, but he had no physical sensation of her presence. "Oh Kate, why are you doing this?"

"Because I need you."

"No, with Crazy Wolf, in the Sun Dance. I know what you're offering."

"Oh, that's just a ritual. I'm here with you now."

"But Kate, don't you see? I've got nothing, and you're everything." He pushed her away, looking down at the fine layer of paint left on his clothes and hands.

"Ah, there's nothing more attractive to a woman than a man who doesn't want her. Is that what you're trying to do?"

"Kate..." Sam didn't know what to say. He felt conflicted, tired, confused.

From back at the farmstead, the sound of a drum beat broke through the quietness. A sudden gust of wind carried a flurry of snowflakes. Kate brought the robe tight around her body.

"I've got to go. Don't say you didn't have your chance." She turned and began to run.

Now Sam felt an instant surge of anger. He could catch her up and keep her here! He could make her his prisoner right now! He saw a dark movement between them and a buffalo pair came out of the trees, the male facing off with Sam, the female pawing the ground and searching the air with her nostrils. The wind picked up. Three more buffalo came into the clearing. The drum beat became louder and more frequent. Sam could see the glow of a large fire, and now the shriek of eagle bone whistles.

The buffalo began to move, face on into the wind and the increasing blizzard of snow fall. Sam fell in behind, not thinking, not remembering what had just happened with Kate or what he might have done if she hadn't come. It was as if he was a brand new person, a calf following the herd, without any past of his own, and a future that lay somewhere beyond the oncoming storm.

25

The buffalo moved with a quiet determination that came from surviving the great storms of Siberia, the high arctic, and down through countless seasons in the mountains, valleys, and plains of the North American continent. Pushing head-on into a storm accelerated its passage and brought the herd into the relative warmth at the tail end. The triple thick layers of curly hair across the animal's head, neck, and shoulders made a perfect battering ram against the wind chill, but it was the powerful instinct in their heart that made the beasts virtually invulnerable to the harsh conditions. They survived mainly out of a powerful will to keep going no matter what.

Sam walked behind the herd, feeling their strength build in his own weakened heart. The snow was blinding in his eyes, but he didn't need to see; the buffalo knew the way. It was very cold, and the snow was beginning to accumulate on the ground. Three buffalo were grouped in a wedge-like triangle ahead, the male at the point, the mother and yearling on either side of his massive flanks. Sam moved forward to join in the wake of the family, their warmth a comfort and the path made by their sets of hooves clearing the way for him to find footing in the growing darkness. Sam had worked around cattle as a teenager and had become accustomed to their smell out on the open range. They certainly weren't pets, but he had grown to appreciate their dumb simplicity, the relentless lowing and the pathetic way they followed him around. Their response to a storm was typically so different from a buffalo: when the wind rose and the snow fell they blew right along with it, following the path of the storm dead into barbed wire or an impassable rimrock where the cold could beat them down. And when they were brought to a cattle yard, the smell that had seemed evocative out in the open, became an unbearable stench, the pens and corrals leading inexorably to the final slaughterhouse. But here on the lower slopes of the Rockies, the smell of buffalo was the aroma of enduring life. With each breath Sam felt stronger, more alive, more committed to staying alive.

He considered throwing his rifle aside, it was so heavy and cold, a thing of death. He shifted the shoulder strap from left to right, then back again, but it was impossible to make it comfortable, and each time his bare hands nearly froze to the blue steel. What good is a rifle with only one bullet, he thought. The barrel was too long for shooting game in a forest, and the firepower was much too large for rabbits or the kind of creatures he might encounter this time of year. He stopped walking and struggled to lift the strap over his head, but it got caught on a jacket button, then the barrel tangled with a low hanging dead branch and he fell backwards into the snow hole at the base of a tree. The shocking cold of snow slipping down his collar brought him out of his plodding sensibility back into full awareness.

"Goddam this thing!" he cursed, ripping the rifle off his shoulder and pitching it away. Free of his cross, he turned to stay with the herd, but they were gone. He saw movement off to the side, smaller than a buffalo. "Wohpe?" he called, thinking perhaps it was the white buffalo calf, but even in the gloom and snow he could tell that this animal was a darker shade of gray. Now there was another beyond; he turned, and the dim light picked up two eyes peering intently at him from beyond a stump.

Sam backed up. The presence of wolves around the edge of the buffalo herd was a given fact of the natural order; he knew that. But the difference between knowing, and respecting, the deadly seriousness of elemental nature was an urban luxury; here in the nearly pure wild, showing a lack of due respect was a form of complacency that could only lead to death. He fell to his knees, scraping in the snow for his rifle. The one bullet wouldn't stop the whole pack, but a single shot might well send them running. He swept the snow with his frozen hands, not wasting even a second to look up. Maybe I could climb a tree, he asked himself. Then answered his own question: Yeah, that would be a fine way to die. Frozen meat hung from a limb.

He felt his fingers freeze to the rifle barrel just as the wolf lunged. He swung around, crunching the butt end into its open jaw. He helicoptered around, hitting a tree branch, then another wolf coming at him from behind. Now they were all around, whining and growling for an opening to make their final charge. He kept moving, backwards in the darkness, the wolves on every side, his feet tripping over a fallen log, kicking it free, rolling down into a spunky trench with the log on top wedged between several rocks, the branches making a sort of curtain through which the wolves snapped and yapped, trying to get a piece of him. He made little punches and kicking motions to hold them at bay, the snow piling up and the darkness now complete, until he heard a commanding yelp from the light-colored leader and the wolves suddenly took off in pursuit of the herd.

Sam lay still, breathing hard. He shifted to move a sharp stick out from piercing through to his kidney. The rifle was at his side. He could touch it with his knuckles, the barrel pointed upwards, the grip down around his knees. His face was a scarce two inches from the log above his face. He could still move his arms a bit, but his legs seemed encased in snow and dirt. It was a nearly perfect grave: cold, quiet, impenetrable.

A wave of claustrophobia washed over him, which combined with a convulsive pulse of shivering to make his situation intolerable. He made a croaking cry for help, the sound absorbed by the snow and wood.

Something deeper than fear welled up in his chest: a choking sense of inevitability and doom. He was alive, but dead, equipped with the facilities to ascertain his complete helplessness. He flailed with his hand to try and bring the rifle into position to pull the trigger. The mechanism was tantalizingly close but there was no way he could reach it. He strained, wiggled his knee, moved his head back and forth, succeeding only in raising his sense of claustrophobia to a new level of terror.

He tried to think. Images of family, childhood friends, Marine buddies, a neighborhood dog that bit him when he was two, all flashed through his mind. He saw the face of his high school girlfriend, who had kept true to her promise to wait, how they'd first made love before he headed out for boot camp, their first kiss at a prom in the high school gym, the way she looked at him when he came back and she said she was leaving him.

A drip of water landed at the base of his nose and ran down into his mouth. The taste of it was earthen, a stone tea backed by pine. He realized how thirsty he was, and hungry. He raised his head and tried to catch another drop, but the log was right there. He licked at it, a spunky taste plus a crunchy bit of something that he chewed into and nearly vomited: a carpenter ant. There was no way to turn his head and spit it out, the bitterness a poison that worked all the way down the back of his throat into his aching stomach.

He thought of Kate. Why hadn't he accepted the offer of her body? Wasn't that what he wanted? The red and white streaks of paint had been surreal but there was no mistaking her curves and supple strength. She seemed so sure of herself, all he had to do was respond. He suddenly felt aroused and laughed out loud. Look at him, laying here all ready to go.

He tried shouting again. The pure absorption of sound magnified the silence. He hoped the end would come quickly. Surely he would freeze to death. He would just lie here and let it come. That was the thing.

Not fight it. He could hear his own heart beating steadily. The sound seemed to catch an echo, a rhythmic beat that was much deeper, pushing a quantity of blood that was as big as a river. The beating was like distant thunder, echoing far across windswept prairies. He saw the thunderclouds racing towards him, but he pressed right into the lighting and chaos, the hail pouring down like stones, tornadoes gyrating at the edge of the microburst. The hail turned to snow covering the world, sheathing him in an icy blanket, but still he pressed on. He could see the light beyond the darkness now; it had always been there, waiting for him. The wind and snow lessened, rain fell, a fog settled behind the rain and now the sun burst out on fields of green pasture, the streams full, tender shoots pushing up from the black earth.

Sam felt a sense of exultation, ceasing his long march to graze on the fertile growth. He was tired and well fed. He lay down beside his mate, their bodies warm in the sun, and slept.

26

Yura worked quickly, painting a large moon on the chest of each of the young men. She handed each a whistle made from the eagle bones, then she instructed John to make the steady beat of the dance drum and they walked towards the Medicine Lodge. Crazy Wolf was already there, standing at the head of the altar: a rainbow pattern leading up to a set of straight lines, then the buffalo skull, painted red, its eyes stuffed with green grass. The men entered the Lodge, with Yura, Little Bull, and finally Kate wrapped in the robe. Crazy Wolf blessed them with cedar incense, directing them to stand at the four corners of the earth. Kate lay down to the side of the altar, her body still enshrouded in the buffalo robe.

"We come together for healing and renewal," he said. "This is a Medicine Lodge because it is the place where we restore the broken wheel, from which all energy flows. When we are broken we are separated from Mother Earth. That is what happened when Medicine Dog was taken by the bear. It was not an accident. We all knew it was coming; the bear acted on our behalf to break the wheel where Medicine Dog was standing. And now we must come together to restore the sacred circle. Each of you has begun a journey within your own tribe. You have fasted, completed a vision quest, sweated in your own lodges, undertaken the Seven Sacred Rites, or Crossed the Four Ridges. You know your own way, but it is a journey we all take as Indians. This is how it was before they came; it is a place to which we must return. This is not an easy journey, and although we travel together, each must carry the weight of his own soul. Today and tonight, we will drum and dance. Tomorrow we will do the same. The next day we will begin the torture. I have taken this journey before." He pulled open his shirt to show them the scars. "I can tell you it is not easy, but *Maheo,* the Cheyenne all-powerful, watches over you and accepts your offering of pain. Stay true to your vision. Believe in your people. Remember your relations."

And with that he motioned for the dancing to begin. Each dancer flexed up and down, swaying back and forth, face turned to the Thunder nest at the top of the center pole, and blew on the whistle in a cycle of four songs repeated four times. The first few minutes seemed easy, the whistles a loud shriek, the men creating a steady rhythm with their legs, hips, and upper bodies. But after an hour the exertion and the steady blowing began to take its toll. The sound decreased, the motions became jerky.

"We're doing this for four days?" Shining Shirt sputtered.

"Silence!" Crazy Wolf commanded. "Hello John, take his place, give him the drum. Think of your vision! Pray for strength from your ancestors! Keep your face turned to the Tree of Life, above which live the Sacred Powers!"

The dancing went until the darkness was complete, then exhausted, the young men returned in silence to their beds. Kate went to check on the buffalo calf; she found Crazy Wolf standing in the place where the buffalo usually spent the night.

"Where's my *Wohpe?*"

"Gone. They're all gone. I can't find any tracks. And Sam with them."

"Well, that's why we're doing the Sun Dance, to bring back the buffalo, isn't that right?" She lowered the robe to her shoulders, like a large body scarf, cascading down below her neck.

"In a large way, yes. But these are our buffalo. This herd is my responsibility."

Kate laughed and shook her hair. "You take yourself too seriously. We should bring the bison in, get them tested. We could probably have them returned to the park and everything would be just fine."

"Fine? To trust them, give them power over us? Woman, you've lived among them too long, you think and sound like one."

"Maybe so, maybe not, but I know something about bison management."

"Mis-management. They kill every chance they get. First it was to kill our food supply, now they claim it's because the buffalo threaten *their* food supply. They'll use any reason or excuse they can find, just as long as it kills our sacred buffalo."

She moved towards him, close enough to brush against him with the robe. "One thing I know about buffalo, they can find their way. You worry too much. How about you come inside this robe and I warm you up?"

She started to draw the robe around him, but he pushed her away. "A Cheyenne woman is modest, or she is nothing!"

"Well that's great, but I'm Lakota, remember?"

"You're a devil! I've sworn to be true to my wife and child, you know this."

"I know that we have to restore and renew the earth in a few days. We might get a bit of practice to make sure we do it right."

From somewhere out in the darkness came the howl of a lone wolf.

"That's what you are," Crazy Wolf said, "a female wolf trying to lead the pack. You're not the only one who has watched how they work, the way they use their sex to keep the pack in line. But it won't work with me."

Kate didn't say anything, but she lowered the robe to her hips, turning slightly to look at him over her bare shoulder. "It's pretty cold out here, want to help me with this robe?"

It took all of Crazy Wolf's will power to resist. He looked away. "I didn't ask for this. You're mis-using the ritual. I'm trying to keep to the old ways to lead our people, but you're just like the Whites, infecting us from the inside."

"C'mon, Brian. Give us both a break. It won't kill you to let me rub you up with a little sacred paint." She could sense in his hesitation that she had him. He stood there, head bowed, as she came closer, whispering "Crazy Wolf" in his ear. She wrapped him in the robe and drew him to her.

27

When Yura saw the residue of Kate's paint smeared on Crazy Wolf's neck and clothes the next morning, she quietly advised him to step aside as the Pledger, but he denied any wrongdoing. He told her that Kate had embraced him in a friendly, supportive fashion, but that nothing improper had occurred and that his vow was intact. Yura looked over at Kate, lying liked a contented cat on her buffalo robe bed. Kate made strong eye contact with her and with Crazy Wolf, then looked away, but with a half-smile that Yura interpreted as an unmistakable expression of female triumph.

"You're sure of this? The renewal of our power and the fate of the buffalo depend on your integrity."

"My honor and integrity are not to be questioned!" he said, resuming his place at the head of the altar. He set a brutal pace for the day's dance, demanding a very strong drumbeat, deep motions and movements, and the loudest possible whistle blowing. He never looked again at Yura or Kate, his eyes fixed on the very top of the Tree of Life, blowing furiously and trying to not even blink.

One after another the young men dropped out of the ritual dancing. First, Shining Shirt fell to the ground, appearing to be in a vision trance. But when Yura leaned over him to initiate the vision interpretation, he looked up and croaked: "Water!" Next, it was Joseph White Bird, who gave a final blast on his eagle bone whistle, spit it out of his mouth, and left the circle, saying that the Nez Perce had never been great practitioners anyway and that he was more interested in the Ghost Dance and the Native American Church peyote rituals. He and Shining Shirt took turns on the drum, or played together, seated and with their eyes on their feet. This left Crazy Wolf, Two Suns, and Hello John. The clouds broke in the afternoon and for a brief period the sun shone through, cold but blindingly bright. Crazy Wolf motioned for a break.

Yura came forward to see why he had broken the dance. "There is much suffering to atone for, we must keep going no matter the pain."

"Don't talk to me about pain," Crazy Wolf said, untying the ropes from the bottom of the center pole. "The appearance of the sun is a sign. We will begin the torture and go on until all have broken free. There is no point in waiting until tomorrow, we will begin at once."

He handed her two fish hooks, each the size of his index finger curved over in a deadly arc. He blew sharply on his whistle and motioned for the boys to step forward. They watched, horrified, as Yura twisted the hooks deep into the skin and muscle of Crazy Wolf's chest, the blood flowing down to his feet. His jaw was tightly clenched, the whistle between his lips, his eyes staring straight into the sun. He stepped backwards until the ropes were taut against the top of the pole, then he motioned again for the drummers to resume, and began to slowly sway back and forth, leaning back, the skin pulled grotesquely out from his chest, the blood coagulated now but the pierced holes large enough for the red flesh beneath to be clearly seen, the skin tearing a bit and bleeding again.

Two Suns looked as though he was going to faint. He staggered, collected himself, shook his head and went over to the drummers. Yura held the two hooks in her hands. She stared at her grandson, not displaying any emotion or suggestion for what he should do. Hello John stopped looking at Crazy Wolf. Very slowly, he spread his arms, stared up at the center beam, and offered his chest to her. She placed the hooks, a bit less deep than for Crazy Wolf, but the blood flowed in a greater quantity and for a much longer period of time. His face drained of color and his eyes took on a wild, crazed aspect as he blew the whistle and stared into the sun, the tears streaming down his face and neck to mix with the blood running down his chest. He began to sway, not copying Crazy Wolf, but with the same gentle flowing motion that made them both appear to be dancing with the Tree of Life.

28

Time stopped for Sam. There was a long grayness that might have been day, but mostly his eyes remained closed. There was nothing to look at on the outside; all feeling had stopped cold; he was an already-dead, contemplative corpse.

An image played over in an endless loop through his mind, the world seen from about two feet above the ground, a landscape of grass and shrubs, the far horizon a boiling mass of dark clouds. The comforting presence of relatives were to either side and behind, giving him a sense of strength that nothing could impede. The howling of wolves coupled with strange, piercing cries accelerated his movement, the ground rushing beneath his feet, but the same sense of invulnerability and powerful heart-strength sustaining him through a steady pounding run, his relatives with him, the world an open plain ahead. This image went on for quite some time, but it always ended the same, with a long corridor of poles and upright sticks funneling him towards a sharp line in the ground, a lake opening up beyond, then with an apnea-form of caught breath, a weightless tumble through clear skies, free now from the herd, his feet losing contact with the ground, and a brief sensation of staring back up at a lone eagle circling above the cliff he had just been driven over, before there was a sharp jolt, and the image looped and replayed.

A new sound interrupted the image, disturbing his sense of peace: a repetitive thumping that triggered a looped image marked by fear and awareness of his claustrophobia. He saw Heydon's face, then the children playing their elementary game of lacrosse, a woman who opened a robe lined with explosives, an orange flash, a woman falling to the ground with a dead baby in her arms. Sam made a convulsive gasp as the image repeated itself. The repetitive sound was replaced by a steady scritch-scratching noise from just beyond his right ear. He tried to turn his head, but the snow had compacted into a perfect bowl matching the contours of his skull, his breath transforming the snow above his face into an icy dome. The scratching became louder and he thought he could hear a deep throated chortling sound that was lower than a growl, and somehow much more menacing. He felt the ice at the right side of his face crack and crumble, give way, and now he could turn and confront not a half-foot away a nightmarish brown and black striped apparition that was all teeth and claws.

Sam let out a barking cry of fear and the face retreated back up its tunnel. Sam squirmed with his face and shoulder, enlarging the hole, now bashing his head to the side to break the sheen of ice and expose the softer more malleable snow behind. He heard a new round of scratching and felt the ice give way down around his hand. Instinctively he waved and screamed, trying to keep it away. A wolverine, he realized, come to eat him alive. He knew a thing or two about these monsters. They dug huge holes on the range and the ranchers hated them only slightly less than they feared them. A wolverine was serious trouble, always on the attack. No one even thought of laying out a bedroll without first making sure there was no den within a thousand yards of camp, and here one was right next to him. Sam squirmed and twisted as if possessed, able now to get his hand around the rifle and smash it up and down in the face of the creature. He succeeded in raising his knee and pushing up against the log, then bench pressing with his left arm and hand to gain a precious couple of inches of space to rotate his body away from the snarling wolverine. It bit him in the butt right on top of his wallet, tearing his pants and going for more. But Sam had freed the rifle enough to give it a mouthful of steel. And with an enormous burst of energy born of pure fear he thrashed and churned his body up and around the log and into the early evening light, the wolverine now tearing at his legs but Sam pounding the rifle butt into the snow and driving it back into the web of tunnels where the devilish animal made its home.

Sam stood upright, gasping and bleeding. He heard a loud mechanical whine and stumbled towards it, crawling and postholing in the deep snow out to a clearing where a snowmobile was racing across, the driver seeing him and turning sharply to come back around and remove his helmet: Big John McLaughlin, smiling and incredulous.

"Why Sam, what the hell you doing a-way out here? And look at you, all snowy and torn up. You've had quite the time of it!"

Sam stared at him in disbelief. "Where are they?" he finally managed to say.

BJ got off the snowmobile, removing his huge gloves and unzipping the collar of his bulky snow suit. "Where's who? Those Indians you been palling around with?"

"I don't care about them!" Sam said, wiping the dirt from his face and trying to shake the life back into his legs. "The buffalo! That's all I care about."

BJ looked carefully at Sam, trying to evaluate his condition. "Can't say that I know. But I can promise you we'll find 'em."

"How's that? I need to find them. Take me there."

BJ didn't move for a moment. "Hey Sam, it's me, John. You remember me?"

The feeling started to return to Sam's limbs, and with it, a searing pain. He burst into tears, blubbering and looking all around. "Where are they? Come back!" he shouted, beginning to tremble uncontrollably.

"How long's it been since you had something to eat or drink? Here, I got some coffee." BJ removed a thermos from beneath the seat, plus a cheese and salami sandwich. Also a lightweight but very warm thermal blanket. "Sit down right here and get yourself sorted out. There ya go. Drink this down. Take a bite." He had Sam sit on the snowmobile and put the blanket over his shoulders, brought the food and drink to his lips. Neither said anything for quite a while. BJ came around to stand right in front of Sam and placed his hands at the base of his neck. "Sam, listen to me. Situation is all screwed up. Ok? You with me here? Those Indians have stirred up a first-class shit storm, and it turns out one of the buff has a tracking device implanted in its shoulder. Chopper's in the air now, scanning the territory, and it won't be long before they find them and that'll be game over. If the Indians are with them, which some folks in high places hope they are, that'll just be their collateral-damage bad luck, because no one wants any survivors on this one. You still with me?"

"They're gonna kill them all?"

"Every motherin' one of them. So you can't be anywhere nearby. You got that? Not within a country mile!"

Sam heard the reverberation of the chopper making a pass somewhere to the south. "Where am I?"

"'Bout two miles west of where you were, most likely. I never saw any tracks, but I heard some weird whistle and drumming sounds over that ridge and checked it out on foot: little farmstead, appeared to be where the Indians were doing some sort of war dance."

"The Sun Dance. They're trying to restore the world and bring back the buffalo."

"Well they better dance hard. It's gonna take a huge piece of magic to save them from annihilation, and double that for the buffalo."

Sam thought as clearly as he could under the circumstances. He took a last gulp of coffee and stood up. He had no idea where the buffalo had gone, but if they were to be found and saved, it would have to be with the natives "You got to understand something, boss," Sam said. "I brought some wounds back from Iraq that aren't ever going to be fixed unless those buffalos live. They live, I live. They die, I'm not even worth burying." He pointed westward. "Over that ridge, you say?"

BJ didn't think about it for more than maybe two seconds, then he pulled on his gloves. "Climb on back and hold on. I'll take you close enough so you can sneak up the rest of the way and they won't know a thing. Meantime we'll figure out something to buy time to find the buff and get rid of that tracker. Ok?"

Sam hung the rifle over his shoulder, got in behind BJ. He laid his head against BJ's back and closed his eyes, trying to rewind the fading image of the buffalo surging across an endless plain towards a cliff with a lone eagle circling against the sun.

29

Crazy Wolf tore first. It took the full day, night, and most of the next day before the hooks ripped out of the muscle and flesh, leaving a pair of ugly, jagged wounds that seemed deep enough to expose his heart. The young men would not look at it, but Kate came over, wrapped in her robe, and tried to measure the depth with her finger. Crazy Wolf was too stunned and exhausted to resist. Yura batted Kate's hand away.

"No, child! These wounds are sacred, and there is the risk of infection. Nothing must touch the wounds while the scars grow."

"But when do we renew the earth? Won't I have to touch them then?"

"You must take care. The ritual is far from over. Our one remaining dancer must complete his ordeal."

"I'm amazed he's still standing. Shouldn't we cut him free? How long can he stand this?"

"As long as it takes. Look at my John. He is dancing with his ancestors."

John had fallen into a fluid, almost poetic motion, swaying with a graceful, ethereal ease, his mind and body far beyond the threshold of pain. The whistle sounds he made were faint, but his gaze was strong and the expression on his face was serene, almost beautiful. It seemed that he could dance forever.

But before the sun set on the third day, first one, then the second hook pulled free. The ropes dangled and settled back against the pole, and John stood in place, his body still moving, his face turned upwards. The whistle fell from his mouth. Yura came to him and held him just before he fell.

"My great warrior!" she whispered in his ear. "You have brought pride to your ancestors, and to your grandmother." She motioned for Shining Shirt to stoke the fire and lay John on a blanket, offering the first water and food he had taken in four days. "Rest, my warrior. We will talk about your journey soon." Now she had Joseph White Bird begin a slow drumbeat, and for Two Suns to sing the renewal song.

"*Wakanyan nawajielo, wakanyan nawajielo*—'I am standing sacred, I am standing sacred,' " he sang to the rhythmic beat.

She went to Kate and tugged the edges of the robe together. "Bring him into the robe with you. Undress him just enough to embrace his manhood. Place your hands on his hips and guide his movements. When his strength is complete release him immediately and do not kiss or speak to him throughout." Walking behind, she pushed and directed Kate towards Crazy Wolf.

"*Kola wamayankiyo, wakanyan nawajielo*—'Friend, take a look at me, I am standing sacred.' "

Everything in Crazy Wolf's body and soul were aligned against this part of the dance. The pain that had been hidden in the stretch and shock of the hooks was now released, and he felt a throbbing agony that resonated within his core and spread out through his extremities. The misery had stripped him of his sense of purpose and cultural pride. All he wanted was to be cared for and consoled by his wife, admired by his son. The vision of Kate approaching him was repugnant. He felt that he would do anything to avoid what came next.

But he was powerless to resist. She looked at him with a predatory interest that demanded his attention and cooperation. In the Army, he had waged war with an indifference and fearlessness that came from accepting he was already dead. Here, he succumbed to an overwhelming force. He couldn't fight; surrender was the only option. The song washed over him:

"*Cannupa wa uha wakanyan nawajielo*—'With this pipe, I am standing sacred.' "

Yura left Kate and went to kneel beside John, stroking his head and not looking up. The young men kept their faces down, eyes on the drum.

Kate stood silhouetted against the fire, her shadow over Crazy Wolf. She felt like she was about to begin a laboratory project, the object of dissection pinned there on the cutting board in front of her. The words of the prayer song were familiar, a reminder of the world she had struggled so hard to leave behind.

"*Wakanyam nawajielo, wamayankiyo*—'I am standing sacred, take a look at me.' "

Brian Thompson, the great Crazy Wolf chief of the Cheyenne, was hardly a commanding figure, she thought, staring down at him. She smiled a sincere look of pity then held him, Pieta-like, gently rocking him in her arms. She played a mind game with herself, imagining that they were walking arm in arm down Bozeman's Main Street, returning from dinner to their hotel room, the people on the street admiring the way he held her arm. She drew him a bit closer, opening her robe, as if opening the door to their room, the bed clean, the lights low. She lay backwards on the robe, him on top, and began to guide him as Yura had instructed. It was really quite easy, he made no effort to resist. She blew a breath of air across his forehead and neck, encouraging his strength. She could feel him beginning to respond. She took him by the hips and made a pulsing motion. This would only take a minute, but she wanted to draw it out, give him something to remember and to come back for more. She closed her eyes to absorb the music and the growing strength of Crazy Wolf.

"*Tunkashila, Tunkashila, Cannupa wa wakanca myacuye, Uni piktelo*—'Grandfather, Grandfather, this pipe you have given me is sacred, we are going to live!' "

The drumming stopped; the wailing chant stuttered and became silent. Kate opened her eyes and saw Sam standing over her, aiming his rifle at the back of Crazy Wolf's head.

"What's all this?" he sputtered. "What are you doing?"

"What's it look like, cowboy?" she said.

Crazy Wolf painfully rolled off her, covered himself, and looked up the barrel at Sam.

"Thank you," he said, closing his eyes.

"This is not your place," Yura said angrily. She tried to pull Sam away, but he stood his ground. "You must go! Go now!"

"My place is with the buffalo. I tried to work it out with you," he said, turning the rifle to Kate, "but look at you."

"Look at you!" she replied. "Put that gun away before you hurt someone. And stop acting so distant and strange."

The words hit Sam between the eyes. The gun quivered in his hands. He stared up at the buffalo skull on the altar, then the top of the center pole with its fluttering crown of eagle feathers. "There was an eagle above the cliff. We were running, I was right in with the herd."

Yura nudged the rifle aside and stared intently into Sam's eyes. "When did you see this?"

"I was lying in a grave; time passed. We went over the side, but it didn't matter, they were all around me."

"An eagle and buffalo in the same vision; that is a great power. You sure you're not part Indian?" she asked.

Sam blinked and rotated his shoulders, trying to get things back into focus. "What I'm sure of is that there's a crew of guys headed your way, gonna waste everything in their path."

Two Suns threw a sucker punch from the side, knocking Sam back. Joseph White Bird got him from behind in a bear hug and lifted him off his feet. Two Suns came around front and wound up to deliver a blow to Sam's face.

"They got a transmitter on the buffalo so it's only a matter of time. You can hear them now!"

Yura held Two Suns' elbow and everyone listened to the distant sound of a helicopter working up and down the ridges.

"Where are they?" Two Suns asked.

"Couple miles north, working a search pattern east to west, moving south." Sam made a wrenching move to free himself from the bear hug. He felt someone grab his ankle and looked down into Crazy Wolf's eyes as he rolled away from Kate and struggled to his feet.

"No, the *tatanka,* our sacred buffalo," Crazy Wolf said.

They squared off face to face. Sam stared at the ragged wounds. Crazy Wolf drew back his shoulders and a look of defiance returned to his face.

"I followed, and then lost them in the storm. Wind's changed. They could be just about anywhere."

Kate tried to step between them, wrapped in the robe. "Don't we have a ritual to complete?"

"I'm the Pledger," Crazy Wolf said with authority, "and I say the circle is complete. Yura, you must see for us. Two Suns, return to drumming and Joseph, complete the song."

Kate could feel her dominance evaporate in the deepening evening cold. "You're making a big mistake to try and continue this escapade. We should get in touch with the authorities; work with them to bring the buffalo in safely."

"There aren't going to be any survivors by the time this gets played out," Sam said. "Deal's already been cut."

"But that was back on the edge of the park. I know how the rules are written. We're in a whole new area with a completely different jurisdiction."

"I don't know, it's still Montana," Sam said.

"It's still America," Crazy Wolf said. "Killing Indians and buffalo might not be the rule of law, but it is the rule of the land; their rule. We will not negotiate. And I swear on my ordeal and on the souls of my wife and son that I will not surrender or be captured alive!" He held his arms out for the others to see the brutal truth of his wounds and words, staring especially hard at Kate. "Yura, sit with me, we need to dream back our buffalo and ask them to invite us to find where they are."

"I will try," she said simply. She squatted on her knees beside the fire, took up a piece of charcoal, and closed her eyes. "Tell the Sacred Offering woman to lay the robe here, at my side."

"But it's freezing," Kate said, pulling the robe tightly around herself.

"You can borrow my jacket if you want," Sam said. He took it off and held it out; she didn't budge; he turned away with the jacket held at arm's length, and now he felt the jacket jerked out of his hand, replaced by the robe. "You're welcome."

Crazy Wolf took the robe and spread it hair side down beside Yura. Her lips were moving and the skin at the edges of her eyes crinkled and quivered.

"I see a storm," she said in a high-pitched tone, her hand beginning to sketch lines and curves on the bare leather. "The clouds move in the shape of a buffalo herd, leading us to a river, past a great rock. Our buffalo are brave, they have no fear of the wolves watching them. They lay down in a place where the wind has blown away the snow, leaving many tracks." She resettled herself, her voice more natural and sure of itself. "And now we move on, a high ridge to the right, a barren ridge to the left. Here, there is an eagle tree." She drew a nest at the top of a lightning blasted stump. "But always, we keep moving, the wind in our face, the rising sun at our back." She drew more details on the robe.

Crazy Wolf, watching, took a piece of charcoal and wrote the word "East" on that side of the map, with an arrow pointing in the direction of travel.

"We cross a low mountain, with three streams coming together at the base. The longer stream is our path, going up to clouds and deep snow." She paused, changed position, then opened her eyes and stared blankly at those standing around. "Where is my grandson? I must see to his wounds." She took Kate by the arm and led her away, leaving Sam and Crazy Wolf alone.

"So, what does your Marine training tell you?" Crazy Wolf asked, leaning back on his elbow.

"I don't know. You're the Army Ranger. I think you pull rank here."

"What I know is that we're out-manned, outgunned, and we have three boys, two women, and your rifle with what, two bullets? Or is it none?"

"One, just enough for a full-out attack."

Crazy Wolf coughed, holding his hand over his wounds. "Oh, I like these odds. This is how the Afghan Al Qaeda kept us in check, making us think we were the ones on the defensive."

Sam opened the breech, looked down the barrel, then closed it, wiping the stock clean of grit and moisture.

"Hey, just so we're clear here, I don't need you guys at my back," Sam said. "I have some personal reasons to do what's necessary to save the buffalo. You want, I can take that robe right now and go get 'em."

"You have a plan?"

"Comes right out of being ambushed over in Iraq."

"Oh, I know, breaking through the weak perimeter, circling around behind."

"Right. Trick here is to pick the right point of trajectory. Plus, we have to immobilize the tracking unit, hopefully knock out their transport. We need to buy us some time to go find those buff."

"Yeah, but don't forget, we have your one bullet." Crazy Wolf held out his hand. "Here, help a disabled old vet up."

Sam hesitated. "I asked you to stay away from Kate."

"Then you asked the wrong person. Should've asked her."

Sam thought about that, nodded, and pulled him to his feet.

Crazy Wolf picked up the robe and held onto it. "I go where the robe goes. The buffalo are my sacred responsibility."

Sam considered jacking it out of his hands and making a run for it. What were the chances this wounded, bow legged Indian could catch him? Pretty damn good, he answered himself.

"Ok, I need to leave for a bit. There's a guy on the outside who told me about the transmitter. He's in a position to give us some help."

"You're sure you can trust him? That I can trust you?"

"Semper Fi," Sam said, making a quick little nod and salute.

30

Lieutenant Walker searched in vain, his chopper cutting a tight pattern three hundred feet above the trees, but he wasn't giving up hope, not by a long shot. He kept the binoculars to his eyes, scanning the forest, only setting them aside to check a blank computer screen resting on his lap with a blinking red dot in the center. He spoke into the microphone attached to his helmet. "Anything?"

The crackly voice of John McLaughlin answered back. "Not a sign of those dirty bison anywhere."

"Damn! Where do you think they got to?"

"Hard to say. My guess is they drifted down the valley trying to get out of the snow. Buffalo's got to eat, and they don't eat snow last time I checked." Which was at least partly true. BJ had seen some shadow tracks filled in by the recent storm, and those indicated the buffalo were headed up the valley.

Walked tried to see BJ through the trees. Other than an injured lone wolf that they'd swooped down onto and blown into bloody pieces, he hadn't seen a single living thing for three days now. The red dot on his computer suddenly started to bounce around and move into the upper right quadrant of the screen.

"No, wait a sec, we got something here. Hey, we got something!" He held the computer over to the pilot. "Take me to that dot!" Then, turning to the door gunner: "Lock and load baby, we got a live target."

"What target?" the pilot asked.

"The blinking fucking dot, that's what." Walker looked at the computer screen. The red dot had disappeared. "Well what the hell?" He shook and pounded on the computer, trying to restore the image.

"You got a fresh battery?" the pilot asked.

"Hey boss," the door gunner said, "check this out: trace of smoke, three-o-clock."

Walker was extremely agitated at losing the tracking signal, but he raised his binoculars and saw the farmstead with a group of brown-skinned people walking around, one a painted-up naked woman, another a young guy that looked remarkably like the little weasel that escaped after being waterboarded, and another carrying a dead animal skin of some kind. His faith in superior technology and unlimited resources was restored. "We got Injuns! Oh yeah! Let's set her down, regroup, and get ready to rumble!"

• • •

Sam heard the helicopter engine recede and fade into silence, a sure sign that it had either passed across a ridge or perhaps landed in preparation of attack. His instincts told him the latter was the more likely possibility. He headed in a northeasterly direction, intending to meet up with BJ at a prearranged spot one and a half miles away. He walked steadily through the crusty snow, looking down to avoid deadwood and wolverine dens, looking up to see if the eagle nest landmark was in sight.

He tried not to think about seeing Kate entwined with Crazy Wolf, but the image filled his mind. There was so little left to cling to. Truth was, the only reason he hadn't shot Crazy Wolf when he had the chance was that he was afraid to use that last bullet on someone other than himself. Fighting now to save the buffalo was all he had left.

He saw movement through the trees and immediately threw himself down on the snow. Wolves, he thought. He slowly raised his head to look from side to side: these wolves moved on two feet and carried government issue rifles and mortars. He did three quick roll-overs to position himself on the down-sight side of their progress: definitely the special-ops unit BJ had described, moving in the direction of the farmstead. He allowed his military training to crowd out the misery and pain caused by Kate. He got up and began to run, bending low, the view of the bushes and stones passing beneath his feet reminiscent of the vision dream he had experienced.

The snag with the eagle nest on top came into sight. He heard the unlikely whistle of a water dipper and followed it to a boulder just beyond the tree. BJ stepped out from behind, motioning for Sam to stay low and follow. He led them to a clearing where the chopper was parked just beyond a line of eight snowmobiles.

"Here's the plan," BJ whispered. "Simple little diversion: get into the chopper and obliterate the snowmobiles. Bleed the chopper fuel lines, toss a match, and get on back to the natives and clear out. No one gets hurt and you're on your way."

"But what about you?"

"You tie me up and I'll claim there's a whole damn native uprising, hundreds of Indians come together to avenge all the wrongs done to their tribes. That should put the fear of god into my kick-ass colleagues."

Sam couldn't help loving the sheer audacity of BJ's plan. "You sure you want to go through with this? I'm the one who's all screwed up. This's taking a pretty big risk."

"Son, I didn't fight for this country and spend my whole adult career as a game warden, so a bunch of pencil-necked nitwits could pull another My Lai on man and beast. I still have some shred of self-respect. Now let's get on with this before one of us comes to our senses."

BJ handed Sam a knife, a cigarette lighter, and a piece of cord rope. Sam tied his hands behind a stout sapling a hundred yards away from the chopper then did exactly as BJ instructed, running over to the chopper open doorway, loading the big gun and in the space of one minute and three-thousand rounds reducing the snowmobiles to a mass of smoking wreckage. He cut the fuel line, spraying high octane gas onto the ground, stepped back and tossed the lighted cigarette lighter onto the spot. The flames flickered, following the gas up into the engine compartment, and before Sam was two-thirds of the way back to BJ, the chopper erupted in a whoosh and fireball. A big smile broke out on Sam's face, and he realized that the gunfire and explosions had a cleansing, exhilarating effect. It felt good to be the perpetrator rather than the victim.

"One last thing," BJ said. "Reach into that pocket there on the side of my jacket; it's a cell phone. You take it, stay in touch. Only one thing I ask."

Sam retrieved the phone, put it in his pocket. "Yeah, what's that?"

"Trade it for that bullet in your rifle."

Sam was taken aback. "You want what?"

"I'm doing everything I can here to save a fellow Marine. There's been too much killing and mayhem. I don't want to go through all this and lose you in the process."

Sam was extremely touched by BJ's sentiment. He opened the breech on his rifle and slowly started to remove the one last bullet. It was like he was being asked by the father he'd never known to step back from the brink. And that in turn rekindled an image from deep in his soul about a pounding, churning charge towards a fast-approaching horizon line then pitching over into a free fall that was at once blessed and fatal. He realized he couldn't do it. "BJ, I'm sorry." Sam closed the breech and stepped back. He stared blankly at BJ. "I'll let you know how things turn out."

"You'll call me before?"

They both knew what he meant by that. Sam nodded. "I gotta go."

"That's right, you got some buffalo to save. But don't think these good ol' boys won't stay after you. I just hope you get yourself some good luck down the road."

Sam choked back the urge to cry, the swing from exhilaration to helplessness filling him with a sense of confusion. It seemed that events had been put in motion from which there was no escape. He began to run. He cut an angle to the direct path between the landing pad and the farmstead, figuring that the noise and smoke would cause the men to return double-time. He used the cover of trees and rocks to avoid detection and saw the whole line of them running madly through the open to get back to their ruined attack base. When he came to the farmstead he waited a full half an hour but didn't see a single sign of intruders. He snuck around behind and found everyone safe inside holding axes, pitchforks, and sharpened sticks. Yura was making a last few marks on the buffalo robe, her grandson curled up on the ground beside her.

"Let's go," Sam said. "We can make a run for the trees then up the valley."

"They'll kill us all," Two Suns said. "Did you see what they were carrying? We can't go up against that."

"It's a good day to die," Little Bull said, gripping her primitive spear. "My great grandfather was a suicide warrior and my vision was of me carrying his shield into battle. I'm not afraid."

"Fear is a powerful medicine," Crazy Wolf said. "We must take it in doses, respect it, but not be controlled by it."

"We should have gone out and negotiated terms," Kate said. "What do you think, that we can run away forever? It is inevitable that the authorities will arrest us, find the buffalo, and put an end to this little escapade. This is the 21st century, not 1865."

"I think she's right," Joseph White Bird said. "Even when our great Chief Joseph led my ancestors up towards Canada there came a point where he knew it was time to give up."

"Exactly!" Kate said.

"No! These buffalo are sacred," Crazy Wolf said. He went to Yura and she handed him the robe which he now held above his head. "Our whole identity as a people is embedded in their living free and being able to follow their destined paths. We will not give up, but we will also not run blindly into their guns. This is not a good day to die."

"The only thing embedded is the tracking device that's stuck in one of the animal's shoulder. We can run but we can't hide."

Sam could see that the room was slowly dividing between the followers of Crazy Wolf, and those of Kate. He recalled the way the wolf pack had responded to the light female leader when they were trying to attack the buffalo calf. This seemed to be the same dynamic. Kate sidled over to Sam and stood close enough for him to feel her warmth.

"What do you think, Sam? You with me or not?"

Sam shut his eyes, but it seemed he could see clearly across a snowy field towards a high pass with a lone eagle leading the way to safety. The eagle was swallowed by a swirling bank of fog. "I think once we get hooked back up with the buffalo we can take it from there. Who knows how this will turn out?" He opened his eyes and brought the rifle around to point at Crazy Wolf. "You can all stay here and argue about this as long as you want, but I'm going to need that map."

Yura helped Hello John to stand. The boy was severely wounded from his ordeal and had lost a lot of blood, but his voice was clear when he spoke: "I have seen the world from a high place, so high the sun was on my shoulder and all the rivers flowed into one. The people were gathered, waiting for spring, a great gathering for the Circle Dance and Round

Dance. All my ancestors were there. We had plenty to eat and drink. It was a happy time. All of you were there as well. But a cloud covered the sun, and thunder and lightning stopped the dance. The rains came and floods poured out of the hills, the water rose, and we had to run up in the hills, farther and farther to escape. The buffalo led the way but in a meadow at the top there was a terrible thing. I couldn't see what it was but we were pulled into it and only when we sang the renewal song were we allowed to fly free, right up into the sky. That is all." He buried his face in Yura's arm. She held him gently and made a slight nod to Sam.

"We must go to our brothers and follow them to safety," she said. "I will walk with my John."

Crazy Wolf turned the robe so the map was facing up. He traced his finger across the charcoal marks on the skin. "We go up the river to the place where two streams come in from the sides. They could be here, or here."

"That's not quite a computerized tracking screen, which they'll have, keyed in to the embedded device," Kate said to the group. "Can't you see where he's leading us? Do any of you really want to follow him?"

Crazy Wolf stood face to face with Kate; she met his stare and stood her ground. The members of the group migrated to stand behind Kate, or Crazy Wolf.

"The buffalo are leading us," he said. "They are the heart of our people and our special link to *Maheo,* the All Powerful. You know this if you listen to your heart and hear them speak through your dreams and visions. But where we go from here is a war party; each must decide for himself. Those who come, come; those who stay, stay."

The ones behind Kate shifted nervously then went to gather their things, leaving her alone.

"Lead on, chief," Sam said, lowering the rifle. "We got no time to lose."

31

When Lieutenant Walker saw the devastation and destruction of his entire fleet of vehicles, his anger was white hot. "Oh, I'll kill them! Every last one of them!" But when BJ informed him that the renegades who had tied him up and laid waste to the helicopter and snowmobiles were the advance party of a much larger group—a Native Uprising across the entire territory—Walker's anger transformed immediately into a nearly paralytic state of fear. "Quick, form a circle and load up! We're outnumbered and they could attack any second! Shoot anything that moves!"

The men huddled behind logs, boulders, and bushes, taking pot shots at the few birds and rabbits that came within view; even that lumbering low-to-the ground wolverine. Several of the cowboys wanted to lie down and shoot themselves rather than be cut to pieces, their genitals stuffed in their mouths, the way they'd heard it generally turned out with rampaging Indians; but Walker told them to "buck up" and try to hold on until the reinforcements arrived.

"Well for kee-rist sakes," Bob Smith said when he took Walker's radio call, "the goal here was the buffalo, not stirring up another Little Big Horn campaign! Can't you sneak out of there and get back on track?"

"Yeah, but here's the thing—when they blew the chopper, my laptop with the tracking signal went up in smoke with it. I got no way to follow them."

"Shee-it!" Bob rolled his eyes and shook his head at Duke and Tino Gugliardi, who were seated across the desk in Bob's office. "We should've put a tracking device on that Crazy Wolf, let *him* lead us to the buff! That guy isn't ever going to let them get away."

Duke laughed; Tino squirmed in his seat, realizing the simple truth of Bob's observation.

"Hey Duke," Bob said, "get the Jet Star. We gotta rescue General Custer here. And contact your police buddies over in Missoula and Lolo, we're going to need some local law enforcement to posse-up, put an end to this uprising. Tino, you want to come along, witness the last great Indian battle on the western frontier?"

Tino stood and moved towards the door. "No, I think maybe it's time I said goodbye and good luck. I've got, uh, a golf handicap to work on. But happy shooting out there."

When he'd left and Duke had finished making his calls, Bob turned to him and said: "You know, I don't think he gives a hoot about those buffalo."

Which if Tino had heard Bob speak, he would have complimented him for the dead-on accuracy of his statement. The buffalo were a distraction, a means to an end. It was too late to wire-up Crazy Wolf; the trick now was to get a police scanner and follow the movement of the agencies on the blood scent of the bison tracking device. They'd find them sooner or later. But if there was any hope to resurrect and sign the all-important, highly lucrative Indian Nations Land Use Enhancement Project contract, he would need to include those filthy, expendable buffalo as part of the signing deal. What happened to them once the contract was signed was totally irrelevant, although the thought did cross his mind that a barbecue would be in order.

32

Crazy Wolf draped the robe over Yura and John's shoulders, and the group followed him out the door and up the valley. They walked in single file, Sam and Kate at the back.

Kate turned to speak to Sam: "You let me down."

"What, did you want me to use my last bullet on him?"

"Don't be ridiculous. I want us to save the bison. You should be able to get behind that."

"I'm behind you now; I think that's all you really care about."

"What's that supposed to mean?"

"You're a wolf expert. You know what I mean."

Crazy Wolf motioned for the group to halt and lay low for a moment while he and Yura checked the robe. She gestured in a slightly different direction, through the trees along a rising slope beside the creek, and the group set out again, with Crazy Wolf dropping back to join Sam and Kate. He pointed to some tracks leading into a gully with a scattering of dirt and deadwood dug out.

"Wolverine den," he said to Sam. "Ever seen one?"

"Only in a dream."

A plume of oily black smoke rose from the far side of the valley, the odor thickly pungent in the still, dense forest. Everyone walked in silence, except for Kate who was positioned between Crazy Wolf and Sam, whispering to Sam but in a voice that was loud enough for Crazy Wolf to hear as well.

"I've had to fight for everything in my life. Do you think it was easy getting off the rez and going to a university? And that I'd look back and romanticize all the crap I'd left behind? Look at us, wandering around in the wilderness with some dream weaver markings to show us where to go, written on a bison robe! You don't have to be a PhD to know the difference between reality and blind madness."

"The reality you embrace *is* madness," Crazy Wolf said. "You don't see it because your eyes have been blinded by *their* way of seeing. But look at Mother Earth: she is rejecting all people and will sweep the world clean to start over fresh. That's the reality you refuse to see."

Kate started to respond but the words wouldn't come. She walked in silence, then: "I don't know. Sam, what do you think?"

"I think you two are fighting for control of this little group; you both want to be the leader but that's the problem with leadership: you either are or you aren't."

"To be a leader is to serve," Crazy Wolf said, "the strongest putting the weakest first, eating last. That is the Cheyenne way, the opposite of your way."

Sam didn't feel like arguing, but a thought occurred to him: "So that's what these buffalo are to you? A way to make you more of a leader?"

"I can see that without them we are nothing. I want my people to survive, so yes, I'm willing to fight to save our sacred buffalo."

"Now, that's where I disagree," Kate said. "You've taken a flesh and blood animal and made it a symbol, like it's some sort of flag worth dying for."

Sam had an immediate recollection of seeing the Marine memorial, those young men raising the flag at Iwo Jima, most of them killed within the month. "There're flags worth fighting for," he said.

"Maybe for you, but look at the price you've paid. What's that last bullet for, anyway?"

Her question took his breath away; the bullet was like that cliff in his dream, drawing closer. He tried to focus on keeping his feet in the narrow trail formed by the others ahead. "So, for you, the buffalo are kind of a laboratory project? Maybe they'll get you a promotion with the Park Service or something when we get back?"

"Maybe. But the point is whether we get back."

Crazy Wolf started to speak, but Sam stopped walking and interrupted him, holding the rifle as if he might shoot either of them. "The point is that both of you want the buffalo for something else!" he said angrily. Everyone up ahead clearly heard him speak and stopped to turn around. "But I'm only here for them, because without them I am finished!" He turned the rifle to his head. "Do you hear me? Finished!"

"They'll hear us!" Two Suns hissed.

"Let him do it," Joseph White Bird said. "We're done for anyway, what difference does it make now or later?"

Sam backed up, not sure of anything anymore.

"Sam, I need you," Kate said. "Stay with me."

"Need me?" For an instant, he made eye contact with Yura and Hello John, both of them holding out their hands to him. But before he could complete his thought or say another word, he fell backwards off a low cliff above the creek, falling through the air and seeing the darkening sky above, exactly as it had appeared in his dream. He landed in a snowdrift and clawed his way out to face the herd of twelve peacefully resting, ruminating buffalo.

33

It was a good hiding place for the entire group, and they stayed the night. Kate felt that they were probably in a radio frequency dark spot, there below the cliff, and that the transmitter would go undetected. For the most part, everyone remained silent, as much to avoid giving voice to their doubts and fears about what lay in store the next day, as to expose themselves to anyone passing by.

Sam curled up beside a rock away from the group but closer to the buffalo. He liked hearing and smelling them, and if he turned his face to the side, then back, he could actually feel their radiated warmth. After the long days buried in the snow, he felt impervious to the cold. He settled into a form of wakeful hibernation and allowed the darkness to wash over him and the memories of his deep dream to come alive.

But a new dream appeared this time: of a woman coming to him and holding him in her arms. She kissed him beneath the chin and on the neck, very gently, the two of them breathing together as one. They didn't speak but communicated on a level where language was unnecessary. The beating of their hearts was the sweat lodge drum, beating in harmony with one another and the deep rhythm of the earth. He felt happy and connected: to her, to the world, and most importantly to himself. Her body was his blanket, and they drifted through the night, her smell hauntingly familiar.

When he stiffly awoke at first light, his immediate impression was of the steam billowing from the nostrils of a grazing buffalo just beyond his feet. The animal took no notice of him, nibbling on the grassy bare spots and sweeping the snow away with its head to get at the emerging green shoots beneath. Sam leaned back and tried to recall any details, but the only sense he could remember was a pleasant smell that he suddenly matched to the sight of Kate, standing above on the cliff. He watched her moving slowly along the edge. Crazy Wolf startled him by coming over and squatting down right next to him.

"Still here, huh?" Crazy Wolf said. "I figured you'd take off in the night."

"And leave a fellow soldier to the *hadji*? That's not the Marine way, chief."

"Oh, so now they're the enemy, and we're what, your new redskin brothers?"

Sam shrugged. "I think we're on the same side of this skirmish. We've got at least one thing in common."

Crazy Wolf carefully examined and held his hand over a low depression in the snow beside Sam. "Such as?"

"The buffalo, what else?"

Crazy Wolf looked up at the cliff. A thick bank of fog had drifted down the canyon, partially obscuring Kate. "She climbed up there so she could examine our buffalo from above, maybe find that tracking device. But I doubt you could find even a tick beneath their fur." He looked back down at the depression. "This just about matches the one next to me."

Sam looked from Crazy Wolf to Kate as the fog closed in and she disappeared altogether. "She was there with you last night?"

"I thought my wife had come to me in a dream, but then I awoke. It was dark; she didn't want to talk or anything; just sit there. But I made her go away. I've taken a vow."

Sam felt his sense of connectedness waver and become obscured by a rising sense of hopelessness. "Why would she come to you, when she could be here with me?"

"Indian blood runs strong, my friend. And the power of a woman is something stronger than any man. We think we're tough, but if they make up their mind to dominate and lead the pack, then all we can do is fall into line. I've seen it with wolves; that's the way of the buffalo too. I hear it's that way with lions. The woman always leads. Look how we go to Yura to see for us, to dream through the buffalo and know where to go."

Sam tried not to show his deep sense of despair. He wanted so much to believe that she was there for him, that she was the one thing he could depend on. "But you don't want to follow Kate?"

"I don't want to but she'll win in the end. They always do. But if we turn ourselves in now those men will kill all our buffalo, and us too if they get the chance." The muffled sound of a helicopter could be heard in the distance. Crazy Wolf stood up, staring into the fog and listening intently, but it was impossible to tell which direction it was headed. "We both know that sound."

"Reinforcements?"

"No. Destiny!"

Yura and John came out of the fog, the robe across their shoulders. "Our buffalo are moving," she said. "We must go."

"But where are we taking them?" John asked.

"They're leading us, the same as when we started," Crazy Wolf said. He held out his hand to Sam and pulled him up. "Come on my friend, it's a good day to die!"

34

Lieutenant Walker wanted to establish a virtual wall across the upper reach of the watershed leading down from Lolo Pass, correctly assuming that was the preferred route of escape. But Bob Smith nixed the idea and insisted on a straight-out attack of the valley below. He didn't want the buffalo to come to him; he wanted the combined forces of the military, police, and cattle association to take the battle to them.

"You understand every hour they're out there it costs me about five mill in lost international sales—those're real dollars Lieutenant; phone number dollars, as in seven figures. So, get a hump on!"

"Only problem is the fog, Mister Smith." Walker's new laptop seemed to be loaded with devil software: the red dot scooted and blinked all over the screen, occasionally and haphazardly filling the screen with brilliant color, only to flash back into an unpredictable moving target.

"Well what about your guys on the ground? What the hell they doing? Drinking coffee and eating donuts?" Bob turned to Duke. "And where's that BJ? I liked him. He was one of us."

Duke shook his head. "Cashed out and went home to Nevada. Said he'd had enough of Walker's bullshit."

"I told you he was one of us, cause that for damn-sure makes two of us."

Walker started giving orders and the teams of police officers from ten jurisdictions and five livestock districts set out in SUVs, ATVs, and horseback on a coordinated sweep of the territory.

"This a shoot-on-sight situation?" someone asked.

"Shoot first and ask later," Walker replied.

"And don't ask, and don't tell," Bob Smith added.

The buffalo were oblivious to the sounds of truck doors slamming, engines firing up, and horses neighing. They pushed forward, heads down, snorting and farting, guided by a compass deep within their brains. But the eerie glow of squad car police lights pulsating through the fog was very upsetting to the disheveled, disoriented, and disharmonious band walking to their side and behind.

"We're done-for!" Shining Shirt said. "Look! There, and there! We're surrounded!"

"Bring it on," Little Bull said.

Yura kept her head high, her arm around John, her eyes transfixed on a distant horizon.

"It would be so much better if we announced we were coming in, rather than surprising them," Kate said. "They'll probably shoot first and ask later."

The sound of gunfire and a yelping dog could be heard off to the right.

"Someone's going to be asking what happened to their dog," Two Suns said.

"They'll shoot anything that moves," Crazy Wolf said. "Be ready!"

Sam felt his mind leave his body. Whatever the rules of engagement were for the battle ahead, it was certain that it would be over quick. He plodded along like the buffalo, feeling invisible and wondering if he would hear the rifle shot that sent a bullet crashing into his body.

The fog became thicker. Two Suns and Shining Shirt sang guttural, chanted war songs; Kate talked angrily to herself, the others seemed resigned to the inevitable fate that awaited them.

The sound of several helicopters circling above; of men calling out orders or cursing the lack of visibility; the occasional random gunfire and shouts of dismay by those who were within range; and now, most surreal of all, the rising roar of an engine that reverberated through the fog with the force of ten thousand horsepower. It passed like a mighty angel right above the buffalo then circled around and came back towards them on a stretch of highway blacktop, yellow fog lights cutting through visibility that was now less than a hundred feet. The group was terrified, but Sam and Crazy Wolf recognized it from their time spent in the mid-east: a private cargo plane, smaller than a C-5, the sort used by military contractors for rapid insertions or extrications of men and equipment in battle zones all around the world, cash up front, a bonus upon delivery live or dead, and no questions asked.

The rear door banged down onto the pavement and Tino Gugliardi came running towards them with a police scanner in one hand, tracking monitor in the other. The pilot and co-pilot ran out the back, scattering a path of alfalfa behind them.

"Let's go, go, go! Load 'em on! We got one minute, and you've already used two!"

The buffalo followed the fragrant trail right up into the plane, the Indians astounded but now whooping it up, urging the beasts forward, then everyone clambered in behind. The door cranked into place even as the engines revved up and the plane roared back down through the smoking fog, barely missing several cars then up, up and away, and gone, leaving Bob Smith to exclaim, angrily but admiringly: "Oh, I like his style!"

35

Tino had thought of everything, even setting boxes with alfalfa and cubed protein bars on the infantry style seats along the sides, and piling bales of loose hay on the floor to snuggle down into. The plane was capable of carrying jeeps, armament, caskets—whatever you wanted and could afford—so the buffalo had plenty of room.

"Anyone want something to eat or drink?" Tino asked once they were aloft. "Sandwiches, pizza? Maybe catch a movie? There's some pop on ice right here in the cooler. What do you guys like?"

"Fry bread and gravy," Shining Shirt said.

"And a cardiologist standing by," Kate said. This was her first time meeting Tino and she knew there had to be a catch. "So, you're like, a zillionaire buffalo lover? But somehow you don't look like Ted Turner, unless you work for him?"

"I wish I had his money," Tino said. "But Crazy-guy here knows what this is about, don't you?" He delivered a playful punch to Crazy Wolf's shoulder.

Crazy Wolf ran his hands through his hair. He looked and felt extremely tired. "Maybe I'll take one of those sandwiches."

"Got it!" Tino snapped his fingers, pointed at Crazy Wolf and smiled with broad insincerity, then went forward to get the food.

Crazy Wolf fell back into a chair. "Bid-ness," he said to Kate. "Tino here wants to do some big time bid-ness."

"Business huh? Sounds like the usual Indian case of one-way exploitation, especially if he's willing to spend the kind of money to pay for all this!" She looked around, shaking her head in disbelief. "Beware a white man bearing gifts, ever heard that one? But I will say I should have trusted your instincts. These buffalo really must be sacred."

Hello John was doing his best to walk slowly down the middle aisle, his arms held out to steady himself from the pitches and rolls of the plane. "Look at me, I'm flying!" He stopped beside a little table where Tino had placed the police scanner and tracking device. "What's this?" He picked up the tracking device and aimed it towards the buffalo, causing a small beeping noise to instantly become much louder.

Kate went to him and looked carefully at the device. "May I?" He handed it to her, and she walked past the buffalo, aiming the device at each, then turning away, trying to assess which one had the embedded transmitter. When she got to the white buffalo calf, sleeping peacefully in its pile of hay, the tracker emitted a continuous, high pitched beep. "It's my *Wohpe!* C'mere girl." She bent down and ran her hands over the calf's body, settling on a small bump just above her shoulder. "John, can you get me a piece of ice? And does one of you have a pocket knife? Blade's got to be extra sharp."

John went over to the cooler and grabbed several ice cubes. Little Bull whipped out a flip knife. He gave them to Kate and she held the ice cubes over the transmitter, numbing the skin. Then, she made a small incision, the calf quiet and not complaining. Kate removed the transmitter and held it up with one hand for all to see. "This is amazing!" She came back down the aisle. "I thought it would be impossible!"

The plane made a violent lurch and Kate was thrown off balance. She fell to the side, landing in Crazy Wolf's lap. She started to get back up, but he held her, whispering into her ear: "These buffalo are like our people, wiped out, massacred, exploited, left for dead, but somehow we're still here. You shouldn't give up being an Indian just because it's impossible."

Kate met his piercing stare, allowing him to hold her, and sinking slowly into his embrace.

Sam sat across from them in the shadows at the very back of the plane, the cold air blowing in from the edges of the door. He was happy that the buffalo were saved, but after the adrenaline and excitement of the escape he felt empty. And now, seeing Kate with Crazy Wolf, he had to wonder if she really needed him at all.

Tino came back with piled high trays of sandwiches and cookies, and a file of papers. He set the food on the cooler and handed the file to Crazy Wolf. Kate got off his lap and allowed them to begin talking about the garbage contract. She tried not to seem nosey but still wanted to listen and moved down the plane, sitting across and just up from Sam.

"So, where do we go from here, Kate?" Sam asked.

She was surprised to see Sam sitting there. "I don't know. Who would've thought we'd get this far?"

"Yeah. Amazing, huh?" She seemed agitated, checking her pockets and patting her shirt as if she'd lost something. Maybe he wasn't the only one who could be distant and strange. "Y'know, I had the weirdest dream last night, I been meaning to tell you about it."

"Don't," she said, continuing to look for some lost thing.

"You were in it. In fact, you were the dream. It's like you were right there beside me. I can remember every detail."

"Sam, this whole trip has been a dream; maybe more of a nightmare, actually." She could see that Tino and Crazy Wolf were starting to argue, their voices rising and falling as they turned pages. And she could tell that Crazy Wolf was tired, but that his strength would not allow Tino to talk over him.

"But I just have to ask; the one thing you said, that you needed me. Is that true? Because baby, I really need you."

Kate stood up, shaking her clothes as if a piece of lost jewelry might fall out. Tino was right in Crazy Wolf's face, screaming for him to sign the contract, not listening to anything Crazy Wolf had to say. She wanted to go to Crazy Wolf, stand at his side. "I don't know, of course I need you. I need everyone on this plane. But what I really need is to find that transmitter device. I thought I had it. Plus, I want to see if I can help Crazy Wolf. He's done so much and brought us so far." She went back up the aisle.

Sam shifted the rifle strap on his shoulder and closed his eyes. That's right, he thought, Crazy Wolf's the undisputed leader now Sam. Good for him. He's earned it: the buffalo, the band of Indians, and now the girl. He's got it all. Sam closed his eyes and felt the dog tags at his neck. But I've got my pain, he thought. No one can take that away, even if they try. The pain will be with me always. That, and my one last bullet.

"Wanta play catch?" a voice said from the darkness.

Sam opened his eyes and saw Hello John standing there, tossing his magic hair ball up and down in his hand. The boy had a ghostly pall to his skin, his eyes sunken but bright as coals. He tossed the ball to Sam, which even in his addled state he managed to catch. He held it for a moment, feeling the warmth and hidden power of so pure and simple a thing, then gently tossed it back. "When we land, we should get some more willow branches, make a proper lacrosse stick."

"Yeah, that would be great!" John said.

They tossed the ball back and forth, John prattling on about every topic on his busy little mind, Sam appearing to listen but focused more on the angry drama unfolding further up the plane. Tino was spitting-mad apoplectic, accusing Crazy Wolf of bad faith and worse, demanding that he sign the contract right this second or there would be holy hell to pay. But Crazy Wolf was not inclined to sign. In fact, it seemed that nothing in the world could induce him to complete the contract. Sam heard words like "Mother Earth" and "Sacred Ancestors" drift back over the engine roar. Kate was right there at his side, her hand on his shoulder, tossing in advice and support on behalf of Crazy Wolf, making Tino even more furious. Yura was also there, standing on the other side, the rest of the natives migrating over to surround Crazy Wolf with their supportive energy and good will; Tino Gugliardi versus all of them. After one last outburst and harangue, he finally gave up and stormed back up the center aisle, kicking each buffalo as he passed and making a roaring ugly face at *Wohpe.* But not a one so much as stirred or paid him any notice. When he was gone, the natives all began trilling and shouting at once, and slapped Crazy Wolf on the shoulders. He was happy to receive their congratulations, but after a while he began pacing up and down the center aisle. The others found a stack of movies Tino had brought along; they tried to decide between *Drums Along the Mohawk* or *The Legend of the Lone Ranger* and settled on the latter.

"What's the problem, chief?" Sam asked Crazy Wolf. "Seems like you won hands-down."

"The battle, not the war. We're being taken to Las Vegas. He's up front now, radioing the cattle association to meet us at the airport. Our sacred buffalo will be hauled to the nearest slaughterhouse and we'll be hauled off to jail."

"Not me," Sam said quietly.

Crazy Wolf stopped pacing and stood in front of Sam. "You have a plan?"

"Never take me alive. Remember anyone saying that?"

Crazy Wolf nodded. "But that was then. We've come a long ways." He looked over at the others, happily eating, drinking, and cheering for Tonto each time he came on screen. "I have to think about them. Someone also said: A Cheyenne chief serves his people. It would be selfish of me to put them at risk to serve my own needs."

"Well, that's your problem, not mine. I've made my decision." Sam shifted the rifle again and squirmed in his seat, trying to get more comfortable. Something uneven with multiple buckles and hard straps was poking him in the back. He turned to smooth it out and saw that it was a very large backpack of some type.

"Just don't put yourself in the line of fire with any of my people, ok? That's all I ask." Crazy Wolf went back up to rejoin the others.

There won't by anyone in the line of fire, Sam thought, except for myself. He felt overcome by tiredness and wanted to close his eyes before they landed and the lights went out forever. But it was impossible to get comfortable. What was with this backpack anyway? He pulled and tugged until it came free from the area behind the chair where it was wedged in. He read down a list of serial and patent numbers, the product Made In China, of course, then in small letters a description of the drop weights and safety parameters of an industrial strength parachute, capable of safely air lifting a pallet of wheat or weapons, a jeep, or—Sam suddenly realized in a flash—a fully grown buffalo!

Sam moved quickly up the length of the plane, counting the available parachutes, twenty in all, which was precisely the total number of buffalo, Indians, and one last chute for himself.

"John! Turn off that movie and lock the door! Kate, you were able to cut a transmitter out of that calf without it going crazy. You're going to need to do the same for all of them."

"What are you saying? There's more than one transmitter?"

Everyone stood up, unsure what Sam wanted, but alarmed and energized by his state of excitement.

"I'm saying it's not a good day to die after all. Here, put this on one of the buffalo. There are plenty more tucked in behind the chairs along the wall. Grab one for yourself and bring the rest to Kate. There should be twelve for the buffalo."

"Twelve what?"

"Parachutes! We're saved! We're going to fly out of here just like in John's vision."

"No way!" Hello John said, pulling out and putting on a parachute pack that was as big as his whole body.

"Oh, big-time yes-way!" Sam said. He looked at Crazy Wolf, who could barely restrain a smile, nodding slightly.

"Nothing's impossible," Crazy Wolf said.

"Except for getting these strapped onto the bison," Kate said. "They may be sacred, but they're still a thousand pounds of wildness topped with a set of horns."

"We'll manage," Sam said, grateful that one last door had opened, leading him away from the brink.

36

Tino sat up front with the pilots on the little fold-out jump seat next to the lavatory, stewing about the pig-headedness of Crazy Wolf. He'd done everything short of licking the guy's toenails to make this deal come together and now time was running out. He figured that the threat to have them all busted and the buffalo ground up into hamburger would be enough to bring Crazy Wolf around. He hoped he was back there right now sweating bullets.

"How much longer?" he asked the pilot.

"Just comin' up on Tahoe; maybe another hour to Vegas. Danged load must be shifting around, plane's all squirrely."

"What exactly do you mean by 'moving around?' "

Tino stood and flipped open a little telescopic spy hole in the cabin door. The view through it was distorted, but there was no question something fishy was going on: most of the buffalo were standing up and they seemed to be equipped like pack animals with huge bags strapped to their backs. "The fuck is this!" He grabbed the door handle and nearly broke his wrist trying to yank it open.

"Hey, careful with the merchandise!" the pilot barked. "You break it, you bought it."

The plane swooned catastrophically nose upwards as the buffalo were herded towards the tail section, thoroughly upsetting the balance and aerodynamics. Tino would have fallen over if he hadn't been holding onto the door.

"Whoa, nelly!" the pilot screamed. A red light flashed on the dashboard and an extremely loud emergency signal commenced beeping.

The co-pilot took his hands off the stick and tried to poke it quiet. "Back bay door's opening up. What the hell's going on back there? We're doomed!"

"His contract just got doubled, that's what the hell's goin' on!" the pilot shouted, wrestling with the stick to keep the plane from doing a backwards barrel loop.

Tino watched in horror through the peep hole as one after another of the buffalo jogged out the door ramp platform, a strap attached to a pulley rail on the ceiling automatically opening the parachute the moment they hit the open air. He squirmed around to see the Indians in the foreground, putting on the same bulky packs and hooking their straps to the rail, following the buffalo out the back. He ripped a fire extinguisher off the wall and smashed at the door handle.

"You are *so into* contract extensions!" the pilot screamed. "And you now *own* that door!"

"There is no bloody way I'm going to let my investment fly off into the void!" The door crashed open and Tino pushed through just in time to see Kate wave back at him and jump clear. Sam and Crazy Wolf were putting on the last two parachutes. Tino grabbed Crazy Wolf from behind. "On no you don't, not 'til you sign that contract!"

Crazy Wolf was struggling to attach a buckle around his waist. He reached over for the contract file, which was underneath the police scanner, and tossed the file towards the hurricane of wind at the back of the plane, the papers swirling away forever. "There's your contract, go get it if you want."

Enraged, Tino pulled the pack off Crazy Wolf's back and hurled it out the rear door. "Oh yeah? I've got a copy! You got another parachute?"

Sam went to the door and looked out at the drifting line of parachutes with the buffalo and Indians floating towards the snowy forest way down below, the contract papers and Crazy Wolf's parachute pack blowing into the jet stream, and realized this was the chance he had been waiting for. Crazy Wolf was grappling with Tino; Sam could jump and have Kate all to himself. He hooked the parachute cord to the rail over his head: all he had to do was take two steps forward, but he better do it now, each second the distance was growing between himself and the others. He turned back to Crazy Wolf; Tino was a street fighter from way back and knew every trick in the book: the dirty little *hadji* was gouging, biting, and kneeing Crazy Wolf into submission. Sam started; stopped; it was time to go, Kate would be down there waiting for him. But Sam's Marine Corp instinct took over his sense of self interest. He couldn't leave a fellow vet behind.

Sam held out his hand to Crazy Wolf. "Come on! The buffalo are leading us. We'll jump together!"

Crazy Wolf managed to push Tino away and ran full force into Sam, body blocking them out the ramp doorway, the world suddenly becoming much quieter and colder, the two of them trying desperately to hold onto one another in the streaming air, Sam cartwheeling and looking back up at the flying away plane with Tino's white hot face disappearing behind the mushroom veil of the parachute fabric.

37

Sam had an instant recollection of his vision dream at the buffalo jump, except that now he was very much not alone. The wind and strong pull of gravity were knives, cutting Crazy Wolf away from the safety of Sam and his parachute. But they clutched one another like a pair of mating crabs, their arms and legs intertwined, chins clamped down on one another's shoulders, using every ounce of strength to keep from separating.

"I got you!" Sam shouted directly into Crazy Wolf's ear.

"Did you see that weasel's face?" Crazy Wolf shouted back, laughing through clenched teeth. "When I threw his shitty little contract out the door?"

"That was so great!"

"Hey, pull the ripcord!"

"What do you mean? Of course I did," Sam said.

"But it feels like we're still falling."

Sam looked up just to make sure it wasn't his imagination that the parachute had deployed. The chute was full, but he had to admit the view down to the ground seemed to be coming at them much faster than he wanted. There were no other parachutes in sight. "I think we're in for a rough landing."

Which was an understatement: they crashed through the upper and understory of a Ponderosa pine tree, stripping branches on the way down, cratering hard in eight feet of snow, the wind knocked out of them but fortunately no broken bones. They were deeply buried and had to fight their way up to the surface. They gave one another high-fives.

"Welcome to wherever!" Crazy Wolf said. "Are we still in America?"

"I don't know," Sam said, looking around. They were in high mountains, but off in the distance, presumably to the east, there seemed to be an expanse of lower, drier land. "I don't see a casino anywhere so we must not be on a rez."

"Oh, you worthless Marine!" Crazy Wolf said, laughing. "I figured we were headed south, and that this must be Nevada, or California, or Oregon, someplace like that. But I sure didn't expect to see so much snow; this is deep!"

He tried to take a step and sank up to his groin. Sam floundered around beside him. It was mid-afternoon and the snow had softened even though it still felt right around freezing.

"We're headed for a cold night, that's for damn sure," Sam said. "I didn't see any houses or roads on the way down."

"Hey, we can cuddle up with one another; we know how to do that!" Crazy Wolf said. He too looked around as if there might be some indication which way to go.

"No, wait!" Sam remembered the cell phone BJ had given him. He found it in a pocket, flipped it open and turned it on. The jingling little bit of music that accompanied activation seemed preposterous given the surroundings. "Perfect, no service." He turned it off and put it back in his pocket.

"Well, we know the others must be off in that direction." Crazy Wolf pointed towards a nearby ridge. "The plane was traveling this-a-way so all we gotta do is fight through the snow that-a-way for about five days and maybe we'll find them."

"Make that six!" Sam said. "Here, let's walk single file and take turns. I'm up to my waist!"

It was slow going but they made better time than Sam had expected, especially as they neared the top of the ridge. In the valley below there was a road and off in the distance Sam could see a large man walking in their general direction, followed by a dozen or more big animals.

"Are those our sacred buffalo?" Crazy Wolf said.

"I think those are cattle. And that guy, it's a long ways, but he looks kind of familiar."

They plowed through the snow as fast as they could, aiming to intersect the stranger on the ice-crusted road. The man walked staring down at his feet, his feet wrapped in burlap and soggy cardboard. Both he and the following Hereford cattle were extremely gaunt and disconsolate.

"Oxnard?" Sam asked.

"You know this guy?" Crazy Wolf said.

"Yeah, sure, it's one of the guys I came up to Montana with. Oxnard, hey buddy, what are you doing out here?"

Oxnard looked up, then back down, like a beaten dog.

"And where the hell are we?" Crazy Wolf asked.

Oxnard coughed; a death rattle. "You're in the inner circle, that's where. You're so close you could be taken up, like that!" He fumbled to snap his fingers, but they wouldn't respond so he put his hands back into his pockets.

"The what?" Sam asked. "You're not making any sense here Ox. You sure you're feeling ok?"

"The Rapture!" he hissed. "Carried up on the wings of eagles leaving famine and destruction, the battle between good and evil for all those poor souls left behind. It's the Arma-fuckin'-geddon, right back up this road. And you are welcome to it!"

The intensity of his statement was unnerving. A cow mooed, its milk bag shriveled and empty.

"You don't want to be Raptured?" Sam asked.

"I don't want to be holy nourishment for a bunch a lunatics. Would you? No, I'll take my chances duking it out with good and evil. I don't mind a fight." He turned to leave.

"Hey Ox, c'mon now, it's me, Sam. You heard anything from BJ?"

Oxnard squinted at Sam, his face as worn out and wrinkled as the cow's bag. "They took my phone; they took everything, said I wouldn't be needing it pretty soon. Even my shoes. I look like I don't need shoes? What the hell you call these piece of shit things on my feet? Shoes? I don't think so!"

He continued on down the road, the cows behind. But when Sam and Crazy Wolf headed the other way, the cows became disoriented, then turned and followed them back up the road.

Sam called to Oxnard one last time: "You see a group of Indians, plus about twelve buffalo?"

He raised his arms in disbelief. "From where?"

"From the sky," Crazy Wolf said. "They were coming down from an airplane."

"Oh no, you got it all wrong," Oxnard shouted back. "The Rapture takes 'em up *into* the sky. From here," pointing at the snow, "to there!" pointing at the sky. Then waved as if in disgust and kept walking.

"Strange guy," Crazy Wolf said.

"Distant and strange," Sam said.

The icy road made for easier walking and around a long turn they saw the first of the parachutes draped in the branches part way up a pine tree. It looked as though a snowplow had driven from beneath the tree over to the road.

"I'm guessing that was one of the buffalo," Sam said.

"Tracks are right here in the road. Plus, that pile there is buffalo shit, not cow manure."

They started counting the other parachutes, left behind in the trees, on bushes, or simply abandoned and blown up against a rock, all the tracks leading to the road and from there, single file in an ever-deepening trail. The wind shifted and the cows started to get spooked, mooing and fidgeting the way they do when they don't want to go any further.

"You smell what I smell?" Crazy Wolf asked.

"Cross between an outhouse and barbecue gone bad."

"And what's that? Singing?"

"Or screaming."

"I got a bad feeling about this," Crazy Wolf said. "Let's get off the road and up that hill, take a look around."

"I'm with you."

They followed a windswept ridge that was relatively clear of snow, the cattle crowded together and following. The sound and smell got stronger the closer they came to the ridgeline. Crazy Wolf motioned to Sam to stay low and crouch behind a rock outcrop that afforded a view into the valley beyond. They saw a farmhouse with broken windows, dozens of cars and trucks buried in snow drifts that appeared from the surrounding debris and filth to be lived in, and a barn that had some kind of bonfire burning inside, the smoke sifting out of cracks in the closed doors, windows, and any number of missing shingles.

"Looks like a vision of hell," Crazy Wolf said.

"I don't see Kate or the others. No wait, look at that!" Sam gestured to the far side of the barn, where a group of men and women were chasing the buffalo with the star pattern on its forehead. They had knives, meat cleavers, and axes, but each time they got close enough to take a swing or make a stab, the buffalo would lunge forward, hook them with its horns, and toss them about twenty feet to the side.

"Those folks must be damn hungry to take that kind of beast down," Sam said.

"I really don't like the looks of this," Crazy Wolf said.

The barn door was opened a crack and a Moses-like, large, bearded man in a flowing robe carrying a tall staff with a crook at the top—the very same Reverend Jones who had cursed the buffalo back on the Gardiner Bridge—came outside, held his arms wide as if parting the seas, and went to the house. A desperate attempt at singing drifted out of the barn, Christian hymns lacking the enthusiasm of a saved people. The people with the knives and meat cleavers gave up on the buffalo and dragged their wounded bodies over to the barn and went inside. The buffalo sniffed the air and moved around to the far side.

"We should work our way to the lee of that barn. I bet the buffalo are just out of sight," Crazy Wolf said.

Sure, let's see if we can get over to that far window, take a peek inside. Maybe everyone's in there."

"I hope not."

"Oh my god, there!" Sam pointed at the house, where the entire group of natives was led out by Reverend Jones, everyone tied to one another with a rope strung from neck to neck, their hands tied behind their backs. A contingent of men and women prodded them forward with sharp sticks. Little Bull shouted an angry tirade at her captors and struggled to break free. Several large men and two women pounced on her, beating her unmercifully.

"Yeah, we're definitely still in America," Crazy Wolf said. "And these are good Indian-hating Christians. Give me your rifle; I'll settle this right here and now."

"Keep a clear head," Sam said. "One bullet's not going to solve anything."

They could hear Little Bull's tirade change to screams of fear and pain. Two Suns tried to come to her aid and Reverend Jones began beating him with the staff.

"No, give it to me. It'll solve this."

Sam took the rifle off his shoulder. He held it in his hands, resisting the impulse to hand it over to Crazy Wolf. "No."

"What do you mean, no?"

The thought of not having that last bullet seemed like too big of a risk to take. "It's mine. I got my own reasons." Crazy Wolf looked intensely at Sam, his expression hardening. His hand darted out and he gripped the rifle, trying to pull it away. "What, so you can shoot me in the back when the time's right?"

"Let go, goddam you!" They struggled, silently and intensely, Sam fighting with all his strength to retain the rifle.

"It's because of her, isn't it?" Crazy Wolf hissed. "Your little Sacajawea fling?"

With a mighty burst of energy Sam elbowed Crazy Wolf in the face and wrested the gun free. He aimed it at him, finger on the trigger and safety off. "You're right! I should shoot you now. She was mine; we were starting to have something together. She needed me."

"She's Indian. She doesn't need you!" Crazy Wolf spat. "None of us needs you. You should turn that rifle around, put the barrel in your mouth, and get it over with right now. You don't even need yourself."

Sam could barely breathe. He staggered back from Crazy Wolf, the gun trembling in his hands. He heard a new sound: Kate's voice, screaming "No!" as if she was calling him back from the darkness.

Sam and Crazy Wolf both turned at once and threw themselves at the edge of the rocks. Kate was at the front of the line, and Reverend Jones had her by the hair, dragging her towards the barn, the others staggering along behind. Sam raised the rifle, aiming at Jones, but Kate was in and out his line of fire. The group came to the front of the barn, the door was thrown open wide, and the singing inside took on a whole new tone of hysterical excitement. Smoke and sparks from the bonfire inside poured out the door. The singing became a chant: "Feed us Lord! Feed us Lord!" The Reverend led his captives inside, and the doors were pulled closed, but the chanting of the believers and the screams of the Indians could be heard echoing over the frozen wilderness.

38

"You're hired," Bob Smith said to Tino, extending a hand to shake on the deal. They stood on the broken, weedy tarmac of an abandoned military airfield, ten miles north of Reno, Nevada.

Tino reached out but did not yet grasp Bob's hand.

"But I work alone, not with any of your dick-head goons." Tino gestured towards Lieutenant Walker, supervising the unloading of ten steel black barrels and a large wooden box from an unmarked government truck. The cargo plane was just beyond, surrounded by a protective network of cattle association pickup trucks and Nevada State police cars. "Plus my finder's fee."

"Got it." Bob tried to grab Tino's hand.

"And expenses." Tino kept his hand out, still avoiding shaking.

Bob wheezed a gasp of exasperation, nodded, kept trying to grab Tino's hand.

"Plus my lost commission. This was a sure thing. I could still make it happen, anytime I want."

"For Christ sakes, yes! A deal's a deal." They shook, both trying to squeeze the blood out of the other's hand. "Whatever works. You know what you got to do. I'm paying for results here, you understand."

They let go and lowered their hands, wiggling fingers to restore circulation.

"Oh, I'll deliver. Bet on it!" Tino made a final adjustment on his hand-held GPS unit and went to a truck with a gun rack on the rear window and a snowmobile in back. He peeled out, heading towards the high mountains to the west. The sun was setting; plumes of wind driven snow drifted above the highest ridges.

"Jeezus, I hate that guy!" Bob said to Duke. "I want him to do the job but I would just love it if he got caught in an avalanche or eaten by a bear along the way."

"You didn't pay him in advance?" Duke replied.

"A check," Bob said, winking. "Can always cancel it unpaid!" He shouted over his shoulder: "Walker! You 'bout ready?"

"Affirmative."

The pilot and co-pilot strolled down the ramp door of the plane, nodded to the police officers, and came over to Walker who had a crowbar and was prying open the wood box. The pilot kicked one of the barrels as the co-pilot lit up a cigarette.

"Hey, take care!" Walker said, jerking the cigarette from the man's mouth and crowding between the pilot and the barrels. He tossed the cigarette on the ground and crushed it with his foot. "You've got to be very, very careful around this stuff."

The pilot lit up two cigarettes and handed one to his co-pilot. "So, when do you want to make this little run? And by the way," he held out his hand, "show me mister green."

Walker removed a thick envelope from his jacket and slapped it in the pilot's hand. "Soon as we load these up," he said, motioning to the barrels, "and get this sonoffagun all wired to go." He lifted the lid off the box and removed a bowl-shaped antenna and a control panel covered with dials and screens.

The pilot counted the money and blew a cloud of smoke in Walker's face. "You sure about this infrared technology?"

"Bombproof," Walker said. "It can pinpoint a cold-blooded terrorist or warm blooded buffalo from ten thousand feet, guaranteed!"

"Yeah well that's fine, but you're short," the pilot said, waving the wad of hundred-dollar bills. "You owe me for one door and twenty parachutes!"

39

The small herd of cows lay sideways in the snow or stood with their heads down, haunches to the wind, too famished to follow Sam or Crazy Wolf any further. Sam didn't wait for Crazy Wolf or care if anyone saw him. He ran full speed down the hill past the rank settlement of deeply buried car dwellers. Excrement and bones were everywhere. The vehicle outlines could be seen popping up through the snow, but some were buried completely, with dark tunnels leading down into the subterranean, foul-smelling hovels. The stripped clean carcasses of dogs, cats, a dismembered cow, and god knows what else were strewn across the snow. No one was about; whoever lived here seemed to be inside the barn.

He went to the far window and turned his head to the side, peering carefully through one eye over the sash. There was a great fire in the center, with rows of boxes, logs, and car seats for the believers to sit or stand upon, all of them chanting "Feed us Lord!" A blood-soaked harvest table was on the other side of the fire. Reverend Jones stood behind it, his staff in one hand, a fierce hunting knife in the other. And behind him was his line of captive Indians. He raised his arms and the chanting stopped.

"Our god is a god of vengeance!" he bellowed. "He loves those who love him and brings justice to those who do not believe. Let me hear you profess!"

The people in the room stood as one, arms raised high, shouting: "I believe! I believe!" The ones who had been gored by the buffalo held one hand over their wounds, the other hand raising their weaponry of cleavers and axes.

Crazy Wolf slid in beside Sam. "You got one bullet, take him out now!"

"But there's more than him," Sam whispered. "What good will that do?"

"He's the leader of this pack; you take him out, the pack falls apart, just like wolves or a herd of buffalo. Plus, I'll grab his staff. Without their symbol of power, they'll have nothing."

The Reverend waved his arms to silence his followers. "We are born to sin and damnation! Only those who are saved shall be fed. Who here is saved?"

The group began screaming again: "I'm saved Lord! I'm saved!"

"I don't know," Sam said. He wanted to take the shot, but what if the group became a mob and fell upon the Indians with whatever weapon was at hand? There were too many of them.

Jones silenced everyone, then boomed: "But those who do not profess, who do not believe, they are unclean in the eyes of the Lord, and shall be brought to justice!"

The group shouted in agreement: "Yes Lord! Yes Lord!"

"All of you profess and believe!" he boomed. "But do these profess and believe?" He turned and swept his staff over the heads of the Indians.

"No Lord! No Lord!" his followers screamed.

"They worship false idols; false gods!"

"False gods! False gods!"

"And what does the Lord ask from us?" he shouted.

"Justice Lord, Justice Lord!"

"And what does he provide?" he shouted, going to the line and slashing at the rope that tied Kate to the group.

"Food, Lord! Food, Lord!"

Reverend Jones grabbed Kate by the hair and dragged her screaming and hysterical to his altar. He forced her on her back, her hands tied behind her, and raised the knife high, mumbling a prayer that only he could hear.

"What are you waiting for?" Crazy Wolf shouted in Sam's ear, his voice lost in the screaming inside the barn. "Take the shot!"

Sam broke the window, stuck the rifle through and aimed, but the believers were on their feet, blocking his view.

"Shoot!"

"I can't, there's no line!"

Crazy Wolf knocked Sam to the ground, seized the rifle and ran around the back of the barn to another window. He brought it up to shoot with a clear bead on the Reverend's head, but in his haste he flipped the safety button to the "on" position and the gun wouldn't fire, just as Kate screamed: "I am not an Indian! I believe! I profess! I'm saved!"

The knife hung in the air; Reverend Jones hesitated. He looked down into Kate's face, trying to discern if she was truly saved, or lying to save her own pathetic life.

"Feed us! Feed us!" the believers shouted less loudly than before, the unity of their chant becoming chaotic and confused by Kate's profession of faith.

Crazy Wolf flipped the button again. He still had a shot, but he held back, hearing Kate scream: "I've never been an Indian! They're heathens and I am a believer! Save me Lord!"

Sam came around the barn. The buffalo were just beyond in the growing darkness, formed up in a protective circle with *Wohpe* in the center. Crazy Wolf appeared to be stunned by Kate's renouncing of her Indianness. Sam pulled the rifle away from Crazy Wolf. "I have a plan," he said. "Go get the cattle, bring them to the barn door and wait for my signal, then drive them inside."

"But what about my people?"

"They'll be free to go. Trust me."

Crazy Wolf thrust both his hands onto the rifle. "Trust my people and the sacred buffalo to a *white man?*"

Sam kept his left hand on the rifle and with his right he flipped out the dog tags and held them towards Crazy Wolf. "No! To *me!*"

Crazy Wolf looked from Sam's eyes to the dog tags and allowed Sam to jerk the gun out of his hands. Sam pushed Crazy Wolf away and went to a back door beside a ladder that led up to the gambrel roof. He scaled the ladder and scooted on all fours over to a cupola window directly above the altar. He looked down at the hellish scene, trying not to cough from the smoke that billowed up from the fire.

Very reluctantly, the Reverend pulled Kate off the altar and motioned for her to join the believers on the other side of the fire, who were clapping and singing, "We believe Lord! Feed us Lord!" She seemed spastic; unable to clap in time, and she would not return the Reverend's leering gaze or look up at the remaining captives.

Reverend Jones walked slowly over to the line of Indians. He strode down the line, carefully examining each, trying to make sure he got a non-believer this time. He stopped in front of Hello John and held the boy's jaw in his hand. "Do you believe, my son?"

John thrust his chest out, showing off his Sun Dance wounds, and kicked Jones hard in the shin. "I believe I'll piss on your grave!"

Jones staggered on one foot, holding his wounded shin, his face glowering. "Oh, you little heathen!" He slashed the rope holding John's neck and dragged him to the altar, lifting him and splaying him out face down, his hand pressing hard on the back of the boy's neck. He cut the ropes holding his wrists and raised the knife high.

"What does the Lord demand we do to heathens?" he called out to his believers.

"Vengeance, Lord! Vengeance!"

Sam turned his face away from the smoke to breathe the cold, clear air blowing across the roof. He could see the first cows stumble over the ridge with Crazy Wolf coming up behind, herding them towards the barn. Sam took a deep breath and brought his face back to the window.

"You have done well, my children!" Sam shouted as loudly as he could in what he imagined to be a god-like voice. "Your Lord is pleased!"

Everyone in the room fell silent. The knife hung in the air, Reverend Jones confused, his head cocked.

"I am your god almighty, and I am pleased with your faith. You profess and believe. I am happy!"

The believers began to smile and fall to their knees. The Reverend's mouth was open, but he was unable to speak.

"You have done well my son, to bring my people here. But let your captives go. I have a greater punishment in store for them. Their suffering will be . . . " Sam searched for the exactly right word, "massive!"

The believers swayed back and forth, listening to god from above. But the Reverend knew all about the devil and his wily ways; he sensed a trap.

"Where are you Lord?" he called out. The knife trembled in his hand. He wanted very much to slaughter this morsel and get on with it. "Show us your face!"

"Silence, worm! It is not for man to know the ways of the Lord!"

At this, many of the believers fell onto the muddy floor on their faces, squirming in the mud, begging for forgiveness. The Reverend was unbowed.

"Then show us a sign, Lord! Show us how to believe and worship your power!"

Sam moved to the icy edge of the roof, scraping with his fingernails to keep from sliding over. Crazy Wolf was down there with all the cattle. Sam waved one arm, Crazy Wolf waved in reply, and Sam scampered back to the cupola. "The Lord provides for those who believe! Release your captives, and uh, have a hamburger on me!"

The barn doors were suddenly flung open and Crazy Wolf made a wolf-howl that went right to the bottom of the cows' fright and flight fear trigger. The animals ran through the doorway and were immediately set upon by the starving horde of believers. Blood began to splatter everywhere as the animals were cut and ripped open, the believers wallowing prayerfully in gore. Hello John pump-kicked a blow straight into Reverend Jones' groin, then grabbed the knife from his hand and slashed across his forehead, blinding the Reverend in his own blood. He rolled off the altar and began cutting the neck ropes on the line of Indians. Crazy Wolf was off to the side motioning frantically for them to make a run for it and they ran out as quickly as they could. Sam came down and shut one door, Crazy Wolf the other, John cutting the last of the ropes from their hands and neck as they ran around the barn towards the buffalo which were already on the move, plowing through the snow in the direction of the far, green lowlands.

It was nearly dark, the stars coming out, the quietness magnifying the outlandishly macabre revel going on back in the barn. The terrified mooing and death wails of the cattle could be heard above the chanting and charismatic hysteria of the believers.

"I'm going back," Sam said to Crazy Wolf.

"Leave her!" Crazy Wolf said. The sound of a plane coming closer could be heard in the distance. A powerful strobe light shown down on the forest as it approached. "Or do as you wish. But we're going on. We have to make the cover of the trees." He ran to catch up with the natives straggling along behind the buffalo.

Sam began to run. He knew Kate was still in there. He went to a window and stared in at the mass of people waving their arms with dripping organs and pieces of raw beef held high and silhouetted against the flames. He saw Kate in the rear of the room, standing in solitary disbelief, the Reverend pushing through the crowd towards her. Sam went to the back door and moved through the darkness, past rotting bales of hay. He saw the wooden handle of a hay hook and uncurled the rusted tool as he passed, striding faster now as the sound and light of the plane passed once over the barn, the feeding frenzy of believers raising their faces to praise the arrival of the Lord.

The Reverend's face was a bloody, furious mess. He came towards Kate, untying his robe as he moved, the staff held forward like a phallic battering ram. He pushed Kate towards the piles of hay where Sam was just now emerging from the darkness, Kate falling back into the mold and rot, the Reverend opening his robe, seeing Sam now for the first time, as Sam swung low, then up, hooking the reverend full in the groin, lifting the man off his feet and seizing his throat to hurl him backwards into a cow dairy stall piled three feet deep with manure, bones, and rotting organs.

"Let's go!" Sam said. He pulled Kate up and practically carried her out the door just as the plane made its second pass. The ramp door was open, and a wired-together line of black barrels was pushed out. They drifted down like an aerial mine field, each barrel containing fifty-five gallons of napalm gel set to ignite four and a half seconds after the ignition was automatically tripped from inside the plane, where Lieutenant Walker viewed an infrared sensor screen indicating that twelve buffalo-like animals and an unknown number of fellow travelers were moving around inside the barn. He had a toggle joystick that allowed him to keep the strobe focused on the barn, which doubled as a target positioning and ignition switch.

"Sayonara, mother fuckers!" he said, pushing the red button.

"The Lord has arrived!" the believers screamed. "Take us in the Rapture!"

Sam heard the pop and saw the flash and threw Kate and himself behind a stump just as the flames erupted in a whoosh and boom, enveloping the entire barn in a fireball that sent a shockwave blasted outwards, then elastically sucking air back in, whipsawing the tops of trees.

Kate was convulsed with fear and humiliation. She gagged, nearly throwing up from the trauma. "Kill me! I don't deserve to live!"

"No, you do!"

"I hate myself!"

"But I love you." Sam held her tightly. "We can do this. We have to keep going. See? There's already a trail, all we have to do is follow it."

"I can't do it."

"You can, I'll go with you."

She wouldn't move so he lifted her in his arms and set off through the snow. The light from the fire illuminated the trees and snow into a terribly beautiful, iridescent sea of gold. It was light for a long ways down the trail, gradually reducing to the soft glow of starlight. He set her down and she was able to walk but wouldn't speak, fearful of what would happen when they joined back up with the group and she would have to confront the full force of her betrayal. But for Sam, the trail had the feel of walking into a dream, the faint odor of the buffalo leading ahead and the breeze carrying a restorative scent of the far-off sage and pinion landscapes of home.

40

Tino set the tracking and GPS devices on the dashboard of the truck and resolved to get as close as possible before resorting to using that monstrosity of a snowmobile in the back. He hated the outdoors, and this was way beyond anything he had bargained for. Although, with the terms he had struck and shaken on with that hayseed of a cattle baron, Bob Smith, it was worth just about anything to finish the deal and claim the commission. He flipped the switch for the overhead panel of track lights. The world ahead became much brighter, almost to a Vegas-scale of outrageous illumination. If a little was good, a lot was better.

He re-calibrated the tracker against the GPS. The red beeping dot had shifted from an uphill to a downhill trend. The trend is always your friend, Tino reminded himself; perhaps the most important rule he had organized his life around. He saw a road leading off in that general direction and gunned it through a snow drift. The temperature gauge on the rearview mirror indicated it was thirty-one degrees outside. He turned up the heater. He knew he had a full tank of petrol; no sense getting even the slightest bit cold.

His cell phone rapped. It was big Bob, his personal ATM. "Yeah?"

"We got 'em. Deal's off."

"The deal's what?"

"I said Walker smoked them. Come on back and bring the keys. Thanks for everything but you're done. And by the way, I cancelled your check."

The phone went dead. Tino stopped the truck and sat there quietly, feeling the rage build like the most virulent of fevers. He seriously considered getting out and torching the vehicle but then realized it would be a long walk home.

Ok, so now I got more than one target, he hissed to himself. First the lying, cheating Indians, even if they didn't have their pestilent herd of animals; they're going down! And now Cowboy Bob and his double-crossing band of losers would get theirs in good time. He rechecked his ammo supply: plenty! Looked through the scope: crystal clear, with very satisfying cross hairs for sighting in on a forehead.

He kept the engine running to keep the heat up and curled back in the driver's seat, darkly muttering a prayer-like litany of curses, as he visualized over and over the pain and suffering he would visit upon his prey come the first light of day.

41

Crazy Wolf walked at the head of the group, embracing the cold and dark, with its pulse of the new day just before dawn. He felt himself cross the Sacred Pledge of Four Ridges—the vivid memory of pledging the Sacred Arrows as a young man, and soon after offering his flesh to the Sacred Buffalo Hat; surviving the ordeal of the Sun Dance ceremony; and now, the fulfillment of his vow of chastity—and imagined how it would be to settle back with his family. The years of abstinence had concentrated his power in his son and now it was time to renew. This trip had been a challenge on so many levels, but he was bringing the buffalo home; the tribal power was restored; he could rest knowing that his people had a spiritual platform on which to build a sustaining future. The dawn would bring a new beginning.

All through the long and luminous night the buffalo plowed a path to follow. They could smell the fresh growth in the lands below the snow. It didn't matter that the Nevada grasses were different from the Montana prairies: the sun's energy locked in the soil and plants was available for grazing, pulling them like metal to a magnet out of the high country and down to the fertile plains surrounding Pyramid Lake.

When Sam and Kate caught up with the group no one turned to welcome them. It was the darkest hour of the night, just before dawn. They had come a long way and the snow was patchy, interspersed with blackened pine needles, white capped mushrooms, and Indian paintbrush plants pushing up through the loam.

Crazy Wolf raised a hand. "We rest," he said, and immediately everyone squatted on their heels or lay on the damp ground, catching a few minutes of sleep.

"I need to go to him," Kate said.

"Stay," Sam said. "Don't punish yourself."

"But I've done everyone so wrong. I can never live that down."

"So, there's your answer. Make a new life with me. You don't need to be a *hadji*." Sam could see her face in the starlight. She was bereft and he realized that nothing he said could change that.

She stood and groped forward past the others and laid her head on Crazy Wolf's knee, not saying anything. He looked away, but after a few minutes Sam could see that he placed his hand on her head.

Sam felt the emptiness build within him. It seemed that nothing he did amounted to anything. He had found a hometown girl who he loved and she loved him, but in the end she moved on; he had served his country but he had come home to an indifferent reception, scarred and filled with doubt; and now, he had embarked on a doomed expedition that had resulted in a measure of salvation for everyone but himself. What was left? The future was a foundation built on quicksand; farming in a dust bowl; a relationship with a non-partner.

"We go," Crazy Wolf said, standing and following the path of the buffalo. Kate tried to walk right behind him, but Two Suns, Shining Shirt, Little Bull, and the others elbowed her out of the way, pushing her to the back of the line.

"So here you are," Sam said, "right back where you started."

Kate plodded along, buffalo-like. "Not exactly. He's allowed me a measure of acceptance. That's enough for me."

"But what do you want?" Sam asked. "You could walk away and say you're Hispanic, or Asian, or Greek. Who would know or care? This is a big world; you can be whatever you want."

"But not what I am. I'm Lakota. I'm an Indian. Nothing can change that."

Sam gave up. It didn't matter what he said; she was what she was, and so was he: distant and strange, a car wreck with a name but no license. He walked bat-like with his eyes closed, hearing the echo location of footsteps ahead and using the buffalo tracks to guide his feet. He raised his head and smelled the rising fragrance of Nevada lowlands. Surely it was after midnight; it was a good day to die.

42

Sunrise broke across the Rapture gathering, revealing a smoldering mass of death and destruction. Bob Smith surveyed the gruesome scene with Lieutenant Walker and pronounced it a qualified success.

"You incinerated a bunch of critters, that's for damn certain," Bob said.

"But is it the *right* critters?" Duke asked. "Plenty of folks among the critters."

"That, to be sure, is the question of the hour," Bob said. "What do you think Walker? This was all your doing. You ready to stand up before a grand jury and swear 'I do'?"

"Hold on there," Walker said, wagging a finger. He walked through the smoking ruins of the barn, kicking at the blackened skulls and ribcages jutting up beneath the charred, chemical smelling timbers. "We're in this together."

"Are we? Seemed to me it was your call all the way. What do you think, Duke?"

"His call."

Bob shrugged, holding up two fingers. "That makes two. Jury'd go with two."

Walker stumbled over a skeleton with a hay hook jammed into its juncture of legs and hip sockets. "I think maybe we should call in a SeaBee reservist crew, bring up some Caterpillar D-9s, and bury everything in place."

"Walker, I take it all back: you're a genius!" Bob said.

"Shoot, shovel, and shut up! Duke added.

"Motto of the new west!" Bob said. "Let's get 'er done!"

43

The sun rose just as the buffalo crossed the snowline and the first meadow unrolled like a golf course green amidst the rough and tumble of the eastern Sierra foothills. In the distance, the tufa formations of the Needles and the Pyramid jutted up from the alkaline waters of Pyramid Lake, like Egyptian sculptures.

"John has an idea," Yura announced.

"Oh yeah, what's that?" Crazy Wolf replied.

Hello John looked like he was about to burst from pride. He held a willow branch in one hand, his magic hair ball in the other.

Yura's arm was over his shoulder. She gently tugged his shirt to expose the scars on his chest to the sun. "That we use native sovereignty rights to protect our sacred buffalo. John's uncle is on the Paiute tribal council. We could talk with him, ask them for grazing rights. Why would they disagree? What agency would dare to interfere?"

Crazy Wolf mulled the idea in his mind. It was his first preference to contact the BIA tribal government back on the Northern Cheyenne reservation in Lame Deer and ask for a resolution of support to truck the buffalo back, make them a test case for Cheyenne Native rights. But you never knew about the Bureau of Indian Affairs. They had a way of twisting everything, first in the favor of some poor ration Indian who thought he had oil under his shack, then in the favor of the last coal strip mine lobbyist who came through the door. The notion of keeping the sacred buffalo right here had its advantages; the issue could be settled without a fight with no one hurt. He liked the sound of that. Plus, he wanted time alone with his wife after these five long years of abstinence. Anything that contributed to some peace of mind was the way to go. He squatted down to look Hello John in the eye.

"Our mighty warrior has counted coup on the enemy, survived the Sun Dance ordeal with scars and a vision to show for it. And now you give us sanctuary with your Paviotso tribe?"

"We are the *Cui Ui Ticutta people,* and once you try some of our *Cui Ui* fish you'll never want to leave. It's the most beautiful place in the world." He tossed Crazy Wolf the buffalo hairball.

Crazy Wolf smiled, holding the ball in his hand. "There is only one beautiful place in the world and every Indian calls that place home." He stood up and surveyed the treeless hills and endless valleys beyond. The buffalo were grazing on the tough but nourishing plants and grasses sheltered by the knee-high sage bushes. "You have a good place, John. Our buffalo will be safe here."

Yura, standing in front of Crazy Wolf, looked past him, her expression changing from a happy patchwork of wrinkles, to a face set in stone. Crazy Wolf did not turn. Hello John walked away, shaping the willow branch into a lacrosse stick.

"I need to talk," Kate said.

"I hear a voice," Crazy Wolf said to Yura. He slowly tossed the hairball in his hand, as if measuring time. "Is there someone speaking to me?"

"No. Not someone. It is no one."

"That is what I thought," Crazy Wolf said. He put the hairball in his pocket and walked off through the sagebrush without turning to look at, speak to, or even acknowledge Kate's presence.

"Grandmother," Kate implored. "I made a mistake, but I'm Lakota, I know that now more than ever." She fell to the ground, crawling forward to prostrate at Yura's feet. "Don't do this to me!"

Yura was unmoved. "We are on a journey; the enemy is all around us. It is a battle where each must help the other to survive. That is the way with our people. It is the way of all life. Look at the buffalo. No one stands alone. If you are alone, if you leave the herd the wolves will take you. That is all, I have spoken. Hey ho."

And she too turned and walked away from Kate, leaving her there on the ground.

Sam considered going to Kate and helping her back up on her feet, but it seemed that whatever he did would be wrong. He turned his face to the sun: it was bright but without warmth. The air had a faint trace of familiar desert smells, but the salient scent was of nothingness. He looked for a place to go where he could put an end to his own sense of emptiness. A rock outcropping on a low bluff seemed like a good resting place. He wondered if anyone had ever bothered to go to such an unremarkable place; it was unlikely anyone would ever find his body up there, which was exactly what he wanted.

He saw Crazy Wolf walking towards the buffalo and thought what a good man he was; what a tough soldier he must have been. He wished he could be that good and tough, but he wasn't. He raised his hand to say goodbye. Crazy Wolf had his right hand in a pocket. He took it out and held his hand in the air, as if returning Sam's gesture, but then Sam realized that he was examining something that he had found in his pocket.

Sam heard the report of gunfire, a single rifle shot, and one of the buffalo dropped to its knees and fell over. Another shot; a second buffalo pitched forward onto its nose.

Now Crazy Wolf was on the run; the buffalo's heads were up, their nostrils searching the air for a clue. The other natives began to run. A third shot; a third buffalo dropped. Sam swung his rifle around and held it as if charging in an attack, but there was nowhere to go, no enemy or shooter to be seen. He ran towards Crazy Wolf. Everyone was converging on the remaining buffalo. A fourth shot.

"What's happening?" Sam shouted.

"Our sacred buffalo," Kate screamed. "We're losing them!"

A fifth shot; the sound could be from anywhere; a sixth. No one knew what to do, where to turn. Sam saw a buffalo fall to the right; instinctively, he turned his eyes to the left, trying to see the line of fire.

Crazy Wolf held a small object up in his hand. "I found this in my pocket."

"Oh no," Kate cried. "It's the transmitter. They must have followed us!"

A seventh; the smell of blood and the sight of buffalo family members falling down in death throes had unsettled the remaining survivors. They stopped and started, trying to confront the unseen enemy.

Sam stepped away from the group, shielding his eyes to estimate the direction from which a shot might have been taken. The only possible vantage point was the rock outcropping on the low bluff. He tried to make out movement, a reflection off a scope or rifle barrel, anything; nothing.

Crazy Wolf grabbed Kate's arm. "When you fell on me in the plane, you were holding this!" He pressed the transmitter in her face.

Now Kate realized what must have happened. "The plane was shaking, it fell out of my hand. I tried to find the transmitter but couldn't. It must have fallen into your pocket!"

He howled in rage and threw the transmitter away. "The buffalo are my people's life! They are the path to *Maheo*, the All Powerful! I can't let this happen!"

The buffalo circled with *Wohpe* in the center. The deadly rhythm of shooting had stopped for a moment and Sam realized that the shooter must be reloading. He got down in a three-point stance, elbows on his knees, feet spread wide. He removed the caps from the scope and searched the rocks but if the shooter was there he was head down. He panned across a wide arc of bushes and alkali mounds looking for anything that suggested a possible target.

The shooting began again, dropping three buffalo out of the circle in quick progression. Only two left, the buffalo with the starred forehead, and last of all: the white buffalo calf.

Sam turned back to the rocks and saw the briefest bit of movement; there! A head rose and a rifle barrel moved to a new position. The scope gave the range: one-thousand two-eight-three yards. Sam licked and raised a finger: slight breeze out of the east. A shot; and the starred buffalo dropped.

Kate was hysterical. "No! Not my *Wohpe!*" She ran towards the calf; it stood its ground, chest thrust out, alone now but not afraid, with Crazy Wolf coming in from the other side, the weight of his entire people's past and infinite future on his shoulders.

Sam could see Tino's face in his scope, the crosshairs twitching at this range. He heard the next shot and saw a flash from the barrel, but he stayed concentrated on his own shot, not thinking that his one last bullet would no longer be available for himself, only that the sacred symbols of a people are what holds them together and makes it possible to be alive. Tino stood up from behind his rocks, aiming again, which made no sense; he'd just taken the twelfth shot, which was all the buffalo, but he was right there in the open. Sam squeezed the trigger and felt the slamming recoil into his shoulder and Tino tumbled back into the rocks.

Sam looked up. Everyone was standing around Crazy Wolf, lying on the ground with a bullet through his chest; Kate and the sacred white buffalo calf standing over him. Crazy Wolf's breath gurgled as the blood filled his lungs, but his eyes were clear as he extended a hand to Kate. Sam went over and heard him say: "You are Katherine Little Coyote, daughter of

Henry Weasel Bear. Your mother's people are Seventh Generation Keepers of the Sacred Pipe. You are Lakota!"

"I am Lakota!" she repeated.

He turned his eyes to the sun; the pupils dilating as his lungs filled. "Laura; my son; my people!" he gasped, his chest convulsing, but then it was over and he lay peacefully, as if in a drowsy sleep, a look of calm settling over his otherwise stricken face.

The calf braced on its front legs. No one spoke. Yura placed her hand on Crazy Wolf's forehead, then stood.

"We must bring our sacred buffalo calf to its new home. John, you are our leader, show us the way. Two Suns, Little Bull, Joseph White Bird, and Shining Shirt, we will bring our Crazy Wolf's body and build a canopy for offering. Take him up."

She motioned towards the far shining waters of Pyramid Lake and the group set out, while Sam went up to the rocks and found Tino. He rolled a boulder onto his chest to prevent the eagles and scavenging creatures from scattering his bones out in the open where they might be found. And then he smashed his own single shot rifle against a rock, breaking it in two, and left the pieces there to rust and be absorbed over endless time by the elements of earth, fire, and water, from which they had been created and where all things would someday return.

He caught up with Kate, who walked with head down, arms tightly folded.

"I'm going back to Montana," she said to Sam in a monotone. "I must speak with his wife and tell him how true he remained to his vow."

"But, what about you?"

"I'm going home to Pine Ridge. I need to start over."

"So do I," Sam said. "So do I."

44

Sam heard a strangely familiar sound as he approached the two-lane highway coursing north to south across western Nevada. He reached in his pocket and removed a cell phone.

"Yeah?"

It was BJ. "Hey ya kid. Where the hell are you?"

Sam looked around, the empty road going to the horizon in both directions. "Right about here. You?"

BJ laughed, coursing along way above the posted speed limit, not a cop, structure, or person in sight. "Same. Never guess who I found walking down the road."

Sam kept walking, appreciating how blue the sky was, the clarity of the air. He breathed deeply and felt the first premonitions of a dream, a vision, and a new life. Then a sound way off in the distance caused him to turn and he saw a beat-up old government-issue truck approaching, two guys in front, one slumped over and ugly as roadkill. "Wouldn't be the Ox-man, would it?"

"That is *exactly* who I got here. How'd you know?"

The truck whizzed past.

"Cause I just saw you drive by, that's how."

The truck braked, backed, and stopped.

"How you doin' there Sam?" BJ asked, all smiles. Oxnard looked up and nodded, then slumped back down.

Sam reached with his right hand to grasp the dog tags around his neck. He pressed his fingers against the Braille-like letters of his own and

Heydon's names, which were now a reassuring presence that kindled a sense of strength rather than panic. And simultaneously with his left hand he reached to adjust the shoulder strap of the single shot rifle that was no longer there, the absence of it a measure of this new day. He took a step forward.

"All sorted out. Take me home."

ACKNOWLEDGEMENTS

Writing this novel has been one of the great adventures and joys of my life, in large part due to the people I met and learned from along the way. My knowledge of Montana begins with my good friend and ranch partner Jim Revoir. Thanks to him my kids learned how to drink whiskey standing on their heads, how to safely operate a hay bailer at midnight, and how to stealthily approach the wiliest trout in the world. Our cattle and wheat ranch near Harlowton had the distinction of having an historic buffalo jump on the bluffs above Deadmans Lake.

Learning about the rich history associated with Rimrock Ranch led me to the Northern Cheyenne. My friendship with Chief Phillip Whiteman Jr (Yellowbird) and his wife Lynette Two Bulls (Scouts the Way Woman) has informed and enriched me on many levels and introduced me to a whole new way of seeing the world, from a sweat lodge with their family, to participating in the Fort Robinson Spiritual Outbreak Run. Their extensive good works with youth and elders through the Yellowbird Lifeways Center is worth supporting.

My lifelong appreciation for native culture began in rural northern California where I learned about the resolute Yahi native survivor, Ishi, and later spent time with the Washoe tribe in Lake Tahoe and Nevada. I took Washoe language classes, rambled about the Great Basin and Columbia plateau homelands of the Paiute and Wanupam, and developed an appreciation for the Dreamer prophet Smoholla, and Jack Wilson, Wovoka, founder of the Ghost Dance religion. Eventually I had the privilege of serving as Chairman of the Museum of the American Indian in Novato, California, where I became the disciple of Colleen Hicks, a deeply wise Cherokee woman who taught me the essential importance of "Spirit".

The power of Spirit ran deep with my inspirational parents, both very literate and outward flowing individuals. My father, Big John, was a proud Navy veteran. Over time I learned that his war years as a late teenager marked and scarred him in profound ways that he carried throughout his life, a plight that is an ongoing deep national shame. A US Department of Defense report in 2021 wrote: "An estimated 30,177 active duty service members and war veterans of the post 9/11 wars have died by suicide, significantly more than the 7,057 killed in Global War on Terror military operations. This marks a failure by the military and U.S. society to manage the mental health cost of our current conflicts."

Despite a long history of government sponsored genocide, native people enlist and serve in disproportionate numbers to their population. Unlike my father, who left for war hungover and without any fanfare from church and community the morning after his senior prom, native people have a myriad of honoring and prayer services with extended families and the tribal community, to celebrate young warriors prior to and upon returning from service. Veteran's groups are generally some of the most robust organizations on any reservation. There is much to learn from the Cheyenne and virtually all other tribes, about how they cherish and heal their warriors.

Spirit runs strong at Sweetgrass Books and Farcountry Press. Big thanks to Erin Turner for providing the kind, professional guidance I needed to bring the book to completion! I owe a large debt of gratitude to my friend and writing mentor, Nancy Ellis, who has been an ally for many years. Also want to thank J. Eddie Thornton III for his expert advice, counsel, and insight. Author of the excellent *Stolen: Stories from a Violent Childhood,* he has much to say about nurturing hope in an unforgiving world. A PTSD survivor and model for moving forward.

They say that the wildest colts make the best horses. I believe that is true, especially seeing the growth of my children, Riley, Jack, Julian, and Maria. Mark Twain once wrote: "When I was a boy of fourteen my father was so ignorant, I could barely stand to have the old man around. But when I got to be twenty-one I was astonished at how much he had learned in seven years." I hope in reading this novel they may find a measure of truth in Twain's words.

ABOUT
THE AUTHOR

John Newman grew up in rural northern California. He worked in agriculture and later owned a working cattle and wheat ranch near Harlowton, Montana, about which he wrote a history, *Tipi Ring Ranch, Before and After the Buffalo* archived at the Montana Historical Society. He studied creative writing and biology at Stanford, worked as a river guide on the great rivers of North America, and for over a decade has been a fire lookout.

His interest in native affairs and culture began at an early age when he helped construct the Ishi trail to honor the last surviving member of the Yahi tribe. He also studied the Washoe language with the tribe near Lake Tahoe, their ancestral home, and for many years served as Chairman of the Museum of the American Indian in Marin County, California. While ranching in Montana he became acquainted with the neighboring Cheyenne tribe, sweated with families, and was invited to participate in the 400-mile Fort Robinson break-out run from Nebraska through Pine Ridge and back to reservation in Lame Deer. His goal as a writer is to create character-based stories set principally in Montana and the west, where natives and anglos confront a spiritually infused world in which predators and prey uneasily coexist, and humans are on equal terms with other creatures; a present day that is primordial on every level. In the process, his characters learn from one another and overcome personal demons and historical trauma. Married and the father of four, John divides his time between Melville, Montana, and northern California. You can contact him at johnsutthoffnewman@gmail.com or visit johnsnewman.com for more information.